GREAT CLASSIC SHORT STORIES

CLASSICS FOR ALL SEASONS

HC CB
HARPERCOLLINS CHILDREN'S BOOKS

First published in 2024 by HarperCollins Children's Books
An imprint of HarperCollins Publishers India
Building No 10, Tower A, 4th Floor, DLF Cyber City, Phase II,
Gurugram – 122002

2 4 6 8 10 9 7 5 3 1

P-ISBN: 978-93-6569-461-1
E-ISBN: 978-93-6569-963-0

To the best of our knowledge, all works included in this collection are out of copyright and available in the public domain. To give a true sense of the genre, themes and sensibilities of the times that they were written in, we have tried to retain the original form and language of the texts.

Typeset in Garamond 11.5 on 15.1, and Courier New 11.5 on 15.1
by Kamal Satyawali

Printed and bound at
Thomson Press (India) Ltd

MIX
Paper | Supporting responsible forestry
FSC® C010615

This book is produced from independently certified FSC® paper to ensure responsible forest management.

CONTENTS

1. The Kidnapped Prime Minister 1
Agatha Christie

2. *From* The Count of Monte Cristo 17
Alexandre Dumas

3. *From* The Tenant of Wildfell Hall 28
Anne Brontë

4. The Lottery Ticket 41
Anton Chekhov

5. *From* The Poison Tree 48
Bankim Chandra Chatterjee

6. The Tale of Peter Rabbit 59
Beatrix Potter

7. *From* Five Children and It 63
E. Nesbit

8. The Witch's Balloons 83
Enid Blyton

9. A Canary for One 86
Ernest Hemingway

10. The Elderbush 93
Hans Christian Andersen

11. *From* A Doll's House 103
Henrik Ibsen

12. That Spot 119
Jack London

13. *From* Three Men in a Boat 131
Jerome K. Jerome

14. To Autumn 140
John Keats

15. *From* Gulliver's Travels 142
Jonathan Swift

16. *From* Twenty Thousand Leagues Under the Sea 154
Jules Verne

17. The Locket 168
Kate Chopin

18. The Fly 176
Katherine Mansfield

19. *From* War and Peace 184
Leo Tolstoy

20. The Jumping Frog 200
Mark Twain

21. *From* Frankenstein 208
Mary Shelley

22. *From* Chitra 224
Rabindranath Tagore

23. The Boy Who Was Caught 234
S. Mukerji

24. *From* Far from the Madding Crowd 246
Thomas Hardy

25. Daffodils 256
William Wordsworth

The Kidnapped Prime Minister

Agatha Christie

Now that war and the problems of war are things of the past, I think I may safely venture to reveal to the world the part which my friend Poirot played in a moment of national crisis. The secret has been well guarded. Not a whisper of it reached the Press. But, now that the need for secrecy has gone by, I feel it is only just that England should know the debt it owes to my quaint little friend, whose marvellous brain so ably averted a great catastrophe.

Coming from a convalescent influenza patient, I hailed the remark as showing a beneficial optimism. I myself had been the first sufferer from the disease. Poirot in his turn had gone down. He was now sitting up in bed, propped up with pillows, his head muffled in a woollen shawl, and was slowly sipping a particularly noxious tisane which I had prepared according to his directions. His eye rested with pleasure upon a neatly graduated row of medicine bottles which adorned the mantelpiece.

"Yes, yes," my little friend continued. "Once more shall I be myself again, the great Hercule Poirot, the terror of evil-doers! Figure to yourself, mon ami, that I have a little paragraph to myself in Society Gossip. But yes! Here it is! 'Go it—criminals—all out! Hercule Poirot—and believe me, girls, he's some Hercules!—our own pet society detective can't get a grip on you. 'Cause why? 'Cause he's got la grippe himself'!"

I laughed.

"Good for you, Poirot. You are becoming quite a public character. And fortunately you haven't missed anything of particular interest during this time."

"That is true. The few cases I have had to decline did not fill me with any regret."

Our landlady stuck her head in at the door.

"There's a gentleman downstairs. Says he must see Monsieur Poirot or you, Captain. Seeing as he was in a great to-do—and with all that quite the gentleman—I brought up 'is card."

She handed me the bit of pasteboard. "Mr Roger Havering," I read.

Poirot motioned with his head towards the bookcase, and I obediently pulled forth "Who's Who". Poirot took it from me and scanned the pages rapidly.

"Second son of fifth Baron Windsor. Married 1913 Zoe, fourth daughter of William Crabb."

"H'm!" I said. "I rather fancy that's the girl who used to act at the Frivolity—only she called herself Zoe Carrisbrook. I remember she married some young man about town just before the War."

"Would it interest you, Hastings, to go down and hear what our visitor's particular little trouble is? Make him all my excuses."

Roger Havering was a man of about forty, well set up and of smart appearance. His face, however, was haggard, and he was evidently labouring under great agitation.

"Captain Hastings? You are Monsieur Poirot's partner, I understand. It is imperative that he should come with me to Derbyshire to-day."

"I'm afraid that's impossible," I replied. "Poirot is ill in bed—influenza."

His face fell.

"Dear me, that is a great blow to me."

"The matter on which you want to consult him is serious?"

"My God, yes! My uncle, the best friend I have in the world, was foully murdered last night."

"Here in London?"

"No, in Derbyshire. I was in town and received a telegram from my wife this morning. Immediately upon its receipt I determined to come round and beg Monsieur Poirot to undertake the case."

"If you will excuse me a minute," I said, struck by a sudden idea.

I rushed upstairs, and in a few brief words acquainted Poirot with the situation. He took any further words out of my mouth.

"I see. I see. You want to go yourself, is it not so? Well, why not? You should know my methods by now. All I ask is that you should report to me fully every day, and follow implicitly any instructions I may wire you."

To this I willingly agreed.

• • •

An hour later I was sitting opposite Mr Havering in a first-class carriage on the Midland Railway, speeding rapidly away from London.

"To begin with, Captain Hastings, you must understand that Hunter's Lodge, where we are going, and where the tragedy took place, is only a small shooting-box in the heart of the Derbyshire moors. Our real home is near Newmarket, and we usually rent a flat in town for the season. Hunter's Lodge is looked after by a housekeeper who is quite capable of doing all we need when we run down for an occasional week-end. Of course, during the shooting season, we take down some of our own servants from Newmarket. My uncle, Mr Harrington Pace (as you may know, my mother was a Miss Pace of New York), has, for the last three years, made his home with us. He never got on well with my father, or my elder brother, and I suspect that my being somewhat of a prodigal son myself rather increased than diminished his affection towards me. Of course I am a poor man, and my uncle was a rich one—in other words, he paid the piper! But, though exacting in many ways, he was not really hard to get on with, and we all three lived very harmoniously together. Two days ago my uncle, rather wearied with some recent gaieties of ours in town, suggested that we should run down to Derbyshire for a day or two. My wife telegraphed to Mrs Middleton, the housekeeper, and we went down that same afternoon. Yesterday evening I was forced to return to town, but my wife and my uncle remained on. This morning I received this telegram." He handed it over to me:

"Come at once uncle Harrington murdered last night bring good detective if you can but do come—Zoe."

"Then, as yet you know no details?"

"No, I suppose it will be in the evening papers. Without doubt the police are in charge."

It was about three o'clock when we arrived at the little station of Elmer's Dale. From there a five-mile drive brought us to a small grey stone building in the midst of the rugged moors.

"A lonely place," I observed with a shiver.

Havering nodded.

"I shall try and get rid of it. I could never live here again."

We unlatched the gate and were walking up the narrow path to the oak door when a familiar figure emerged and came to meet us.

"Japp!" I ejaculated.

The Scotland Yard inspector grinned at me in a friendly fashion before addressing my companion.

"Mr Havering, I think? I've been sent down from London to take charge of this case, and I'd like a word with you, if I may, sir."

"My wife—"

"I've seen your good lady, sir—and the housekeeper. I won't keep you a moment, but I'm anxious to get back to the village now that I've seen all there is to see here."

"I know nothing as yet as to what—"

"Ex-actly," said Japp soothingly. "But there are just one or two little points I'd like your opinion about all the same. Captain Hastings here, he knows me, and he'll go on up to the house and tell them you're coming. What have you done with the little man, by the way, Captain Hastings?"

"He's ill in bed with influenza."

"Is he now? I'm sorry to hear that. Rather the case of the cart without the horse, your being here without him, isn't it?"

And on his rather ill-timed jest I went on to the house. I rang the bell, as Japp had closed the door behind him. After some moments it was opened to me by a middle-aged woman in black.

"Mr Havering will be here in a moment," I explained. "He has been detained by the inspector. I have come down with him from London to look into the case. Perhaps you can tell me briefly what occurred last night."

"Come inside, sir." She closed the door behind me, and we stood in the dimly-lighted hall. "It was after dinner last night, sir, that the man came. He asked to see Mr Pace, sir, and, seeing that he spoke the same way, I thought it was an American gentleman friend of Mr Pace's and I showed him into the gun-room, and then went to tell Mr Pace. He wouldn't give any name, which, of course, was a bit odd, now I come to think of it. I told Mr Pace, and he seemed puzzled like, but he said to the mistress: 'Excuse me, Zoe, while I just see what this fellow wants.' He went off to the gun-room, and I went back to the kitchen, but after a while I heard loud voices, as if they were quarrelling, and I came out into the hall. At the same time, the mistress she comes out too, and just then there was a shot and then a dreadful silence. We both ran to the gun-room door, but it was locked and we had to go round to the window. It was open, and there inside was Mr Pace, all shot and bleeding."

"What became of the man?"

"He must have got away through the window, sir, before we got to it."

"And then?"

"Mrs Havering sent me to fetch the police. Five miles to walk it was. They came back with me, and the constable he stayed all night, and this morning the police gentleman from London arrived."

"What was this man like who called to see Mr Pace?"

The housekeeper reflected.

"He had a black beard, sir, and was about middle-aged, and had on a light overcoat. Beyond the fact that he spoke like an American I didn't notice much about him."

"I see. Now I wonder if I can see Mrs Havering?"

"She's upstairs, sir. Shall I tell her?"

"If you please. Tell her that Mr Havering is outside with Inspector Japp, and that the gentleman he has brought back with him from London is anxious to speak to her as soon as possible."

"Very good, sir."

I was in a fever of impatience to get at all the facts. Japp had two or three hours' start on me, and his anxiety to be gone made me keen to be close at his heels.

Mrs Havering did not keep me waiting long. In a few minutes I heard a light step descending the stairs, and looked up to see a very handsome young woman coming towards me. She wore a flame-coloured jumper, that set off the slender boyishness of her figure. On her dark head was a little hat of flame-coloured leather. Even the present tragedy could not dim the vitality of her personality.

I introduced myself, and she nodded in quick comprehension.

"Of course I have often heard of you and your colleague, Monsieur Poirot. You have done some wonderful things together, haven't you? It was very clever of my husband to get you so promptly. Now will you ask me questions? That is the easiest way, isn't it, of getting to know all you want to about this dreadful affair?"

"Thank you, Mrs Havering. Now what time was it that this man arrived?"

"It must have been just before nine o'clock. We had finished dinner, and were sitting over our coffee and cigarettes."

"Your husband had already left for London?"

"Yes, he went up by the 6.15."

"Did he go by car to the station, or did he walk?"

"Our own car isn't down here. One came out from the garage in Elmer's Dale to fetch him in time for the train."

"Was Mr Pace quite his usual self?"

"Absolutely. Most normal in every way."

"Now, can you describe this visitor at all?"

"I'm afraid not. I didn't see him. Mrs Middleton showed him straight into the gun-room and then came to tell my uncle."

"What did your uncle say?"

"He seemed rather annoyed, but went off at once. It was about five minutes later that I heard the sound of raised voices. I ran out into the hall and almost collided with Mrs Middleton. Then we heard the shot. The gun-room door was locked on the inside, and we had to go right round the house to the window. Of course that took some time, and the murderer had been able to get well away. My poor uncle"—her voice faltered—"had been shot through the head. I saw at once that he was dead. I sent Mrs Middleton for the police. I was careful to touch nothing in the room but to leave it exactly as I found it."

I nodded approval.

"Now, as to the weapon?"

"Well, I can make a guess at it, Captain Hastings. A pair of revolvers of my husband's were mounted upon the wall. One of them is missing. I pointed this out to the police, and they took the other one away with them. When they have extracted the bullet, I suppose they will know for certain."

"May I go to the gun-room?"

"Certainly. The police have finished with it. But the body has been removed."

She accompanied me to the scene of the crime. At that moment Havering entered the hall, and with a quick apology his wife ran to him. I was left to undertake my investigations alone.

I may as well confess at once that they were rather disappointing. In detective novels clues abound, but here I could find nothing that struck me as out of the ordinary except a large bloodstain on the carpet where I judged the dead man had fallen. I examined everything with painstaking care and took a couple of pictures of the room with my little camera which I had brought with me. I also examined the ground outside the window, but it appeared to have been so heavily trampled underfoot that I judged it was useless to waste time over it. No, I had seen all that Hunter's Lodge had to show me. I must go back to Elmer's Dale and get into touch with Japp. Accordingly I took leave of the Haverings, and was driven off in the car that had brought us up from the station.

I found Japp at the Matlock Arms and he took me forthwith to see the body. Harrington Pace was a small, spare clean-shaven man, typically American in appearance. He had been shot through the back of the head, and the revolver had been discharged at close quarters.

"Turned away for a moment," remarked Japp, "and the other fellow snatched up a revolver and shot him. The one Mrs Havering handed over to us was fully loaded and I suppose the other one was also. Curious what darn fool things people do. Fancy keeping two loaded revolvers hanging up on your wall."

"What do you think of the case?" I asked, as we left the gruesome chamber behind us.

"Well, I'd got my eye on Havering to begin with. Oh, yes!" noting my exclamation of astonishment. "Havering has one or two shady incidents in his past. When he was a boy at Oxford there was some funny business about the signature on one of his father's cheques. All hushed up of course. Then, he's pretty heavily in debt now, and they're the kind of debts he wouldn't like to go to his uncle about, whereas you may be sure the uncle's will would be in his favour. Yes, I'd got my eye on him, and that's why I wanted to speak to him before he saw his wife, but their statements dovetail all right, and I've been to the station and there's no doubt whatever that he left by the 6.15. That gets up to London about 10.30. He went straight to his club, he says, and if that's confirmed all right—why, he couldn't have been shooting his uncle here at nine o'clock in a black beard!"

"Ah, yes, I was going to ask you what you thought about that beard?"

Japp winked.

"I think it grew pretty fast—grew in the five miles from Elmer's Dale to Hunter's Lodge. Americans that I've met are mostly clean-shaven. Yes, it's amongst Mr Pace's American associates that we'll have to look for the murderer. I questioned the housekeeper first, and then her mistress, and their stories agree all right, but I'm sorry Mrs Havering didn't get a look at the fellow. She's a smart woman, and she might have noticed something that would set us on the track."

I sat down and wrote a minute and lengthy account to Poirot. I was able to add various further items of information before I posted the letter.

The bullet had been extracted and was proved to have been fired from a revolver identical with the one held by the police. Furthermore, Mr Havering's movements on the night in question had been checked and verified, and it was proved beyond doubt that he had actually arrived in London by the train in question. And, thirdly, a sensational development had occurred. A city gentleman, living at Ealing, on crossing Haven Green to get to the District Railway Station that morning, had observed a brown-paper parcel stuck between the railings. Opening it, he found that it contained a revolver. He handed the parcel over to the local police station, and before night it was proved to be the one we were in search of, the fellow to that given us by Mrs Havering. One bullet had been fired from it.

All this I added to my report. A wire from Poirot arrived whilst I was at breakfast the following morning:

"Of course black bearded man was not Havering only you or Japp would have such an idea wire me description of housekeeper and what clothes she wore this morning same of Mrs Havering do not waste time taking photographs of interiors they are underexposed and not in the least artistic."

It seemed to me that Poirot's style was unnecessarily facetious. I also fancied he was a shade jealous of my position on the spot with full facilities for handling the case. His request for a description of the clothes worn by the two women appeared to me to be simply ridiculous, but I complied as well as I, a mere man, was able to.

At eleven a reply wire came from Poirot:

"Advise Japp arrest housekeeper before it is too late."

Dumbfounded, I took the wire to Japp. He swore softly under his breath.

"He's the goods, Monsieur Poirot! If he says so, there's something in it. And I hardly noticed the woman. I don't know that I can go so far as arresting her, but I'll have her watched. We'll go up right away, and take another look at her."

But it was too late. Mrs Middleton, that quiet middle-aged woman, who had appeared so normal and respectable, had vanished into thin air. Her box had been left behind. It contained only ordinary wearing apparel. There was no clue in it to her identity, or as to her whereabouts.

From Mrs Havering we elicited all the facts we could:

"I engaged her about three weeks ago when Mrs Emery, our former housekeeper, left. She came to me from Mrs Selbourne's Agency in Mount Street—a very well-known place. I get all my servants from there. They sent several women to see me, but this Mrs Middleton seemed much the nicest, and had splendid references. I engaged her on the spot, and notified the Agency of the fact. I can't believe that there was anything wrong with her. She was such a nice quiet woman."

The thing was certainly a mystery. Whilst it was clear that the woman herself could not have committed the crime, since at the moment the shot was fired Mrs Havering was with her in the hall, nevertheless she must have some connection with the murder, or why should she suddenly take to her heels and bolt? I wired the latest development to Poirot and suggested returning to London and making inquiries at Selbourne's Agency.

Poirot's reply was prompt:

"Useless to inquire at agency they will never have heard of her find out what vehicle took her up to hunters lodge when she first arrived there."

Though mystified, I was obedient. The means of transport in Elmer's Dale were limited. The local garage had two battered Ford cars, and there were two station flies. None of these had been requisitioned on the date in question. Questioned, Mrs Havering explained that she had given the woman the money for her fare down to Derbyshire and sufficient to hire a car or fly to take her up to Hunter's Lodge. There was usually one of the Fords at the station on the chance of its being required. Taking into consideration the further fact that nobody at the station had noticed the arrival of a stranger, black-bearded or otherwise, on the fatal evening, everything seemed to point to the conclusion that the murderer had come to the spot in a car, which had been waiting near at hand to aid his escape, and that the same car had brought the mysterious housekeeper to her new post. I may mention that inquiries at the Agency in London bore out Poirot's prognostication. No such woman as "Mrs Middleton" had ever been on their books. They had received the Hon. Mrs Havering's application for a housekeeper, and had sent her various applicants for the post. When she sent them the engagement fee, she omitted to mention which woman she had selected.

Somewhat crestfallen, I returned to London. I found Poirot established in an arm-chair by the fire in a garish, silk dressing-gown. He greeted me with much affection.

"Mon ami Hastings! But how glad I am to see you. Veritably I have for you a great affection. And you have enjoyed yourself? You have run to and fro with the good Japp? You have interrogated and investigated to your heart's content?"

"Poirot," I cried, "the thing's a dark mystery! It will never be solved."

"It is true that we are not likely to cover ourselves with glory over it."

"No, indeed. It's a hard nut to crack."

"Oh, as far as that goes, I am very good at cracking the nuts! A veritable squirrel! It is not that which embarrasses me. I know well enough who killed Mr Harrington Pace."

"You know? How did you find out?"

"Your illuminating answers to my wires supplied me with the truth. See here, Hastings, let us examine the facts methodically and in order. Mr Harrington Pace is a man with a considerable fortune which at his death will doubtless pass to his nephew. Point No. 1. His nephew is known to be desperately hard up. Point No. 2. His nephew is also known to be—shall we say a man of rather loose moral fibre? Point No. 3."

"But Roger Havering is proved to have journeyed straight up to London."

"Précisément—and therefore, as Mr Havering left Elmer's Dale at 6.15, and since Mr Pace cannot have been killed before he left, or the doctor would have spotted the time of the crime as being given wrongly when he examined the body, we conclude quite rightly, that Mr Havering did not shoot his uncle. But there is a Mrs Havering, Hastings."

"Impossible! The housekeeper was with her when the shot was fired."

"Ah, yes, the housekeeper. But she has disappeared."

"She will be found."

"I think not. There is something peculiarly elusive about that housekeeper, don't you think so, Hastings? It struck me at once."

"She played her part, I suppose, and then got out in the nick of time."

"And what was her part?"

"Well, presumably to admit her confederate, the black-bearded man."

"Oh, no, that was not her part! Her part was what you have just mentioned, to provide an alibi for Mrs Havering at the moment the shot was fired. And no one will ever find her, mon ami, because she does not exist! 'There's no sech person,' as your so great Shakespeare says."

"It was Dickens," I murmured, unable to suppress a smile. "But what do you mean, Poirot?"

"I mean that Zoe Havering was an actress before her marriage, that you and Japp only saw the housekeeper in a dark hall, a dim middle-aged figure in black with a faint subdued voice, and finally that neither you nor Japp, nor the local police whom the housekeeper fetched, ever saw Mrs Middleton and her mistress at one and the same time. It was child's play for that clever and daring woman. On the pretext of summoning her mistress, she runs upstairs, slips on a bright jumper and a hat with black curls attached which she jams down over the grey transformation. A few deft touches, and the make-up is removed, a slight dusting of rouge, and the brilliant Zoe Havering comes down with her clear ringing voice. Nobody looks particularly at the housekeeper.

Why should they? There is nothing to connect her with the crime. She, too, has an alibi."

"But the revolver that was found at Ealing? Mrs Havering could not have placed it there?"

"No, that was Roger Havering's job—but it was a mistake on their part. It put me on the right track. A man who has committed a murder with a revolver which he found on the spot would fling it away at once, he would not carry it up to London with him. No, the motive was clear, the criminals wished to focus the interest of the police on a spot far removed from Derbyshire they were anxious to get the police away as soon as possible from the vicinity of Hunter's Lodge. Of course the revolver found at Ealing was not the one with which Mr Pace was shot. Roger Havering discharged one shot from it, brought it up to London, went straight to his club to establish his alibi, then went quickly out to Ealing by the district, a matter of about twenty minutes only, placed the parcel where it was found and so back to town. That charming creature, his wife, quietly shoots Mr Pace after dinner—you remember he was shot from behind? Another significant point, that!—reloads the revolver and puts it back in its place, and then starts off with her desperate little comedy."

"It's incredible," I murmured, fascinated, "and yet—"

"And yet it is true. Bien sur, my friend, it is true. But to bring that precious pair to justice, that is another matter. Well, Japp must do what he can—I have written him fully—but I very much fear, Hastings, that we shall be obliged to leave them to Fate, or le bon Dieu, whichever you prefer."

"The wicked flourish like a green bay tree," I reminded him.

"But at a price, Hastings, always at a price, croyez-moi!"

Poirot's forebodings were confirmed. Japp, though convinced of the truth of his theory, was unable to get together the necessary evidence to ensure a conviction.

Mr Pace's huge fortune passed into the hands of his murderers. Nevertheless, Nemesis did overtake them, and when I read in the paper that the Hon. Roger and Mrs Havering were amongst those killed in the crashing of the Air Mail to Paris I knew that Justice was satisfied.

~

Agatha Christie (1890–1976) is known throughout the world as the Queen of Crime. Her books have sold over a billion copies. She is the author of eighty crime novels and short-story collections, nineteen plays and six novels written under the pseudonym Mary Westmacott.

From The Count of Monte Cristo

Alexandre Dumas

Through the journey of its main character Edmond Dantès, who is unfairly accused of being a Bonapartist and arrested in Marseilles, The Count of Monte Cristo *explores themes such as justice, betrayal and trust, moving across France, Italy and the Mediterranean islands.*

The King's Closet at the Tuileries

We will leave Villefort on the road to Paris, travelling—thanks to trebled fees—with all speed, and passing through two or three apartments, enter at the Tuileries the little room with the arched window, so well known as having been the favourite closet of Napoleon and Louis XVIII, and now of Louis Philippe.

There, seated before a walnut table he had brought with him from Hartwell, and to which, from one of those fancies not uncommon to great people, he was particularly attached, the king, Louis XVIII, was carelessly listening to a man of fifty or fifty-two years of age, with gray hair, aristocratic bearing, and exceedingly gentlemanly attire, and meanwhile making a marginal note in a volume of Gryphius's rather inaccurate, but much sought-after, edition of Horace—a work which was much indebted to the sagacious observations of the philosophical monarch.

"You say, sir—" said the king.

"That I am exceedingly disquieted, sire."

"Really, have you had a vision of the seven fat kine and the seven lean kine?"

"No, sire, for that would only betoken for us seven years of plenty and seven years of scarcity; and with a king as full of foresight as your majesty, scarcity is not a thing to be feared."

"Then of what other scourge are you afraid, my dear Blacas?"

"Sire, I have every reason to believe that a storm is brewing in the south."

"Well, my dear duke," replied Louis XVIII, "I think you are wrongly informed, and know positively that, on the contrary, it is very fine weather in that direction." Man of ability as he was, Louis XVIII liked a pleasant jest.

"Sire," continued M. de Blacas, "if it only be to reassure a faithful servant, will your majesty send into Languedoc, Provence, and Dauphiné, trusty men, who will bring you back a faithful report as to the feeling in these three provinces?"

"*Canimus surdis*," replied the king, continuing the annotations in his Horace.

"Sire," replied the courtier, laughing, in order that he might seem to comprehend the quotation, "your majesty may be perfectly right in relying on the good feeling of France, but I fear I am not altogether wrong in dreading some desperate attempt."

"By whom?"

"By Bonaparte, or, at least, by his adherents."

"My dear Blacas," said the king, "you with your alarms prevent me from working."

"And you, sire, prevent me from sleeping with your security."

"Wait, my dear sir, wait a moment; for I have such a delightful note on the *Pastor quum traheret*—wait, and I will listen to you afterwards."

There was a brief pause, during which Louis XVIII wrote, in a hand as small as possible, another note on the margin of his Horace, and then looking at the duke with the air of a man who thinks he has an idea of his own, while he is only commenting upon the idea of another, said:

"Go on, my dear duke, go on—I listen."

"Sire," said Blacas, who had for a moment the hope of sacrificing Villefort to his own profit, "I am compelled to tell you that these are not mere rumours destitute of foundation which thus disquiet me; but a serious-minded man, deserving all my confidence, and charged by me to watch over the south" (the duke hesitated as he pronounced these words), "has arrived by post to tell me that a great peril threatens the king, and so I hastened to you, sire."

"*Mala ducis avi domum*," continued Louis XVIII, still annotating.

"Does your majesty wish me to drop the subject?"

"By no means, my dear duke; but just stretch out your hand."

"Which?"

"Whichever you please—there to the left."

"Here, sire?"

"I tell you to the left, and you are looking to the right; I mean on my left—yes, there. You will find yesterday's report of the minister of police. But here is M. Dandré himself;" and M. Dandré, announced by the chamberlain-in-waiting, entered.

"Come in," said Louis XVIII, with repressed smile, "come in, Baron, and tell the duke all you know—the latest news of M. de Bonaparte; do not conceal anything, however serious,—let us see, the Island of Elba is a volcano, and we may expect to have issuing thence flaming and bristling war—*bella, horrida bella*."

M. Dandré leaned very respectfully on the back of a chair with his two hands, and said:

"Has your majesty perused yesterday's report?"

"Yes, yes; but tell the duke himself, who cannot find anything, what the report contains—give him the particulars of what the usurper is doing in his islet."

"Monsieur," said the baron to the duke, "all the servants of his majesty must approve of the latest intelligence which we have from the Island of Elba. Bonaparte—"

M. Dandré looked at Louis XVIII, who, employed in writing a note, did not even raise his head. "Bonaparte," continued the baron, "is mortally wearied, and passes whole days in watching his miners at work at Porto-Longone."

"And scratches himself for amusement," added the king.

"Scratches himself?" inquired the duke, "what does your majesty mean?"

"Yes, indeed, my dear duke. Did you forget that this great man, this hero, this demigod, is attacked with a malady of the skin which worries him to death, *prurigo*?"

"And, moreover, my dear duke," continued the minister of police, "we are almost assured that, in a very short time, the usurper will be insane."

"Insane?"

"Raving mad; his head becomes weaker. Sometimes he weeps bitterly, sometimes laughs boisterously, at other time he passes hours on the seashore, flinging stones in the water and when the flint makes 'duck-and-drake' five or six times, he appears as delighted as if he had gained another Marengo or Austerlitz. Now, you must agree that these are indubitable symptoms of insanity."

"Or of wisdom, my dear baron—or of wisdom," said Louis XVIII, laughing; "the greatest captains of antiquity amused themselves by casting pebbles into the ocean—see Plutarch's life of Scipio Africanus."

M. de Blacas pondered deeply between the confident monarch and the truthful minister. Villefort, who did not choose to reveal the whole secret, lest another should reap all the benefit of the disclosure, had yet communicated enough to cause him the greatest uneasiness.

"Well, well, Dandré," said Louis XVIII, "Blacas is not yet convinced; let us proceed, therefore, to the usurper's conversion." The minister of police bowed.

"The usurper's conversion!" murmured the duke, looking at the king and Dandré, who spoke alternately, like Virgil's shepherds. "The usurper converted!"

"Decidedly, my dear duke."

"In what way converted?"

"To good principles. Tell him all about it, baron."

"Why, this is the way of it," said the minister, with the gravest air in the world: "Napoleon lately had a review, and as two or three of his old veterans expressed a desire to return to France, he gave them their dismissal, and exhorted them to 'serve the good king.' These were his own words, of that I am certain."

"Well, Blacas, what think you of this?" inquired the king triumphantly, and pausing for a moment from the voluminous scholiast before him.

"I say, sire, that the minister of police is greatly deceived or I am; and as it is impossible it can be the minister of police as he has the guardianship of the safety and honour of your majesty, it is probable that I am in error. However, sire, if I might advise, your majesty will interrogate the person of whom I spoke to you, and I will urge your majesty to do him this honour."

"Most willingly, duke; under your auspices I will receive any person you please, but you must not expect me to be too confiding. Baron, have you any report more recent than this, dated 20 February, and this is 3 March?"

"No, sire, but I am hourly expecting one; it may have arrived since I left my office."

"Go thither, and if there be none—well, well," continued Louis XVIII, "make one; that is the usual way, is it not?" and the king laughed facetiously.

"Oh, sire," replied the minister, "we have no occasion to invent any; every day our desks are loaded with most circumstantial denunciations, coming from hosts of people who hope for some return for services which they seek to render, but cannot; they trust to fortune, and rely upon some unexpected event in some way to justify their predictions."

"Well, sir, go," said Louis XVIII, "and remember that I am waiting for you."

"I will but go and return, sire; I shall be back in ten minutes."

"And I, sire," said M. de Blacas, "will go and find my messenger."

"Wait, sir, wait," said Louis XVIII. "Really, M. de Blacas, I must change your armorial bearings; I will give you an eagle with outstretched wings, holding in its claws a prey which tries in vain to escape, and bearing this device—*Tenax*."

"Sire, I listen," said De Blacas, biting his nails with impatience.

"I wish to consult you on this passage, '*Molli fugiens anhelitu*,' you know it refers to a stag flying from a wolf. Are you not a sportsman and a great wolf-hunter? Well, then, what do you think of the *molli anhelitu*?"

"Admirable, sire; but my messenger is like the stag you refer to, for he has posted two hundred and twenty leagues in scarcely three days."

"Which is undergoing great fatigue and anxiety, my dear duke, when we have a telegraph which transmits messages in three or four hours, and that without getting in the least out of breath."

"Ah, sire, you recompense but badly this poor young man, who has come so far, and with so much ardour, to give your majesty useful information. If only for the sake of M. de Salvieux, who recommends him to me, I entreat your majesty to receive him graciously."

"M. de Salvieux, my brother's chamberlain?"

"Yes, sire."

"He is at Marseilles."

"And writes me thence."

"Does he speak to you of this conspiracy?"

"No; but strongly recommends M. de Villefort, and begs me to present him to your majesty."

"M. de Villefort!" cried the king, "is the messenger's name M. de Villefort?"

"Yes, sire."

"And he comes from Marseilles?"

"In person."

"Why did you not mention his name at once?" replied the king, betraying some uneasiness.

"Sire, I thought his name was unknown to your majesty."

"No, no, Blacas; he is a man of strong and elevated understanding, ambitious, too, and, *pardieu!* you know his father's name!"

"His father?"

"Yes, Noirtier."

"Noirtier the Girondin?—Noirtier the senator?"

"He himself."

"And your majesty has employed the son of such a man?"

"Blacas, my friend, you have but limited comprehension. I told you Villefort was ambitious, and to attain this ambition Villefort would sacrifice everything, even his father."

"Then, sire, may I present him?"

"This instant, duke! Where is he?"

"Waiting below, in my carriage."

"Seek him at once."

"I hasten to do so."

The duke left the royal presence with the speed of a young man; his really sincere royalism made him youthful again. Louis XVIII remained alone, and turning his eyes on his half-opened Horace, muttered:

"*Justum et tenacem propositi virum.*"

M. de Blacas returned as speedily as he had departed, but in the antechamber he was forced to appeal to the king's authority. Villefort's dusty garb, his costume, which was not of courtly cut, excited the susceptibility of M. de Brezé, who was all astonishment at finding that this young man had the audacity to enter before the king in such attire. The duke, however, overcame all difficulties with a word—his majesty's order; and, in spite of the protestations which the master of ceremonies made for the honour of his office and principles, Villefort was introduced.

The king was seated in the same place where the duke had left him. On opening the door, Villefort found himself facing him, and the young magistrate's first impulse was to pause.

"Come in, M. de Villefort," said the king, "come in."

Villefort bowed, and advancing a few steps, waited until the king should interrogate him.

"M. de Villefort," said Louis XVIII, "the Duc de Blacas assures me you have some interesting information to communicate."

"Sire, the duke is right, and I believe your majesty will think it equally important."

"In the first place, and before everything else, sir, is the news as bad in your opinion as I am asked to believe?"

"Sire, I believe it to be most urgent, but I hope, by the speed I have used, that it is not irreparable."

"Speak as fully as you please, sir," said the king, who began to give way to the emotion which had showed itself in Blacas's face and affected Villefort's voice. "Speak, sir, and pray begin at the beginning; I like order in everything."

"Sire," said Villefort, "I will render a faithful report to your majesty, but I must entreat your forgiveness if my anxiety leads to some obscurity in my language." A glance at the king after this discreet and subtle exordium, assured Villefort of the benignity of his august auditor, and he went on:

"Sire, I have come as rapidly to Paris as possible, to inform your majesty that I have discovered, in the exercise of my duties, not a commonplace and insignificant plot, such as is every day got up in the lower ranks of the people and in the army, but an actual conspiracy—a storm which menaces no less than your majesty's throne. Sire, the usurper is arming three ships, he meditates some project, which, however mad, is yet, perhaps, terrible. At this moment he will have left Elba, to go whither I know not, but assuredly to attempt a landing either at Naples, or on the coast of Tuscany, or perhaps on the shores of France. Your majesty is well aware that the sovereign of the Island of Elba has maintained his relations with Italy and France?"

"I am, sir," said the king, much agitated; "and recently we have had information that the Bonapartist clubs have had meetings in the Rue Saint-Jacques. But proceed, I beg of you. How did you obtain these details?"

"Sire, they are the results of an examination which I have made of a man of Marseilles, whom I have watched for some time, and arrested on the day of my departure. This person, a sailor, of turbulent character, and whom I suspected of Bonapartism, has been secretly to the Island of Elba. There he saw the grand-marshal, who charged him with an oral message to a Bonapartist in Paris, whose name I could not extract from him; but this mission was to prepare men's minds for a return (it is the man who says this, sire)—a return which will soon occur."

"And where is this man?"

"In prison, sire."

"And the matter seems serious to you?"

"So serious, sire, that when the circumstance surprised me in the midst of a family festival, on the very day of my betrothal, I left my bride and friends, postponing everything, that I might hasten to lay at your majesty's feet the fears which impressed me, and the assurance of my devotion."

"True," said Louis XVIII, "was there not a marriage engagement between you and Mademoiselle de Saint-Méran?"

"Daughter of one of your majesty's most faithful servants."

"Yes, yes; but let us talk of this plot, M. de Villefort."

"Sire, I fear it is more than a plot; I fear it is a conspiracy."

"A conspiracy in these times," said Louis XVIII, smiling, "is a thing very easy to meditate, but more difficult to conduct to an end, inasmuch as, re-established so recently on the throne of our ancestors, we have our eyes open at once upon the past, the present, and the future. For the last ten months my ministers have redoubled their vigilance, in order to watch the shore of the Mediterranean. If Bonaparte landed at Naples, the whole coalition would be on foot before he could even reach Piombino; if he land in Tuscany, he will be in an unfriendly territory; if he land in France, it must be with a handful of men, and the result of that is easily foretold, execrated as he is by the population. Take courage, sir; but at the same time rely on our royal gratitude."

"Ah, here is M. Dandré!" cried de Blacas. At this instant the minister of police appeared at the door, pale, trembling, and as if ready to faint. Villefort was about to retire, but M. de Blacas, taking his hand, restrained him.

~

Alexandre Dumas (1802–1870) was a celebrated French writer best known for his classic novels *The Count of Monte Cristo* and *The Three Musketeers*, which are to this day studied and read widely around the world. In addition to novels spanning the genres of history, adventure and fantasy, Dumas has written plays, journal/magazine articles and travelogues.

From The Tenant of Wildfell Hall

Anne Brontë

Narrated mainly by the farmer Gilbert Markham, The Tenant of Wildfell Hall *is the tale of Helen Graham, an enigmatic tenant who takes up residence at a country house and immediately becomes the talk of the town. The novel is a critique on the patriarchial society of the time.*

You must go back with me to the autumn of 1827.

My father, as you know, was a sort of gentleman farmer; and I, by his express desire, succeeded him in the same quiet occupation, not very willingly, for ambition urged me to higher aims, and self-conceit assured me that, in disregarding its voice, I was burying my talent in the earth, and hiding my light under a bushel. My mother had done her utmost to persuade me that I was capable of great achievements; but my father, who thought ambition was the surest road to ruin, and change but another word for destruction, would listen to no scheme for bettering either my own condition, or that of my fellow mortals. He assured me it was all rubbish, and exhorted me, with his dying breath, to continue in the good old way, to follow his steps, and those of his father before him, and let my highest ambition be to walk honestly through the world, looking neither to the right hand nor to the left, and to transmit the paternal acres to my children in, at least, as flourishing a condition as he left them to me.

"Well! An honest and industrious farmer is one of the most useful members of society; and if I devote my talents to the cultivation of my farm, and the improvement of agriculture in general, I shall thereby benefit, not only my own immediate connections and dependants, but, in some degree, mankind at large—hence I shall not have lived in vain."

With such reflections as these I was endeavouring to console myself, as I plodded home from the fields, one cold, damp, cloudy evening towards the close of October. But the gleam of a bright red fire through the parlour window had more effect in cheering my spirits, and rebuking my thankless repinings, than all the sage reflections and good resolutions I had forced my mind to frame—for I was young then, remember—only four-and-twenty—and had not acquired half the rule over my own spirit that I now possess—trifling as that may be.

However, that haven of bliss must not be entered till I had exchanged my miry boots for a clean pair of shoes, and my rough surtout for a respectable coat, and made myself generally presentable before decent society; for my mother, with all her kindness, was vastly particular on certain points.

In ascending to my room I was met upon the stairs by a smart, pretty girl of nineteen, with a tidy, dumpy figure, a round face, bright, blooming cheeks, glossy, clustering curls, and little merry brown eyes. I need not tell you this was my sister Rose. She is,

I know, a comely matron still, and, doubtless, no less lovely—in *your* eyes—than on the happy day you first beheld her. Nothing told me then that she, a few years hence, would be the wife of one entirely unknown to me as yet, but destined hereafter to become a closer friend than even herself, more intimate than that unmannerly lad of seventeen, by whom I was collared in the passage, on coming down, and well-nigh jerked off my equilibrium, and who, in correction for his impudence, received a resounding whack over the sconce, which, however, sustained no serious injury from the infliction; as, besides being more than commonly thick, it was protected by a redundant shock of short, reddish curls, that my mother called auburn.

On entering the parlour we found that honoured lady seated in her arm-chair at the fireside, working away at her knitting, according to her usual custom, when she had nothing else to do. She had swept the hearth, and made a bright blazing fire for our reception; the servant had just brought in the tea-tray; and Rose was producing the sugar-basin and tea-caddy from the cupboard in the black oak side-board, that shone like polished ebony, in the cheerful parlour twilight.

"Well! Here they both are," cried my mother, looking round upon us without retarding the motion of her nimble fingers and glittering needles. "Now shut the door, and come to the fire, while Rose gets the tea ready; I'm sure you must be starved—and tell me what you've been about all day—I like to know what my children have been about."

"I've been breaking in the grey colt—no easy business that—directing the ploughing of the last wheat stubble—for the ploughboy has not the sense to direct himself—and carrying out a plan for the extensive and efficient draining of the low meadowlands."

"That's my brave boy! And Fergus, what have you been doing?"

"Badger-baiting."

And here he proceeded to give a particular account of his sport, and the respective traits of prowess evinced by the badger and the dogs; my mother pretending to listen with deep attention, and watching his animated countenance with a degree of maternal admiration I thought highly disproportioned to its object.

"It's time you should be doing something else, Fergus," said I, as soon as a momentary pause in his narration allowed me to get in a word.

"What *can* I do?" replied he; "my mother won't let me go to sea or enter the army; and I'm determined to do nothing else—except make myself such a nuisance to you all, that you will be thankful to get rid of me on any terms."

Our parent soothingly stroked his stiff, short curls. He growled, and tried to look sulky, and then we all took our seats at the table, in obedience to the thrice-repeated summons of Rose.

"Now take your tea," said she; "and I'll tell you what *I've* been doing. I've been to call on the Wilsons; and it's a *thousand* pities you didn't go with me, Gilbert, for Eliza Millward was there!"

"Well! What of her?"

"Oh, nothing—I'm not going to tell you about her—only that she's a nice, amusing little thing, when she is in a merry humour, and I shouldn't mind calling her—"

"Hush, hush, my dear! your brother has no such idea!" whispered my mother earnestly, holding up her finger.

"Well," resumed Rose; "I was going to tell you an important piece of news I heard there—I have been bursting with it ever since. You know it was reported a month ago, that somebody was going to take Wildfell Hall—and—what do you think? It has actually been inhabited above a week! And we never knew!"

"Impossible!" cried my mother.

"Preposterous!!!" shrieked Fergus.

"It has indeed—and by a single lady!"

"Good gracious, my dear! The place is in ruins!"

"She has had two or three rooms made habitable; and there she lives, all alone—except an old woman for a servant!"

"Oh, dear! that spoils it—I'd hoped she was a witch," observed Fergus, while carving his inch-thick slice of bread and butter.

"Nonsense, Fergus! But isn't it strange, mamma?"

"Strange! I can hardly believe it."

"But you may believe it; for Jane Wilson has seen her. She went with her mother, who, of course, when she heard of a stranger being in the neighbourhood, would be on pins and needles till she had seen her and got all she could out of her. She is called Mrs Graham, and she is in mourning—not widow's weeds, but slightish mourning—and she is quite young, they say—not above five or six and twenty—but *so* reserved! They tried all they could to find out who she was and where she came from, and, all about her, but neither Mrs Wilson, with her pertinacious and impertinent home-thrusts, nor Miss Wilson, with her skilful manœuvring, could manage to elicit a single satisfactory answer, or even a casual remark, or chance expression calculated to allay their curiosity, or throw the faintest ray of light upon her history, circumstances, or connections. Moreover, she was barely civil to them, and evidently better pleased to say 'good-bye', than 'how do you do'. But Eliza Millward says her father intends to call upon her soon, to offer some pastoral advice, which he fears she needs, as, though she is known to have entered the neighbourhood early last week, she did not make her appearance at church on Sunday; and she—Eliza, that is—will beg to accompany him, and is sure *she* can succeed in wheedling something out of her—you know, Gilbert, *she* can do anything. And *we* should call some time, mamma; it's only proper, you know."

"Of course, my dear. Poor thing! How lonely she must feel!"

"And pray, be quick about it; and mind you bring me word how much sugar she puts in her tea, and what sort of caps and aprons she wears, and all about it; for I don't know how I can live till I know," said Fergus, very gravely.

But if he intended the speech to be hailed as a master-stroke of wit, he signally failed, for nobody laughed. However, he was not much disconcerted at that; for when he had taken a mouthful of bread and butter and was about to swallow a gulp of tea, the humour of the thing burst upon him with such irresistible force, that he was obliged to jump up from the table, and rush snorting and choking from the room; and a minute after, was heard screaming in fearful agony in the garden.

As for me, I was hungry, and contented myself with silently demolishing the tea, ham, and toast, while my mother and sister went on talking, and continued to discuss the apparent or non-apparent circumstances, and probable or improbable history of the mysterious lady; but I must confess that, after my brother's misadventure, I once or twice raised the cup to my lips, and put it down again without daring to taste the contents, lest I should injure my dignity by a similar explosion.

The next day my mother and Rose hastened to pay their compliments to the fair recluse; and came back but little wiser than they went; though my mother declared she did not regret the journey, for if she had not gained much good, she flattered herself she had imparted some, and that was better: she had given some useful advice, which, she hoped, would not be thrown away; for Mrs Graham, though she said little to any purpose, and appeared somewhat self-opinionated, seemed not incapable of reflection—though she did not know where she had been all her life, poor thing, for she betrayed a lamentable ignorance on certain points, and had not even the sense to be ashamed of it.

"On what points, mother?" asked I.

"On household matters, and all the little niceties of cookery, and such things, that every lady ought to be familiar with, whether she be required to make a practical use of her knowledge or not. I gave her some useful pieces of information, however, and several excellent receipts, the value of which she evidently could not appreciate, for she begged I would not trouble myself, as she lived in such a plain, quiet way, that she was sure she should never make use of them. 'No matter, my dear,' said I; 'it is what every respectable female ought to know—and besides, though you are alone now, you will not be always so; you *have* been married, and probably—I might say almost certainly—will be again.' 'You are mistaken there, ma'am,' said she, almost haughtily; 'I am certain I never shall.'—But I told her *I* knew better."

"Some romantic young widow, I suppose," said I, "come there to end her days in solitude, and mourn in secret for the dear departed—but it won't last long."

"No, I think not," observed Rose; "for she didn't seem *very* disconsolate after all; and she's excessively pretty—handsome rather—you must see her, Gilbert; you will call her a perfect beauty, though you could hardly pretend to discover a resemblance between her and Eliza Millward."

"Well, I can imagine many faces more beautiful than Eliza's, though not more charming. I allow she has small claims to perfection; but then, I maintain that, if she were more perfect, she would be less interesting."

"And so you prefer her faults to other people's perfections?"

"Just so—saving my mother's presence."

"Oh, my dear Gilbert, what nonsense you talk!—I know you don't mean it; it's quite out of the question," said my mother, getting up, and bustling out of the room, under pretence of household business, in order to escape the contradiction that was trembling on my tongue.

After that Rose favoured me with further particulars respecting Mrs Graham. Her appearance, manners, and dress, and the very furniture of the room she inhabited, were all set before me, with rather more clearness and precision than I cared to see them; but, as I was not a very attentive listener, I could not repeat the description if I would.

The next day was Saturday; and, on Sunday, everybody wondered whether or not the fair unknown would profit by the vicar's remonstrance, and come to church. I confess I looked with some interest myself towards the old family pew, appertaining to Wildfell Hall, where the faded crimson cushions and lining had been unpressed and unrenewed so many years, and the grim escutcheons, with their lugubrious borders of rusty black cloth, frowned so sternly from the wall above.

And there I beheld a tall, lady-like figure, clad in black. Her face was towards me, and there was something in it which, once seen, invited me to look again. Her hair was raven black, and disposed in long glossy ringlets, a style of coiffure rather unusual in those days, but always graceful and becoming; her complexion was clear and pale; her eyes I could not see, for, being bent upon her prayer-book, they were concealed by their drooping lids and long black lashes, but the brows above were expressive and well defined; the forehead was lofty and intellectual, the nose, a perfect aquiline and the features, in general, unexceptionable—only there was a slight hollowness about the cheeks and eyes, and the lips, though finely formed, were a little too thin, a little too firmly compressed, and had something about them that betokened, I thought, no very soft or amiable temper; and I said in my heart—"I would rather admire you from this distance, fair lady, than be the partner of your home."

Just then she happened to raise her eyes, and they met mine; I did not choose to withdraw my gaze, and she turned again to her book, but with a momentary, indefinable expression of quiet scorn, that was inexpressibly provoking to me.

"She thinks me an impudent puppy," thought I. "Humph—she shall change her mind before long, if I think it worth while."

But then it flashed upon me that these were very improper thoughts for a place of worship, and that my behaviour, on the present occasion, was anything but what it ought to be. Previous, however, to directing my mind to the service, I glanced round the church to see if any one had been observing me;—but no,—all, who were not attending to their prayer-books, were attending to the strange lady,—my good mother and sister among the rest, and Mrs Wilson and her daughter; and even Eliza Millward was slily glancing from the corners of her eyes towards the object of general attraction. Then she glanced at me, simpered a little, and blushed, modestly looked at her prayer-book, and endeavoured to compose her features.

Here I was transgressing again; and this time I was made sensible of it by a sudden dig in the ribs, from the elbow of my pert brother. For the present, I could only resent the insult by pressing my foot upon his toes, deferring further vengeance till we got out of church.

Now, Halford, before I close this letter, I'll tell you who Eliza Millward was: she was the vicar's younger daughter, and a very engaging little creature, for whom I felt no small degree of partiality;—and she knew it, though I had never come to any direct explanation, and had no definite intention of so doing, for my mother, who maintained there was no one good enough for me within twenty miles round, could not bear the thoughts of my marrying that insignificant little thing, who, in addition to her numerous other disqualifications, had not twenty pounds to call her own. Eliza's figure was at once slight and plump, her face small, and nearly as round as my sister's—complexion, something similar to hers, but more delicate and less decidedly blooming—nose, *retroussé*—features, generally irregular; and, altogether, she was rather charming than pretty. But her eyes—I must not forget those remarkable features, for therein her chief attraction lay—in outward aspect at least—they were long and narrow in shape, the irids black, or very dark brown, the expression various, and ever changing, but always either preternaturally—I had almost said *diabolically*—wicked, or irresistibly bewitching—often both. Her voice was gentle and childish, her tread light and soft as that of a cat—but her manners more frequently resembled those of a pretty playful kitten, that is now pert and roguish, now timid and demure, according to its own sweet will.

Her sister, Mary, was several years older, several inches taller, and of a larger, coarser build—a plain, quiet, sensible girl, who had patiently nursed their mother, through her last long, tedious illness, and been the housekeeper, and family drudge, from thence to the present time. She was trusted and valued by her father, loved and courted by all dogs, cats, children, and poor people, and slighted and neglected by everybody else.

The Reverend Michael Millward himself was a tall, ponderous elderly gentleman, who placed a shovel hat above his large, square, massive-featured face, carried a stout walking-stick in his hand, and incased his still powerful limbs in knee-breeches and gaiters—or black silk stockings on state occasions. He was a man of fixed principles, strong prejudices, and regular habits, intolerant of dissent in any shape, acting under a firm conviction that *his* opinions were always right, and whoever differed from them must be either most deplorably ignorant, or wilfully blind.

In childhood, I had always been accustomed to regard him with a feeling of reverential awe—but lately, even now, surmounted, for, though he had a fatherly kindness for the well-behaved, he was a strict disciplinarian, and had often sternly reproved our juvenile failings and peccadilloes; and moreover, in those days, whenever he called upon our parents, we had to stand up before him, and say our catechism, or repeat, "How doth the little busy bee," or some other hymn, or—worse than all—be questioned about his last text, and the heads of the discourse, which we never could remember. Sometimes, the worthy gentleman would reprove my mother for being over-indulgent to her sons, with a reference to old Eli, or David and Absalom, which was particularly galling to her feelings; and, very highly as she respected him, and all his sayings, I once heard her exclaim, "I wish to goodness he had a son himself! He wouldn't be so ready with his advice to other people then—he'd see what it is to have a couple of boys to keep in order."

He had a laudable care for his own bodily health—kept very early hours, regularly took a walk before breakfast, was vastly particular about warm and dry clothing, had never been known to preach a sermon without previously swallowing a raw egg—albeit he was gifted with good lungs and a powerful voice—and was, generally, extremely particular about what he ate and drank, though by no means abstemious, and having a mode of dietary peculiar to himself—being a great despiser of tea and such slops, and a patron of malt liquors, bacon and eggs, ham, hung beef, and other strong meats, which agreed well enough with his digestive organs, and therefore were maintained by him to be good and wholesome for everybody, and confidently recommended to the most delicate convalescents or dyspeptics, who, if they failed to derive the promised benefit from his prescriptions, were told it was because they had not persevered, and if they complained of inconvenient results therefrom, were assured it was all fancy.

I will just touch upon two other persons whom I have mentioned, and then bring this long letter to a close. These are Mrs Wilson and her daughter. The former was the widow of a substantial farmer, a narrow-minded, tattling old gossip, whose character is not worth describing. She had two sons, Robert, a rough countrified farmer, and Richard, a retiring, studious young man, who was studying the classics with the vicar's assistance, preparing for college, with a view to enter the church.

Their sister Jane was a young lady of some talents, and more ambition. She had, at her own desire, received a regular boarding-school education, superior to what any member of the family had obtained before. She had taken the polish well, acquired considerable elegance of manners, quite lost her provincial accent, and could boast of more accomplishments than the vicar's daughters. She was considered a beauty besides; but never for a moment could she number me amongst her admirers. She was about six and twenty, rather tall and very slender, her hair was neither chestnut nor auburn, but a most decided bright, light red; her complexion was remarkably fair and brilliant, her head small, neck long, chin well turned, but very short, lips thin and red, eyes clear hazel, quick, and penetrating, but entirely destitute of poetry or feeling. She had, or might have had, many suitors in her own rank of life, but scornfully repulsed or rejected them all; for none but a gentleman could please her refined taste, and none but a rich one could satisfy her soaring ambition. One gentleman there was, from whom she had lately received some rather pointed attentions, and upon whose heart, name, and fortune, it was whispered, she had serious designs. This was Mr Lawrence, the young squire, whose family had formerly occupied Wildfell Hall, but had deserted it, some fifteen years ago, for a more modern and commodious mansion in the neighbouring parish.

Now, Halford, I bid you adieu for the present. This is the first instalment of my debt. If the coin suits you, tell me so, and I'll send you the rest at my leisure: if you would rather remain my creditor than stuff your purse with such ungainly, heavy pieces—tell me still, and I'll pardon your bad taste, and willingly keep the treasure to myself.

Yours immutably,

GILBERT MARKHAM

~

The youngest of the Brontë sisters, Anne Brontë (1820–1849) was an English poet and novelist best known for her works of fiction *Agnes Grey*, *The Professor* and *The Tenant of Wildfell Hall*, and has contributed to several works of poetry. She is lauded for her honest, realistic characters and feminist, progressive writing.

The Lottery Ticket

Anton Chekhov

Ivan Dmitritch, a middle-class man who lived with his family on an income of twelve hundred a year and was very well satisfied with his lot, sat down on the sofa after supper and began reading the newspaper.

"I forgot to look at the newspaper today," his wife said to him as she cleared the table. "Look and see whether the list of drawings is there."

"Yes, it is," said Ivan Dmitritch; "but hasn't your ticket lapsed?"

"No; I took the interest on Tuesday."

"What is the number?"

"Series 9,499, number 26."

"All right... we will look... 9,499 and 26."

Ivan Dmitritch had no faith in lottery luck, and would not, as a rule, have consented to look at the lists of winning numbers, but now, as he had nothing else to do and as the newspaper was before his eyes, he passed his finger downwards along the column of numbers. And immediately, as though in mockery of his scepticism, no further than the second line from the top, his eye was caught by the figure 9,499! Unable to believe his eyes, he hurriedly dropped the paper on his knees without looking to see the number of the ticket, and, just as though some one had given him a douche of cold water, he felt an agreeable chill in the pit of the stomach; tingling and terrible and sweet!

"Masha, 9,499 is there!" he said in a hollow voice.

His wife looked at his astonished and panic-stricken face, and realized that he was not joking.

"9,499?" she asked, turning pale and dropping the folded tablecloth on the table.

"Yes, yes... it really is there!"

"And the number of the ticket?"

"Oh, yes! There's the number of the ticket too. But stay... wait! No, I say! Anyway, the number of our series is there! Anyway, you understand..."

Looking at his wife, Ivan Dmitritch gave a broad, senseless smile, like a baby when a bright object is shown it. His wife smiled too; it was as pleasant to her as to him that he only mentioned the series, and did not try to find out the number of the winning ticket. To torment and tantalize oneself with hopes of possible fortune is so sweet, so thrilling!

"It is our series," said Ivan Dmitritch, after a long silence. "So there is a probability that we have won. It's only a probability, but there it is!"

"Well, now look!"

"Wait a little. We have plenty of time to be disappointed. It's on the second line from the top, so the prize is seventy-five thousand. That's not money, but power, capital! And in a minute I shall look at the list, and there—26! Eh? I say, what if we really have won?"

The husband and wife began laughing and staring at one another in silence. The possibility of winning bewildered them; they could not have said, could not have dreamed, what they both needed that seventy-five thousand for, what they would buy, where they would go. They thought only of the figures 9,499 and 75,000 and pictured them in their imagination, while somehow they could not think of the happiness itself which was so possible.

Ivan Dmitritch, holding the paper in his hand, walked several times from corner to corner, and only when he had recovered from the first impression began dreaming a little.

"And if we have won," he said—"why, it will be a new life, it will be a transformation! The ticket is yours, but if it were mine I should, first of all, of course, spend twenty-five thousand on real property in the shape of an estate; ten thousand on immediate expenses, new furnishing... travelling... paying debts, and so on... The other forty thousand I would put in the bank and get interest on it."

"Yes, an estate, that would be nice," said his wife, sitting down and dropping her hands in her lap.

"Somewhere in the Tula or Oryol provinces... In the first place we shouldn't need a summer villa, and besides, it would always bring in an income."

And pictures came crowding on his imagination, each more gracious and poetical than the last. And in all these pictures he saw himself well-fed, serene, healthy, felt warm, even hot! Here, after eating a summer soup, cold as ice, he lay on his back on the burning sand close to a stream or in the garden under a lime-tree... It is hot... His little boy and girl are crawling about near him, digging in the sand or catching ladybirds in the grass.

He dozes sweetly, thinking of nothing, and feeling all over that he need not go to the office today, tomorrow, or the day after. Or, tired of lying still, he goes to the hayfield, or to the forest for mushrooms, or watches the peasants catching fish with a net. When the sun sets he takes a towel and soap and saunters to the bathing-shed, where he undresses at his leisure, slowly rubs his bare chest with his hands, and goes into the water. And in the water, near the opaque soapy circles, little fish flit to and fro and green water-weeds nod their heads. After bathing there is tea with cream and milk rolls... In the evening a walk or *vint* with the neighbours.

"Yes, it would be nice to buy an estate," said his wife, also dreaming, and from her face it was evident that she was enchanted by her thoughts.

Ivan Dmitritch pictured to himself autumn with its rains, its cold evenings, and its St. Martin's summer. At that season he would have to take longer walks about the garden and beside the river, so as to get thoroughly chilled, and then drink a big glass of vodka and eat a salted mushroom or a soused cucumber, and then—drink another... The children would come running from the kitchen-garden, bringing a carrot and a radish smelling of fresh earth... And then, he would lie stretched full length on the sofa, and in leisurely fashion turn over the pages of some illustrated magazine, or, covering his face with it and unbuttoning his waistcoat, give himself up to slumber.

The St. Martin's summer is followed by cloudy, gloomy weather. It rains day and night, the bare trees weep, the wind is damp and cold. The dogs, the horses, the fowls—all are wet, depressed, downcast. There is nowhere to walk; one can't go out for days together; one has to pace up and down the room, looking despondently at the grey window. It is dreary!

Ivan Dmitritch stopped and looked at his wife.

"I should go abroad, you know, Masha," he said.

And he began thinking how nice it would be in late autumn to go abroad somewhere to the South of France... to Italy... to India!

"I should certainly go abroad too," his wife said. "But look at the number of the ticket!"

"Wait, wait!"

He walked about the room and went on thinking. It occurred to him: what if his wife really did go abroad? It is pleasant to travel alone, or in the society of light, careless women who live in the present, and not such as think and talk all the journey about nothing but their children, sigh, and tremble with dismay over every farthing. Ivan Dmitritch imagined his wife in the train with a multitude of parcels, baskets, and bags; she would be sighing over something, complaining that the train made her head ache, that she had spent so much money... At the stations he would continually be having to run for boiling water, bread and butter... She wouldn't have dinner because of its being too dear...

"She would begrudge me every farthing," he thought, with a glance at his wife. "The lottery ticket is hers, not mine! Besides, what is the use of her going abroad? What does she want there? She would shut herself up in the hotel, and not let me out of her sight... I know!"

And for the first time in his life his mind dwelt on the fact that his wife had grown elderly and plain, and that she was saturated through and through with the smell of cooking, while he was still young, fresh, and healthy, and might well have got married again.

"Of course, all that is silly nonsense," he thought; "but... why should she go abroad? What would she make of it? And yet she would go, of course... I can fancy... In reality it is all one to her, whether it is Naples or Klin. She would only be in my way. I should be dependent upon her. I can fancy how, like a regular woman, she will lock the money up as soon as she gets it... She will hide it from me... She will look after her relations and grudge me every farthing."

Ivan Dmitritch thought of her relations. All those wretched brothers and sisters and aunts and uncles would come crawling about as soon as they heard of the winning ticket, would begin whining like beggars, and fawning upon them with oily, hypocritical smiles. Wretched, detestable people! If they were given anything, they would ask for more; while if they were refused, they would swear at them, slander them, and wish them every kind of misfortune.

Ivan Dmitritch remembered his own relations, and their faces, at which he had looked impartially in the past, struck him now as repulsive and hateful.

"They are such reptiles!" he thought.

And his wife's face, too, struck him as repulsive and hateful. Anger surged up in his heart against her, and he thought malignantly:

"She knows nothing about money, and so she is stingy. If she won it she would give me a hundred roubles, and put the rest away under lock and key."

And he looked at his wife, not with a smile now, but with hatred. She glanced at him too, and also with hatred and anger. She had her own daydreams, her own plans, her own reflections; she understood perfectly well what her husband's dreams were. She knew who would be the first to try and grab her winnings.

"It's very nice making daydreams at other people's expense!" is what her eyes expressed. "No, don't you dare!"

Her husband understood her look; hatred began stirring again in his breast, and in order to annoy his wife he glanced quickly, to spite her at the fourth page on the newspaper and read out triumphantly:

"Series 9,499, number 46! Not 26!"

Hatred and hope both disappeared at once, and it began immediately to seem to Ivan Dmitritch and his wife that their rooms were dark and small and low-pitched, that the supper they had been eating was not doing them good, but lying heavy on their stomachs, that the evenings were long and wearisome...

"What the devil's the meaning of it?" said Ivan Dmitritch, beginning to be ill-humoured. "Wherever one steps there are bits of paper under one's feet, crumbs, husks. The rooms are never swept! One is simply forced to go out. Damnation take my soul entirely! I shall go and hang myself on the first aspen-tree!"

~

Anton Chekhov (1860–1904) was a Russian writer who is considered a master of the short story form. He also wrote plays such as *The Cherry Orchard*, *Uncle Vanya* and *The Seagull*. He once famously said that when writing a story, every detail included must be essential: if a gun appears, it must eventually be fired. This principle is now known as Chekhov's Gun.

From The Poison Tree

Bankim Chandra Chatterjee

The Poison Tree *is a novel set in the rural Bengal of the late nineteenth century. The story revolves around zamindars Nagendra and his wife Surja Mukhi and the challenges they face as they navigate love, loss and duty in the traditional Bengali society of the time.*

Nagendra's Journey by Boat

Nagendra Natha Datta is about to travel by boat. It is the month Joisto (May–June), the time of storms. His wife, Surja Mukhi, had adjured him, saying, "Be careful; if a storm arises be sure you fasten the boat to the shore. Do not remain in the boat." Nagendra had consented to this, otherwise Surja Mukhi would not have permitted him to leave home; and unless he went to Calcutta his suits in the Courts would not prosper.

Nagendra Natha was a young man, about thirty years of age, a wealthy *zemindar* (landholder) in Zillah Govindpur. He dwelt in a small village which we shall call Haripur. He was travelling in his own boat. The first day or two passed without obstacle. The river flowed smoothly on—leaped, danced, cried out, restless, unending, playful. On shore, herdsmen were grazing their oxen—one sitting under a tree singing, another smoking, some fighting, others eating. Inland, husbandmen were driving the plough, beating the oxen, lavishing abuse upon them, in which the owner shared. The wives of the husbandmen, bearing vessels of water, some carrying a torn quilt, or a dirty mat, wearing a silver amulet round the neck, a ring in the nose, bracelets of brass on the arm, with unwashed garments, their skins blacker than ink, their hair unkempt, formed a chattering crowd. Among them one beauty was rubbing her head with mud, another beating a child, a third speaking with a neighbour in abuse of some nameless person, a fourth beating clothes on a plank. Further on, ladies from respectable villages adorned the *ghâts* (landing-steps) with their appearance—the elders conversing, the middle-aged worshipping *Siva*, the younger covering their faces and plunging into the water; the boys and girls screaming, playing with mud, stealing the flowers offered in worship, swimming, throwing water over every one, sometimes stepping up to a lady, snatching away the image of *Siva* from her, and running off with it. The Brahmans, good tranquil men, recited the praises of *Ganga* (the sacred river Ganges) and performed their worship, sometimes, as they wiped their streaming hair, casting glances at the younger women.

In the sky, the white clouds float in the heated air. Below them fly the birds, like black dots. In the coconut trees, kites, like ministers of state, look around to see on what they can pounce; the cranes, being only small fry, stand raking in the mud; the *dahuk* (coloured herons), merry creatures, dive in the water; other birds of a lighter kind merely fly about. Market-boats sail along at good speed on their own behalf; ferry-boats creep along at elephantine pace to serve the needs of others only: cargo boats make no progress at all—that is the owners' concern.

On the third day of Nagendra's journey clouds arose and gradually covered the sky. The river became black, the tree-tops drooped, the paddy birds flew aloft, the water became motionless. Nagendra ordered the *manji* (boatman) to run the boat in shore and make it fast. At that moment the steersman, Rahamat Mullah, was saying his prayers, so he made no answer. Rahamat knew nothing of his business. His mother's father's sister was the daughter of a boatman; on that plea he had become a hanger-on of boatmen, and accident favoured his wishes; but he learned nothing, his work was done as fate willed. Rahamat was not backward in speech, and when his prayers were ended he turned to the Babu and said, "Do not be alarmed, sir, there is no cause for fear." Rahamat was thus brave because the shore was close at hand, and could be reached without delay, and in a few minutes the boat was secured.

Surely the gods must have had a quarrel with Rahamat Mullah, for a great storm came up quickly. First came the wind; then the wind, having wrestled for some moments with the boughs of the trees, called to its brother the rain, and the two began a fine game. Brother Rain, mounting on brother Wind's shoulders, flew along. The two together, seizing the tree-tops, bent them down, broke the boughs, tore off the creepers, washed away the flowers, cast up the river in great waves, and made a general tumult. One brother flew off with Rahamat Mullah's head-gear; the other made a fountain of his beard. The boatmen lowered the sail, the Babu closed the windows, and the servants put the furniture under shelter.

Nagendra was in a great strait. If, in fear of the storm, he should leave the boat, the men would think him a coward; if he remained he would break his word to Surja Mukhi. Some may ask, What harm if he did? We know not, but Nagendra thought it harm. At this moment Rahamat Mullah said, "Sir, the rope is old; I do not know what may happen. The storm has much increased; it will be well to leave the boat." Accordingly Nagendra got out.

No one can stand on the river bank without shelter in a heavy storm of rain. There was no sign of abatement; therefore Nagendra, thinking it necessary to seek for shelter, set out to walk to the village, which was at some distance from the river, through miry paths. Presently the rain ceased, the wind abated slightly, but the sky was still thickly covered with clouds; therefore both wind and rain might be expected at night. Nagendra went on, not turning back.

Though it was early in the evening, there was thick darkness, because of the clouds. There was no sign of village, house, plain, road, or river; but the trees, being surrounded by myriads of fireflies, looked like artificial trees studded with diamonds. The lightning goddess also still sent quick flashes through the now silent black and white clouds. A woman's anger does not die away suddenly. The assembled frogs, rejoicing in the newly fallen rain, held high festival; and if you listened attentively the voice of the cricket might be heard, like the undying crackle of Ravana's funeral pyre. Amid the sounds might be distinguished the fall of the rain-drops on the leaves of the trees, and that of the leaves into the pools beneath; the noise of jackals' feet on the wet paths, occasionally that of the birds on the trees shaking the water from their drenched feathers, and now and then the moaning of the almost subdued wind. Presently Nagendra saw a light in the distance. Traversing the flooded earth, drenched by the drippings from the trees, and frightening away the jackals, he approached the light; and on nearing it with much difficulty, saw that it proceeded from an old brick-built house, the door of which was open. Leaving his servant outside, Nagendra entered the house, which he found in a frightful condition.

It was not quite an ordinary house, but it had no sign of prosperity. The door-frames were broken and dirty; there was no trace of human occupation—only owls, mice, reptiles, and insects gathered there. The light came only from one side. Nagendra saw some articles of furniture for human use; but everything indicated poverty. One or two cooking vessels, a broken oven, three or four brass dishes—these were the sole ornaments of the place. The walls were black; spiders' webs hung in the corners; cockroaches, spiders, lizards, and mice, scampered about everywhere. On a dilapidated bedstead lay an old man who seemed to be at death's door; his eyes were sunk, his breath hurried, his lips trembling. By the side of his bed stood an earthen lamp upon a fragment of brick taken from the ruins of the house. In it the oil was deficient; so also was it in the body of the man. Another lamp shone by the bedside—a girl of faultlessly fair face, of soft, starry beauty.

Whether because the light from the oil-less lamp was dim, or because the two occupants of the house were absorbed in thinking of their approaching separation, Nagendra's entrance was unseen. Standing in the doorway, he heard the last sorrowful words that issued from the mouth of the old man. These two, the old man and the young girl, were friendless in this densely peopled world. Once they had had wealth, relatives, men and maid servants—abundance of all kinds; but by the fickleness of fortune, one after another, all had gone. The mother of the family, seeing the faces of her son and daughter daily fading like the dew-drenched lotus from the pinch of poverty, had early sunk upon the bed of death. All the other stars had been extinguished with that moon. The support of the race, the jewel of his mother's eye, the hope of his father's age, even he had been laid on the pyre before his father's eyes. No one remained save the old man and this enchanting girl. They dwelt in this ruined, deserted house in the midst of the forest. Each was to the other the only helper.

Kunda Nandini was of marriageable age; but she was the staff of her father's blindness, his only bond to this world. While he lived he could give her up to no one. "There are but a few more days; if I give away Kunda where can I abide?" were the old man's thoughts when the question of giving her in marriage arose in his mind. Had it never occurred to him to ask himself what would become of Kunda when his summons came? Now the messenger of death stood at his bedside; he was about to leave the world; where would Kunda be on the morrow?

The deep, indescribable suffering of this thought expressed itself in every failing breath. Tears streamed from his eyes, ever restlessly closing and opening, while at his head sat the thirteen-year-old girl, like a stone figure, firmly looking into her father's face, covered with the shadows of death. Forgetting herself, forgetting to think where she would go on the morrow, she gazed only on the face of her departing parent. Gradually the old man's utterance became obscure, the breath left the throat, the eyes lost their light, the suffering soul obtained release from pain. In that dark place, by that glimmering lamp, the solitary Kunda Nandini, drawing her father's dead body on to her lap, remained sitting. The night was extremely dark; even now rain-drops fell, the leaves of the trees rustled, the wind moaned, the windows of the ruined house flapped noisily. In the house, the fitful light of the lamp flickered momentarily on the face of the dead, and again left it in darkness. The lamp had long been exhausted of oil; now, after two or three flashes, it went out. Then Nagendra, with noiseless steps, went forth from the doorway.

Coming Events Cast Their Shadows Before

It was night. In the ruined house Kunda Nandini sat by her father's corpse. She called "Father!" No one made reply. At one moment Kunda thought her father slept, again that he was dead, but she could not bring that thought clearly into her mind. At length she could no longer call, no longer think. The fan still moved in her hand in the direction where her father's once living body now lay dead. At length she resolved that he slept, for if he were dead what would become of her?

After days and nights of watching amid such sorrow, sleep fell upon her. In that exposed, bitterly cold house, the palm-leaf fan in her hand, Kunda Nandini rested her head upon her arm, more beauteous than the lotus-stalk, and slept; and in her sleep she saw a vision. It seemed as if the night were bright and clear, the sky of a pure blue—that glorious blue when the moon is encircled by a halo. Kunda had never seen the halo so large as it seemed in her vision. The light was splendid, and refreshing to the eyes. But in the midst of that magnificent halo there was no moon; in its place Kunda saw the figure of a goddess of unparalleled brilliance. It seemed as if this brilliant goddess-ruled halo left the upper sky and descended gradually lower, throwing out a thousand rays of light, until it stood over Kunda's head. Then she saw that the central beauty, crowned with golden hair, and decked with jewels, had the form of a woman. The beautiful, compassionate face had a loving smile upon its lips. Kunda recognized, with mingled joy and fear, in this compassionate being the features of her long-dead mother. The shining, loving being, raising Kunda from the earth, took her into her bosom, and the orphan girl could for a long period do nought but utter the sweet word "Mother!"

Then the shining figure, kissing Kunda's face, said to her: "Child, thou hast suffered much, and I know thou hast yet more to suffer; thou so young, thy tender frame cannot endure such sorrow. Therefore abide not here; leave the earth and come with me."

Kunda seemed to reply: "Whither shall I go?"

Then the mother, with uplifted finger indicating the shining constellations, answered, "There!"

Kunda seemed, in her dream, to gaze into the timeless, shoreless ocean of stars, and to say, "I have no strength; I cannot go so far."

Hearing this, the mother's kind and cheerful but somewhat grave face saddened, her brows knitted a little, as she said in grave, sweet tones:

"Child, follow thy own will, but it would be well for thee to go with me. The day will come when thou wilt gaze upon the stars, and long bitterly to go thither. I will once more appear to thee; when, bowed to the dust with affliction, thou rememberest me, and weepest to come to me, I will return. Then do thou come. But now do thou, looking on the horizon, follow the design of my finger. I will show thee two human figures. These two beings are in this world the arbiters of thy destiny. If possible, when thou meetest them turn away as from venomous snakes. In their paths walk thou not."

Then the shining figure pointed to the opposite sky. Kunda, following the indication, saw traced on the blue vault the figure of a man more beautiful than a god. Beholding his high, capacious forehead, his sincere kindly glance, his swan-like neck a little bent, and other traits of a fine man, no one would have believed that from him there was anything to be feared.

Then the figure dissolving as a cloud in the sky, the mother said—

"Forget not this god-like form. Though benevolent, he will be the cause of thy misery; therefore avoid him as a snake."

Again pointing to the heavens she continued—

"Look hither."

Kunda, looking, saw a second figure sketched before her, not this time that of a man, but a young woman of bright complexion and lotus-shaped eyes. At this sight she felt no fear; but the mother said—

"This dark figure in a woman's dress is a *Rakshasi*. When thou seest her, flee from her."

As she thus spoke the heavens suddenly became dark, the halo disappeared from the sky, and with it the bright figure in its midst.

Then Kunda awoke from her sleep.

Nagendra went to the village, the name of which he heard was Jhunjhunpur. At his recommendation and expense, some of the villagers performed the necessary rites for the dead, one of the female neighbours remaining with the bereaved girl. When Kunda saw that they had taken her father away, she became convinced of his death, and gave way to ceaseless weeping.

In the morning the neighbour returned to her own house, but sent her daughter Champa to comfort Kunda Nandini.

Champa was of the same age as Kunda, and her friend. She strove to divert her mind by talking of various matters, but she saw that Kunda did not attend. She wept constantly, looking up every now and then into the sky as though in expectation.

Champa jestingly asked, "What do you see that you look into the sky a hundred times?"

Kunda replied, "My mother appeared to me yesterday, and bade me go with her, but I feared to do so; now I mourn that I did not. If she came again I would go: therefore I look constantly into the sky."

Champa said, "How can the dead return?"

To which Kunda replied by relating her vision.

Greatly astonished, Champa asked, "Are you acquainted with the man and woman whose forms you saw in the sky?"

"No, I had never seen them. There cannot be anywhere a man so handsome; I never saw such beauty."

On rising in the morning, Nagendra inquired of the people in the village what would become of the dead man's daughter, where she would live, and whether she had any relatives. He was told that there was no dwelling-place for her, and that she had no relatives.

Then Nagendra said, "Will not some of you receive her and give her in marriage? I will pay the expense, and so long as she remains amongst you I will pay so much a month for her board and lodging."

If he had offered ready money many would have consented to his proposal; but after he had gone away Kunda would have been reduced to servitude, or turned out of the house. Nagendra did not act in so foolish a manner; therefore, money not being forthcoming, no one consented to his suggestion.

At length one, seeing him at the end of his resources, observed: "A sister of her mother's lives at Sham Bazar; Binod Ghosh is the husband's name. You are on you way to Calcutta; if you take her with you and place her with her aunt, then this *Kaystha* girl will be cared for, and you will have done your duty to your caste."

Seeing no other plan, Nagendra adopted this suggestion, and sent for Kunda to acquaint her with the arrangement.

Champa accompanied Kunda. As they were coming, Kunda, seeing Nagendra from afar, suddenly stood still like one stunned.

Her feet refused to move; she stood looking at him with eyes full of astonishment.

Champa asked, "Why do you stand thus?"

Kunda, pointing with her finger, said, "It is he!"

"He! Who?" said Champa.

"He whom last night my mother pictured in the heavens."

Then Champa also stood frightened and astonished. Seeing that the girls shrank from approaching, Nagendra came near and explained everything. Kunda was unable to reply; she could only gaze with eyes full of surprise.

~

Bankim Chandra Chatterjee (1838–1894) was a Bengali novelist, essayist, poet and thinker. His popular works include *Anandamath* and *The Posion Tree*, originally written in Bengali, and *Rajmohan's Wife*, a novella written in English. He is also the writer of Vande Mātaram, the national song of India, which appears in *Anandamath*.

The Tale Of Peter Rabbit

Beatrix Potter

Once upon a time there were four little Rabbits, and their names were—Flopsy, Mopsy, Cottontail, and Peter.

They lived with their Mother in a sand-bank, underneath the root of a very big fir tree.

"Now, my dears," said old Mrs Rabbit one morning, "you may go into the fields or down the lane, but don't go into Mr McGregor's garden: your Father had an accident there; he was put in a pie by Mrs McGregor."

"Now run along, and don't get into mischief. I am going out."

Then old Mrs Rabbit took a basket and her umbrella, to the baker's. She bought a loaf of brown bread and five currant buns.

Flopsy, Mopsy, and Cottontail, who were good little bunnies, went down the lane to gather blackberries.

But Peter, who was very naughty, ran straight away to Mr McGregor's garden and squeezed under the gate!

First he ate some lettuces and some French beans; and then he ate some radishes;

And then, feeling rather sick, he went to look for some parsley.

But round the end of a cucumber frame, whom should he meet but Mr McGregor!

Mr McGregor was on his hands and knees planting out young cabbages, but he jumped up and ran after Peter, waving a rake and calling out, “Stop thief!”

Peter was most dreadfully frightened; he rushed all over the garden, for he had forgotten the way back to the gate.

He lost one of his shoes among the cabbages, and the other shoe amongst the potatoes.

After losing them, he ran on four legs and went faster, so that I think he might have got away altogether if he had not unfortunately run into a gooseberry net, and got caught by the large buttons on his jacket. It was a blue jacket with brass buttons, quite new.

Peter gave himself up for lost, and shed big tears; but his sobs were overheard by some friendly sparrows, who flew to him in great excitement, and implored him to exert himself.

Mr McGregor came up with a sieve, which he intended to pop upon the top of Peter; but Peter wriggled out just in time, leaving his jacket behind him.

And rushed into the toolshed, and jumped into a can. It would have been a beautiful thing to hide in, if it had not had so much water in it.

Mr McGregor was quite sure that Peter was somewhere in the toolshed, perhaps hidden underneath a flower-pot. He began to turn them over carefully, looking under each.

Presently Peter sneezed—"Kertyschoo!" Mr McGregor was after him in no time, and tried to put his foot upon Peter, who jumped out of a window, upsetting three plants. The window was too small for Mr McGregor, and he was tired of running after Peter. He went back to his work.

Peter sat down to rest; he was out of breath and trembling with fright, and he had not the least idea which way to go. Also he was very damp with sitting in that can.

After a time he began to wander about, going lippity—lippity—not very fast, and looking all around.

He found a door in a wall; but it was locked, and there was no room for a fat little rabbit to squeeze underneath.

An old mouse was running in and out over the stone doorstep, carrying peas and beans to her family in the wood. Peter asked her the way to the gate, but she had such a large pea in her mouth that she could not answer. She only shook her head at him. Peter began to cry.

Then he tried to find his way straight across the garden, but he became more and more puzzled. Presently, he came to a pond where Mr McGregor filled his water-cans. A white cat was staring at some gold-fish; she sat very, very still, but now and then the tip of her tail twitched as if it were alive. Peter thought it best to go away without speaking to her; he had heard about cats from his cousin, little Benjamin Bunny.

He went back towards the tool-shed, but suddenly, quite close to him, he heard the noise of a hoe—scr-r-ritch, scratch, scratch, scritch. Peter scuttered underneath the bushes. But presently, as nothing happened, he came out, and climbed upon a wheelbarrow, and peeped over. The first thing he saw was Mr McGregor hoeing onions. His back was turned towards Peter, and beyond him was the gate!

Peter got down very quietly off the wheelbarrow, and started running as fast as he could go, along a straight walk behind some black-currant bushes.

Mr McGregor caught sight of him at the corner, but Peter did not care. He slipped underneath the gate, and was safe at last in the wood outside the garden.

Mr McGregor hung up the little jacket and the shoes for a scare-crow to frighten the blackbirds.

Peter never stopped running or looked behind him till he got home to the big fir-tree.

He was so tired that he flopped down upon the nice soft sand on the floor of the rabbit-hole, and shut his eyes. His mother was busy cooking; she wondered what he had done with his clothes. It was the second little jacket and pair of shoes that Peter had lost in a fortnight!

I am sorry to say that Peter was not very well during the evening.

His mother put him to bed, and made some camomile tea; and she gave a dose of it to Peter.

"One table-spoonful to be taken at bed-time."

But Flopsy, Mopsy, and Cotton-tail had bread and milk and blackberries for supper.

~

Beatrix Potter (1866–1943) was an English illustrator and author of children's books. Her most popular works include *The Tale of Peter Rabbit*, *The Tale of Benjamin Bunny* and *The Tale of Squirrel Nutkin*, and the animal characters Jeremy Fisher, Jemima Puddle-Duck, Mrs Tiggy-Winkle and others. She illustrated all her own books.

From Five Children and It

E. Nesbit

Five Children and It *is a fantasy novel about five children and their adventures with a wish-granting sand-fairy which they discover when they move to the countryside from London.*

Beautiful as the Day

The house was three miles from the station, but, before the dusty hired hack had rattled along for five minutes, the children began to put their heads out of the carriage window and say, "Aren't we nearly there?" And every time they passed a house, which was not very often, they all said, "Oh, is this it?" But it never was, till they reached the very top of the hill, just past the chalk-quarry and before you come to the gravel-pit. And then there was a white house with a green garden and an orchard beyond, and mother said, "Here we are!"

"How white the house is," said Robert.

"And look at the roses," said Anthea.

"And the plums," said Jane.

"It is rather decent," Cyril admitted.

The Baby said, "Wanty go walky;" and the hack stopped with a last rattle and jolt.

Everyone got its legs kicked or its feet trodden on in the scramble to get out of the carriage that very minute, but no one seemed to mind. Mother, curiously enough, was in no hurry to get out; and even when she had come down slowly and by the step, and with no jump at all, she seemed to wish to see the boxes carried in, and even to pay the driver, instead of joining in that first glorious rush round the garden and orchard and the thorny, thistly, briery, brambly wilderness beyond the broken gate and the dry fountain at the side of the house. But the children were wiser, for once. It was not really a pretty house at all; it was quite ordinary, and mother thought it was rather inconvenient, and was quite annoyed at there being no shelves, to speak of, and hardly a cupboard in the place. Father used to say that the iron-work on the roof and coping was like an architect's nightmare. But the house was deep in the country, with no other house in sight, and the children had been in London for two years, without so much as once going to the seaside even for a day by an excursion train, and so the White House seemed to them a sort of Fairy Palace set down in an Earthly Paradise. For London is like prison for children, especially if their relations are not rich.

Of course there are the shops and theatres, and entertainments and things, but if your people are rather poor you don't get taken to the theatres, and you can't buy things out of the shops; and London has none of those nice things that children may play with without hurting the things or themselves—such as trees and sand and woods and waters. And nearly everything in London is the wrong sort of shape—all straight lines and flat streets, instead of being all sorts of odd shapes, like things are in the country. Trees are all different, as you know, and I am sure some tiresome person must have told you that there are no two blades of grass exactly alike. But in streets, where the blades of grass don't grow, everything is like everything else. This is why many children who live in the towns are so extremely naughty. They do not know what is the matter with them, and no more do their fathers and mothers, aunts, uncles, cousins, tutors, governesses, and nurses; but I know. And so do you, now. Children in the country are naughty sometimes, too, but that is for quite different reasons.

The children had explored the gardens and the outhouses thoroughly before they were caught and cleaned for tea, and they saw quite well that they were certain to be happy at the White House. They thought so from the first moment, but when they found the back of the house covered with jasmine, all in white flower, and smelling like a bottle of the most expensive perfume that is ever given for a birthday present; and when they had seen the lawn, all green and smooth, and quite different from the brown grass in the gardens at Camden Town; and when they found the stable with a loft over it and some old hay still left, they were almost certain; and when Robert had found the broken swing and tumbled out of it and got a bump on his head the size of an egg, and Cyril had nipped his finger in the door of a hutch that seemed made to keep rabbits in, if you ever had any, they had no longer any doubts whatever.

The best part of it all was that there were no rules about not going to places and not doing things. In London almost everything is labelled "You mustn't touch," and though the label is invisible it's just as bad, because you know it's there, or if you don't you very soon get told.

The White House was on the edge of a hill, with a wood behind it—and the chalk-quarry on one side and the gravel-pit on the other. Down at the bottom of the hill was a level plain, with queer-shaped white buildings where people burnt lime, and a big red brewery and other houses; and when the big chimneys were smoking and the sun was setting, the valley looked as if it was filled with golden mist, and the limekilns and hop-drying houses glimmered and glittered till they were like an enchanted city out of the *Arabian Nights.*

Now that I have begun to tell you about the place, I feel that I could go on and make this into a most interesting story about all the ordinary things that the children did,—just the kind of things you do yourself, you know, and you would believe every word of it; and when I told about the children's being tiresome, as you are sometimes, your aunts would perhaps write in the margin of the story with a pencil, "How true!" or "How like life!" and you would see it and would very likely be annoyed. So I will only tell you the really astonishing things that happened, and you may leave the book about quite safely, for no aunts and uncles either are likely to write "How true!" on the edge of the story. Grown-up people find it very difficult to believe really wonderful things, unless they have what they call proof. But children will believe almost anything, and grown-ups know this. That is why they tell you that the earth is round like an orange, when you can see perfectly well that it is flat and lumpy; and why they say that the earth goes round the sun, when you can see for yourself any day that the sun gets up in the morning and goes to bed at night like a good sun as it is, and the earth knows its place, and lies as still as a mouse. Yet I daresay you believe all that about the earth and the sun, and if so you will find it quite easy to believe that before Anthea and Cyril and the others had been a week in the country they had found a fairy. At least they called it that, because that was what it called itself;

and of course it knew best, but it was not at all like any fairy you ever saw or heard of or read about.

It was at the gravel-pits. Father had to go away suddenly on business, and mother had gone away to stay with Granny, who was not very well. They both went in a great hurry, and when they were gone the house seemed dreadfully quiet and empty, and the children wandered from one room to another and looked at the bits of paper and string on the floors left over from the packing, and not yet cleared up, and wished they had something to do. It was Cyril who said—

"I say, let's take our spades and dig in the gravel-pits. We can pretend it's seaside."

"Father says it was once," Anthea said; "he says there are shells there thousands of years old."

So they went. Of course they had been to the edge of the gravel-pit and looked over, but they had not gone down into it for fear father should say they mustn't play there, and it was the same with the chalk-quarry. The gravel-pit is not really dangerous if you don't try to climb down the edges, but go the slow safe way round by the road, as if you were a cart.

Each of the children carried its own spade, and took it in turns to carry the Lamb. He was the baby, and they called him that because "Baa" was the first thing he ever said. They called Anthea "Panther," which seems silly when you read it, but when you say it it sounds a little like her name.

The gravel-pit is very large and wide, with grass growing round the edges at the top, and dry stringy wildflowers, purple and yellow. It is like a giant's washbowl. And there are mounds of gravel, and holes in the sides of the bowl where gravel has been taken out, and high up in the steep sides there are the little holes that are the little front doors of the little bank-martins' little houses.

The children built a castle, of course, but castle-building is rather poor fun when you have no hope of the swishing tide ever coming in to fill up the moat and wash away the drawbridge, and, at the happy last, to wet everybody up to the waist at least.

Cyril wanted to dig out a cave to play smugglers in, but the others thought it might bury them alive, so it ended in all spades going to work to dig a hole through the castle to Australia. These children, you see, believed that the world was round, and that on the other side the little Australian boys and girls were really walking wrong way up, like flies on the ceiling, with their heads hanging down into the air.

The children dug and they dug and they dug, and their hands got sandy and hot and red, and their faces got damp and shiny. The Lamb had tried to eat the sand, and had cried so hard when he found that it was not, as he had supposed, brown sugar, that he was now tired out, and was lying asleep in a warm fat bunch in the middle of the half-finished castle. This left his brothers and sisters free to work really hard, and the hole that was to come out in Australia soon grew so deep that Jane, who was called Pussy for short, begged the others to stop.

"Suppose the bottom of the hole gave way suddenly," said she, "and you tumbled out among the little Australians, all the sand would get in their eyes."

"Yes," said Robert; "and they would hate us, and throw stones at us, and not let us see the kangaroos, or opossums, or bluegums, or Emu Brand birds, or anything."

Cyril and Anthea knew that Australia was not quite so near as all that, but they agreed to stop using the spades and to go on with their hands. This was quite easy, because the sand at the bottom of the hole was very soft and fine and dry, like sea-sand. And there were little shells in it.

"Fancy it having been wet sea here once, all sloppy and shiny," said Jane, "with fishes and conger-eels and coral and mermaids."

"And masts of ships and wrecked Spanish treasure. I wish we could find a gold doubloon, or something," Cyril said.

"How did the sea get carried away?" Robert asked.

"Not in a pail, silly," said his brother.

"Father says the earth got too hot underneath, as you do in bed sometimes, so it just hunched up its shoulders, and the sea had to slip off, like the blankets do us, and the shoulder was left sticking out, and turned into dry land. Let's go and look for shells; I think that little cave looks likely, and I see something sticking out there like a bit of wrecked ship's anchor, and it's beastly hot in the Australian hole."

The others agreed, but Anthea went on digging. She always liked to finish a thing when she had once begun it. She felt it would be a disgrace to leave that hole without getting through to Australia.

The cave was disappointing, because there were no shells, and the wrecked ship's anchor turned out to be only the broken end of a pick-axe handle, and the cave party were just making up their minds that sand makes you thirstier when it is not by the seaside, and someone had suggested that they all go home for lemonade, when Anthea suddenly screamed—

"Cyril! Come here! Oh, come quick—It's alive! It'll get away! Quick!"

They all hurried back.

"It's a rat, I shouldn't wonder," said Robert. "Father says they infest old places—and this must be pretty old if the sea was here thousands of years ago."

"Perhaps it is a snake," said Jane, shuddering.

"Let's look," said Cyril, jumping into the hole. "I'm not afraid of snakes. I like them. If it is a snake I'll tame it, and it will follow me everywhere, and I'll let it sleep round my neck at night."

"No, you won't," said Robert firmly. He shared Cyril's bedroom. "But you may if it's a rat."

"Oh, don't be silly!" said Anthea; "it's not a rat, it's *much* bigger. And it's not a snake. It's got feet; I saw them; and fur! No—not the spade. You'll hurt it! Dig with your hands."

"And let *it* hurt *me* instead! That's so likely, isn't it?" said Cyril, seizing a spade.

"Oh, don't!" said Anthea. "Squirrel, *don't*. I—it sounds silly, but it said something. It really and truly did."

"What?"

"It said, 'You let me alone.'"

But Cyril merely observed that his sister must have gone off her head, and he and Robert dug with spades while Anthea sat on the edge of the hole, jumping up and down with hotness and anxiety. They dug carefully, and presently everyone could see that there really was something moving in the bottom of the Australian hole.

Then Anthea cried out, "*I'm* not afraid. Let me dig," and fell on her knees and began to scratch like a dog does when he has suddenly remembered where it was that he buried his bone.

"Oh, I felt fur," she cried, half laughing and half crying. "I did indeed! I did!" when suddenly a dry husky voice in the sand made them all jump back, and their hearts jumped nearly as fast as they did.

"Let me alone," it said. And now everyone heard the voice and looked at the others to see if they had heard it too.

"But we want to see you," said Robert bravely.

"I wish you'd come out," said Anthea, also taking courage.

"Oh, well—if that's your wish," the voice said, and the sand stirred and spun and scattered, and something brown and furry and fat came rolling out into the hole, and the sand fell off it, and it sat there yawning and rubbing the ends of its eyes with its hands.

"I believe I must have dropped asleep," it said, stretching itself.

The children stood round the hole in a ring, looking at the creature they had found. It was worth looking at. Its eyes were on long horns like a snail's eyes, and it could move them in and out like telescopes; it had ears like a bat's ears, and its tubby body was shaped like a spider's and covered with thick soft fur; its legs and arms were furry too, and it had hands and feet like a monkey's.

"What on earth is it?" Jane said. "Shall we take it home?"

The thing turned its long eyes to look at her, and said—

"Does she always talk nonsense, or is it only the rubbish on her head that makes her silly?"

It looked scornfully at Jane's hat as it spoke.

"She doesn't mean to be silly," Anthea said gently; "we none of us do, whatever you may think! Don't be frightened; we don't want to hurt you, you know."

"Hurt *me*!" it said. "*Me* frightened? Upon my word! Why, you talk as if I were nobody in particular." All its fur stood out like a cat's when it is going to fight.

"Well," said Anthea, still kindly, "perhaps if we knew who you are in particular we could think of something to say that wouldn't make you angry. Everything we've said so far seems to have done so. Who are you? And don't get angry! Because really we don't know."

"You don't know?" it said. "Well, I knew the world had changed—but—well, really—Do you mean to tell me seriously you don't know a Psammead when you see one?"

"A Sammyadd? That's Greek to me."

"So it is to everyone," said the creature sharply. "Well, in plain English, then, a *Sand-fairy*. Don't you know a Sand-fairy when you see one?"

It looked so grieved and hurt that Jane hastened to say, "Of course I see you are, *now*. It's quite plain now one comes to look at you."

"You came to look at me, several sentences ago," it said crossly, beginning to curl up again in the sand.

"Oh—don't go away again! Do talk some more," Robert cried. "I didn't know you were a Sand-fairy, but I knew directly I saw you that you were much the wonderfullest thing I'd ever seen."

The Sand-fairy seemed a shade less disagreeable after this.

"It isn't talking I mind," it said, "as long as you're reasonably civil. But I'm not going to make polite conversation for you. If you talk nicely to me, perhaps I'll answer you, and perhaps I won't. Now say something."

Of course no one could think of anything to say, but at last Robert thought of "How long have you lived here?" and he said it at once.

"Oh, ages—several thousand years," replied the Psammead.

"Tell us about it. Do."

"It's all in books."

"*You* aren't!" Jane said. "Oh, tell us everything you can about yourself! We don't know anything about you, and you *are* so nice."

The Sand-fairy smoothed his long rat-like whiskers and smiled between them.

"Do please tell!" said the children all together.

It is wonderful how quickly you get used to things, even the most astonishing. Five minutes before, the children had had no more idea than you had that there was such a thing as a Sand-fairy in the world, and now they were talking to it as though they had known it all their lives.

It drew its eyes in and said—

"How very sunny it is—quite like old times! Where do you get your Megatheriums from now?"

"What?" said the children all at once. It is very difficult always to remember that "what" is not polite, especially in moments of surprise or agitation.

"Are Pterodactyls plentiful now?" the Sand-fairy went on.

The children were unable to reply.

"What do you have for breakfast?" the Fairy said impatiently, "and who gives it to you?"

"Eggs and bacon, and bread and milk, and porridge and things. Mother gives it to us. What are Mega-what's-its-names and Ptero-what-do-you-call-thems? And does anyone have them for breakfast?"

"Why, almost everyone had Pterodactyl for breakfast in my time! Pterodactyls were something like crocodiles and something like birds—I believe they were very good grilled. You see, it was like this: of course there were heaps of Sand-fairies then, and in the morning early you went out and hunted for them, and when you'd found one it gave you your wish. People used to send their little boys down to the seashore in the morning before breakfast to get the day's wishes, and very often the eldest boy in the family would be told to wish for a Megatherium, ready jointed for cooking. It was as big as an elephant, you see, so there was a good deal of meat on it. And if they wanted fish, the Ichthyosaurus was asked for—he was twenty to forty feet long, so there was plenty of him. And for poultry there was the Plesiosaurus; there were nice pickings on that too. Then the other children could wish for other things. But when people had dinner-parties it was nearly always Megatheriums; and Ichthyosaurus, because his fins were a great delicacy and his tail made soup."

"There must have been heaps and heaps of cold meat left over," said Anthea, who meant to be a good housekeeper some day.

"Oh no," said the Psammead, "that would never have done. Why, of course at sunset what was left over turned into stone. You find the stone bones of the Megatherium and things all over the place even now, they tell me."

"Who tell you?" asked Cyril; but the Sand-fairy frowned and began to dig very fast with its furry hands.

"Oh, don't go!" they all cried; "tell us more about when it was Megatheriums for breakfast! Was the world like this then?"

It stopped digging.

"Not a bit," it said; "it was nearly all sand where I lived, and coal grew on trees, and the periwinkles were as big as tea-trays—you find them now; they're turned into stone. We Sand-fairies used to live on the seashore, and the children used to come with their little flint-spades and flint-pails and make castles for us to live in. That's thousands of years ago, but I hear that children still build castles on the sand. It's difficult to break yourself of a habit."

"But why did you stop living in the castles?" asked Robert.

"It's a sad story," said the Psammead gloomily. "It was because they *would* build moats to the castles, and the nasty wet bubbling sea used to come in, and of course as soon as a Sand-fairy got wet it caught cold, and generally died. And so there got to be fewer and fewer, and, whenever you found a fairy and had a wish, you used to wish for a Megatherium, and eat twice as much as you wanted, because it might be weeks before you got another wish."

"And did *you* get wet?" Robert inquired.

The Sand-fairy shuddered. "Only once," it said; "the end of the twelfth hair of my top left whisker—I feel the place still in damp weather. It was only once, but it was quite enough for me. I went away as soon as the sun had dried my poor dear whisker. I scurried away to the back of the beach, and dug myself a house deep in warm dry sand, and there I've been ever since. And the sea changed its lodgings afterwards. And now I'm not going to tell you another thing."

"Just one more, please," said the children. "Can you give wishes now?"

"Of course," said it; "didn't I give you yours a few minutes ago? You said, 'I wish you'd come out,' and I did."

"Oh, please, mayn't we have another?"

"Yes, but be quick about it. I'm tired of you."

I daresay you have often thought what you would do if you had three wishes given you, and have despised the old man and his wife in the black-pudding story, and felt certain that if you had the chance you could think of three really useful wishes without a moment's hesitation. These children had often talked this matter over, but, now the chance had suddenly come to them, they could not make up their minds.

"Quick," said the Sand-fairy crossly. No one could think of anything, only Anthea did manage to remember a private wish of her own and Jane's which they had never told the boys. She knew the boys would not care about it—but still it was better than nothing.

"I wish we were all as beautiful as the day," she said in a great hurry.

The children looked at each other, but each could see that the others were not any better-looking than usual. The Psammead pushed out his long eyes, and seemed to be holding its breath and swelling itself out till it was twice as fat and furry as before. Suddenly it let its breath go in a long sigh.

"I'm really afraid I can't manage it," it said apologetically; "I must be out of practice."

The children were horribly disappointed.

"Oh, *do* try again!" they said.

"Well," said the Sand-fairy, "the fact is, I was keeping back a little strength to give the rest of you your wishes with. If you'll be contented with one wish a day among the lot of you I daresay I can screw myself up to it. Do you agree to that?"

"Yes, oh yes!" said Jane and Anthea. The boys nodded. They did not believe the Sand-fairy could do it. You can always make girls believe things much easier than you can boys.

It stretched out its eyes farther than ever, and swelled and swelled and swelled.

"I do hope it won't hurt itself," said Anthea.

"Or crack its skin," Robert said anxiously.

Everyone was very much relieved when the Sand-fairy, after getting so big that it almost filled up the hole in the sand, suddenly let out its breath and went back to its proper size.

"That's all right," it said, panting heavily. "It'll come easier to-morrow."

"Did it hurt much?" said Anthea.

"Only my poor whisker, thank you," said he, "but you're a kind and thoughtful child. Good day."

It scratched suddenly and fiercely with its hands and feet, and disappeared in the sand.

Then the children looked at each other, and each child suddenly found itself alone with three perfect strangers, all radiantly beautiful.

They stood for some moments in silence. Each thought that its brothers and sisters had wandered off, and that these strange children had stolen up unnoticed while it was watching the swelling form of the Sand-fairy. Anthea spoke first—

"Excuse me," she said very politely to Jane, who now had enormous blue eyes and a cloud of russet hair, "but have you seen two little boys and a little girl anywhere about?"

"I was just going to ask you that," said Jane. And then Cyril cried—

"Why, it's *you*! I know the hole in your pinafore! You *are* Jane, aren't you? And you're the Panther; I can see your dirty handkerchief that you forgot to change after you'd cut your thumb! The wish *has* come off, after all. I say, am I as handsome as you are?"

"If you're Cyril, I liked you much better as you were before," said Anthea decidedly. "You look like the picture of the young chorister, with your golden hair; you'll die young, I shouldn't wonder. And if that's Robert, he's like an Italian organ-grinder. His hair's all black."

"You two girls are like Christmas cards, then—that's all—silly Christmas cards," said Robert angrily. "And Jane's hair is simply carrots."

It was indeed of that Venetian tint so much admired by artists.

"Well, it's no use finding fault with each other," said Anthea; "let's get the Lamb and lug it home to dinner. The servants will admire us most awfully, you'll see."

Baby was just waking up when they got to him, and not one of the children but was relieved to find that he at least was not as beautiful as the day, but just the same as usual.

"I suppose he's too young to have wishes naturally," said Jane. "We shall have to mention him specially next time."

Anthea ran forward and held out her arms.

"Come, then," she said.

The Baby looked at her disapprovingly, and put a sandy pink thumb in his mouth. Anthea was his favourite sister.

"Come, then," she said.

"G'way 'long!" said the Baby.

"Come to own Pussy," said Jane.

"Wants my Panty," said the Lamb dismally, and his lip trembled.

"Here, come on, Veteran," said Robert, "come and have a yidey on Yobby's back."

"Yah, narky narky boy," howled the Baby, giving way altogether. Then the children knew the worst. *The Baby did not know them!*

They looked at each other in despair, and it was terrible to each, in this dire emergency, to meet only the beautiful eyes of perfect strangers, instead of the merry, friendly, commonplace, twinkling, jolly little eyes of its own brothers and sisters.

"This is most truly awful," said Cyril when he had tried to lift up the Lamb, and the Lamb had scratched like a cat and bellowed like a bull! "We've got to *make friends* with him! I can't carry him home screaming like that. Fancy having to make friends with our own baby—it's too silly."

That, however, was exactly what they had to do. It took over an hour, and the task was not rendered any easier by the fact that the Lamb was by this time as hungry as a lion and as thirsty as a desert.

At last he consented to allow these strangers to carry him home by turns, but as he refused to hold on to such new acquaintances he was a dead weight, and most exhausting.

"Thank goodness, we're home!" said Jane, staggering through the iron gate to where Martha, the nursemaid, stood at the front door shading her eyes with her hand and looking out anxiously. "Here! Do take Baby!"

Martha snatched the Baby from her arms.

"Thanks be, *he's* safe back," she said. "Where are the others, and whoever to goodness gracious are all of you?"

"We're *us*, of course," said Robert.

"And who's Us, when you're at home?" asked Martha scornfully.

"I tell you it's *us*, only we're beautiful as the day," said Cyril. "I'm Cyril, and these are the others, and we're jolly hungry. Let us in, and don't be a silly idiot."

Martha merely dratted Cyril's impudence and tried to shut the door in his face.

"I know we *look* different, but I'm Anthea, and we're so tired, and it's long past dinner-time."

"Then go home to your dinners, whoever you are; and if our children put you up to this play-acting you can tell them from me they'll catch it, so they know what to expect!" With that she did bang the door. Cyril rang the bell violently. No answer. Presently cook put her head out of a bedroom window and said—

"If you don't take yourselves off, and that precious sharp, I'll go and fetch the police." And she slammed down the window.

"It's no good," said Anthea. "Oh, do, do come away before we get sent to prison!"

The boys said it was nonsense, and the law of England couldn't put you in prison for just being as beautiful as the day, but all the same they followed the others out into the lane.

"We shall be our proper selves after sunset, I suppose," said Jane.

"I don't know," Cyril said sadly; "it mayn't be like that now—things have changed a good deal since Megatherium times."

"Oh," cried Anthea suddenly, "perhaps we shall turn into stone at sunset, like the Megatheriums did, so that there mayn't be any of us left over for the next day."

She began to cry, so did Jane. Even the boys turned pale. No one had the heart to say anything.

It was a horrible afternoon. There was no house near where the children could beg a crust of bread or even a glass of water. They were afraid to go to the village, because they had seen Martha go down there with a basket, and there was a local constable. True, they were all as beautiful as the day, but that is a poor comfort when you are as hungry as a hunter and as thirsty as a sponge.

Three times they tried in vain to get the servants in the White House to let them in and listen to their tale. And then Robert went alone, hoping to be able to climb in at one of the back windows and so open the door to the others. But all the windows were out of reach, and Martha emptied a toilet-jug of cold water over him from a top window, and said—

"Go along with you, you nasty little Eye-talian monkey."

It came at last to their sitting down in a row under the hedge, with their feet in a dry ditch, waiting for sunset, and wondering whether, when the sun *did* set, they would turn into stone, or only into their own old natural selves; and each of them still felt lonely and among strangers, and tried not to look at the others, for, though their voices were their own, their faces were so radiantly beautiful as to be quite irritating to look at.

"I don't believe we *shall* turn to stone," said Robert, breaking a long miserable silence, "because the Sand-fairy said he'd give us another wish to-morrow, and he couldn't if we were stone, could he?"

The others said "No," but they weren't at all comforted.

Another silence, longer and more miserable, was broken by Cyril's suddenly saying, "I don't want to frighten you girls, but I believe it's beginning with me already. My foot's quite dead. I'm turning to stone, I know I am, and so will you in a minute."

"Never mind," said Robert kindly, "perhaps you'll be the only stone one, and the rest of us will be all right, and we'll cherish your statue and hang garlands on it."

But when it turned out that Cyril's foot had only gone to sleep through his sitting too long with it under him, and when it came to life in an agony of pins and needles, the others were quite cross.

"Giving us such a fright for nothing!" said Anthea.

The third and miserablest silence of all was broken by Jane. She said—

"If we *do* come out of this all right, we'll ask the Sammyadd to make it so that the servants don't notice anything different, no matter what wishes we have."

The others only grunted. They were too wretched even to make good resolutions.

At last hunger and fright and crossness and tiredness—four very nasty things—all joined together to bring one nice thing, and that was sleep. The children lay asleep in a row, with their beautiful eyes shut and their beautiful mouths open. Anthea woke first. The sun had set, and the twilight was coming on.

Anthea pinched herself very hard, to make sure, and when she found she could still feel pinching she decided that she was not stone, and then she pinched the others. They, also, were soft.

"Wake up," she said, almost in tears for joy; "it's all right, we're not stone. And oh, Cyril, how nice and ugly you do look, with your old freckles and your brown hair and your little eyes. And so do you all!" she added, so that they might not feel jealous.

When they got home they were very much scolded by Martha, who told them about the strange children.

"A good-looking lot, I must say, but that impudent."

"I know," said Robert, who knew by experience how hopeless it would be to try to explain things to Martha.

"And where on earth have you been all this time, you naughty little things, you?"

"In the lane."

"Why didn't you come home hours ago?"

"We couldn't because of *them*," said Anthea.

"Who?"

"The children who were as beautiful as the day. They kept us there till after sunset. We couldn't come back till they'd gone. You don't know how we hated them! Oh, do, do give us some supper—we are so hungry."

"Hungry! I should think so," said Martha angrily; "out all day like this. Well, I hope it'll be a lesson to you not to go picking up with strange children—down here after measles, as likely as not! Now mind, if you see them again, don't you speak to them—not one word nor so much as a look—but come straight away and tell me. I'll spoil their beauty for them!"

"If ever we *do* see them again we'll tell you," Anthea said; and Robert, fixing his eyes fondly on the cold beef that was being brought in on a tray by cook, added in heartfelt undertones—

"And we'll take jolly good care we never *do* see them again."

And they never have.

~

Edith Nesbit (1858–1924), popularly known to readers as E. Nesbit, was a British poet and author who wrote mainly for children. She is best known for her novels *Five Children and It*, *The Enchanted Castle* and *The Railway Children*. Nesbit credited her success to being one of those people who feel "that they are children in a grown-up world".

The Witch's Balloons

Enid Blyton

Opposite the nursery sat a woman old and
brown,
I should think she was the very oldest person
in the town,
She sold balloons to children as they passed
her corner there,
She was very cross and horrid and she had
a nasty stare.

I looked at her one morning, on a very
windy day,
And she saw me and she stared at me in such
a nasty way,
I felt afraid, and certain sure that she must be
a witch,
And keep all sorts of stolen treasures hidden
in a ditch.

And as I looked at her, and she was staring up
at me,
I saw a fairy flying low from out the chestnut
tree,
She held a little knife, and oh, she cut the
strings right through,
That held the big balloons together, then away
she flew!

And off went all the purple ones and off went
all the pink,
A-flying in the air as high as ever you could
think,
Around the chimney pots, and right away up
in the sky,
Until they bumped into the clouds, a-sailing
slowly by.

And then I looked to see what that old woman
had to say,
But there wasn't any sign of her, she'd
vanished right away,
She *must* have been a wicked witch, and by
the fairies slain,
For tho' I've looked each morning, she has
never come again.

~

One of the most beloved children's novelists whose books have been translated into several languages and have sold millions of copies worldwide, Enid Blyton (1897–1968) is most famous for her Magic Faraway Tree, Famous Five, Secret Seven and Adventure series. Lesser known is the fact that the British author was also a prolific poet and columnist.

A Canary For One

Ernest Hemingway

THE train passed very quickly a long, red stone house with a garden and four thick palm-trees with tables under them in the shade. On the other side was the sea. Then there was a cutting through red stone and clay, and the sea was only occasionally and far below against rocks.

"I bought him in Palermo," the American lady said. "We only had an hour ashore and it was Sunday morning. The man wanted to be paid in dollars and I gave him a dollar and a half. He really sings very beautifully."

It was very hot in the train and it was very hot in the *lit salon* compartment. There was no breeze came through the open window. The American lady pulled the window-blind down and there was no more sea, even occasionally. On the other side there was glass, then the corridor, then an open window, and outside the window were dusty trees and an oiled road and flat fields of grapes, with gray-stone hills behind them.

There was smoke from many tall chimneys—coming into Marseilles, and the train slowed down and followed one track through many others into the station. The train stayed twenty-five minutes in the station at Marseilles and the American lady bought a copy of *The Daily Mail* and a half-bottle of Evian water. She walked a little way along the station platform, but she stayed near the steps of the car because at Cannes, where it stopped for twelve minutes, the train had left with no signal of departure and she had only gotten on just in time. The American lady was a little deaf and she was afraid that perhaps signals of departure were given and that she did not hear them.

The train left the station in Marseilles and there was not only the switch-yards and the factory smoke but, looking back, the town of Marseilles and the harbor with stone hills behind it and the last of the sun on the water. As it was getting dark the train passed a farmhouse burning in a field. Motor-cars were stopped along the road and bedding and things from inside the farmhouse were spread in the field. Many people were watching the house burn. After it was dark the train was in Avignon. People got on and off. At the news-stand Frenchmen, returning to Paris, bought that day's French papers. On the station platform were negro[1] soldiers. They wore brown uniforms and were tall and their faces shone, close under the electric light. Their faces were very black and they were too tall to stare. The train left Avignon station with the negroes standing there. A short white sergeant was with them.

Inside the *lit salon* compartment the porter had pulled down the three beds from inside the wall and prepared them for sleeping.

1 Author's original text; all such instances retained for authenticity

In the night the American lady lay without sleeping because the train was a *rapide* and went very fast and she was afraid of the speed in the night. The American lady's bed was the one next to the window. The canary from Palermo, a cloth spread over his cage, was out of the draft in the corridor that went into the compartment wash-room. There was a blue light outside the compartment, and all night the train went very fast and the American lady lay awake and waited for a wreck.

In the morning the train was near Paris, and after the American lady had come out from the wash-room, looking very wholesome and middle-aged and American in spite of not having slept, and had taken the cloth off the birdcage and hung the cage in the sun, she went back to the restaurant-car for breakfast. When she came back to the *lit salon* compartment again, the beds had been pushed back into the wall and made into seats, the canary was shaking his feathers in the sunlight that came through the open window, and the train was much nearer Paris.

"He loves the sun," the American lady said. "He'll sing now in a little while."

The canary shook his feathers and pecked into them. "I've always loved birds," the American lady said. "I'm taking him home to my little girl. There—he's singing now."

The canary chirped and the feathers on his throat stood out, then he dropped his bill and pecked into his feathers again. The train crossed a river and passed through a very carefully tended forest. The train passed through many outside of Paris towns. There were tram-cars in the towns and big advertisements for the Belle Jardinière and Dubonnet and Pernod on the walls toward the train. All that the train passed through looked as though it were before breakfast. For several minutes I had not listened to the American lady, who was talking to my wife.

"Is your husband American too?" asked the lady.

"Yes," said my wife. "We're both Americans."

"I thought you were English."

"Oh, no."

"Perhaps that was because I wore braces," I said. I had started to say suspenders and changed it to braces in the mouth, to keep my English character. The American lady did not hear. She was really quite deaf; she read lips, and I had not looked toward her. I had looked out of the window. She went on talking to my wife.

"I'm so glad you're Americans. American men make the best husbands," the American lady was saying. "That was why we left the Continent, you know. My daughter fell in love with a man in Vevey." She stopped. "They were simply madly in love." She stopped again. "I took her away, of course."

"Did she get over it?" asked my wife.

"I don't think so," said the American lady. "She wouldn't eat anything and she wouldn't sleep at all. I've tried so very hard, but she doesn't seem to take an interest in anything. She doesn't care about things. I couldn't have her marrying a foreigner." She paused. "Some one, a very good friend, told me once, 'No foreigner can make an American girl a good husband.' "

"No," said my wife, "I suppose not."

The American lady admired my wife's travelling-coat, and it turned out that the American lady had bought her own clothes for twenty years now from the same maison de couturier in the Rue Saint Honoré. They had her measurements, and a vendeuse who knew her and her tastes picked the dresses out for her and they were sent to America. They came to the post-office near where she lived up-town in New York, and the duty was never exorbitant because they opened the dresses there in the post-office to appraise them and they were always very simple-looking and with no gold lace nor ornaments that would make the dresses look expensive. Before the present vendeuse, named Thérèse, there had been another vendeuse, named Amélie. Altogether there had only been these two in the twenty years. It had always been the same couturier. Prices, however, had gone up. The exchange, though, equalized that. They had her daughter's measurements now too. She was grown up and there was not much chance of their changing now.

The train was now coming into Paris. The fortifications were levelled but grass had not grown. There were many cars standing on tracks—brown wooden restaurant-cars and brown wooden sleeping-cars that would go to Italy at five o'clock that night, if that train still left at five; the cars were marked Paris-Rome, and cars, with seats on the roofs, that went back and forth to the suburbs with, at certain hours, people in all the seats and on the roofs, if that were the way it were still done, and passing were the white walls and many windows of houses. Nothing had eaten any breakfast.

"Americans make the best husbands," the American lady said to my wife. I was getting down the bags. "American men are the only men in the world to marry."

"How long ago did you leave Vevey?" asked my wife.

"Two years ago this fall. It's her, you know, that I'm taking the canary to."

"Was the man your daughter was in love with a Swiss?"

"Yes," said the American lady. "He was from a very good family in Vevey. He was going to be an engineer. They met there in Vevey. They used to go on long walks together."

"I know Vevey," said my wife. "We were there on our honeymoon."

"Were you really? That must have been lovely. I had no idea, of course, that she'd fall in love with him."

"It was a very lovely place," said my wife.

"Yes," said the American lady. "Isn't it lovely? Where did you stop there?"

"We stayed at the Trois Couronnes," said my wife.

"It's such a fine old hotel," said the American lady.

"Yes," said my wife. "We had a very fine room and in the fall the country was lovely."

"Were you there in the fall?"

"Yes," said my wife.

We were passing three cars that had been in a wreck. They were splintered open and the roofs sagged in.

"Look," I said. "There's been a wreck."

The American lady looked and saw the last car. "I was afraid of just that all night," she said. "I have terrific presentiments about things sometimes. I'll never travel on a *rapide* again at night. There must be other comfortable trains that don't go so fast."

Then the train was in the dark of the Gare de Lyons, and then stopped and porters came up to the windows. I handed bags through the windows, and we were out on the dim longness of the platform, and the American lady put herself in charge of one of three men from Cook's who said: "Just a moment, madame, and I'll look for your name."

The porter brought a truck and piled on the baggage, and my wife said good-by and I said good-by to the American lady, whose name had been found by the man from Cook's on a typewritten page in a sheaf of typewritten pages which he replaced in his pocket.

We followed the porter with the truck down the long cement platform beside the train. At the end was a gate and a man took the tickets.

We were returning to Paris to set up separate residences.

~

Ernest Hemingway (1899–1961) was an American novelist, short-story writer and journalist. He served at the front in the First World War, and war became a theme in several of his works. Known for *The Old Man and the Sea*, *For Whom the Bell Tolls* and *A Farewell to Arms*, he was awarded the Nobel Prize in 1954.

The Elderbush

Hans Christian Andersen

Once upon a time there was a little boy who had taken cold. He had gone out and got his feet wet; though nobody could imagine how it had happened, for it was quite dry weather. So his mother undressed him, put him to bed, and had the tea-pot brought in, to make him a good cup of Elderflower tea. Just at that moment the merry old man came in who lived up a-top of the house all alone; for he had neither wife nor children—but he liked children very much, and knew so many fairy tales, that it was quite delightful.

"Now drink your tea," said the boy's mother; "then, perhaps, you may hear a fairy tale."

"If I had but something new to tell," said the old man. "But how did the child get his feet wet?"

"That is the very thing that nobody can make out," said his mother.

"Am I to hear a fairy tale?" asked the little boy.

"Yes, if you can tell me exactly—for I must know that first—how deep the gutter is in the little street opposite, that you pass through in going to school."

"Just up to the middle of my boot," said the child; "but then I must go into the deep hole."

"Ah, ah! That's where the wet feet came from," said the old man. "I ought now to tell you a story; but I don't know any more."

"You can make one in a moment," said the little boy. "My mother says that all you look at can be turned into a fairy tale: and that you can find a story in everything."

"Yes, but such tales and stories are good for nothing. The right sort come of themselves; they tap at my forehead and say, 'Here we are.'"

"Won't there be a tap soon?" asked the little boy. And his mother laughed, put some Elder-flowers in the tea-pot, and poured boiling water upon them.

"Do tell me something! Pray do!"

"Yes, if a fairy tale would come of its own accord; but they are proud and haughty, and come only when they choose. Stop!" said he, all on a sudden. "I have it! Pay attention! There is one in the tea-pot!"

And the little boy looked at the tea-pot. The cover rose more and more; and the Elder-flowers came forth so fresh and white, and shot up long branches. Out of the spout even did they spread themselves on all sides, and grew larger and larger; it was a splendid Elderbush, a whole tree; and it reached into the very bed, and pushed the curtains aside. How it bloomed! And what an odour! In the middle of the bush sat a friendly-looking old woman in a most strange dress. It was quite green, like the leaves of the elder, and was trimmed with large white Elder-flowers;

so that at first one could not tell whether it was a stuff, or a natural green and real flowers.

"What's that woman's name?" asked the little boy.

"The Greeks and Romans," said the old man, "called her a Dryad; but that we do not understand. The people who live in the New Booths have a much better name for her; they call her 'old Granny'—and she it is to whom you are to pay attention. Now listen, and look at the beautiful Elderbush.

"Just such another large blooming Elder Tree stands near the New Booths. It grew there in the corner of a little miserable court-yard; and under it sat, of an afternoon, in the most splendid sunshine, two old people; an old, old seaman, and his old, old wife. They had great-grand-children, and were soon to celebrate the fiftieth anniversary of their marriage; but they could not exactly recollect the date: and old Granny sat in the tree, and looked as pleased as now. 'I know the date,' said she; but those below did not hear her, for they were talking about old times.

"'Yes, can't you remember when we were very little,' said the old seaman, 'and ran and played about? It was the very same court-yard where we now are, and we stuck slips in the ground, and made a garden.'

"'I remember it well,' said the old woman; 'I remember it quite well. We watered the slips, and one of them was an Elderbush. It took root, put forth green shoots, and grew up to be the large tree under which we old folks are now sitting.'

"'To be sure,' said he. 'And there in the corner stood a waterpail, where I used to swim my boats.'

"'True; but first we went to school to learn somewhat,' said she; 'and then we were confirmed. We both cried; but in the afternoon we went up the Round Tower, and looked down on Copenhagen, and far, far away over the water; then we went to Friedericksberg, where the King and the Queen were sailing about in their splendid barges.'

"'But I had a different sort of sailing to that, later; and that, too, for many a year; a long way off, on great voyages.'

"'Yes, many a time have I wept for your sake,' said she. 'I thought you were dead and gone, and lying down in the deep waters. Many a night have I got up to see if the wind had not changed: and changed it had, sure enough; but you never came. I remember so well one day, when the rain was pouring down in torrents, the scavengers were before the house where I was in service, and I had come up with the dust, and remained standing at the door—it was dreadful weather—when just as I was there, the postman came and gave me a letter. It was from you! What a tour that letter had made! I opened it instantly and read: I laughed and wept. I was so happy. In it I read that you were in warm lands where the coffee-tree grows. What a blessed land that must be! You related so much, and I saw it all the while the rain was pouring down, and I standing there with the dust-box. At the same moment came someone who embraced me.'

"'Yes; but you gave him a good box on his ear that made it tingle!'

"'But I did not know it was you. You arrived as soon as your letter, and you were so handsome—that you still are—and had a long yellow silk handkerchief round your neck, and a bran new hat on; oh, you were so dashing! Good heavens! What weather it was, and what a state the street was in!'

"'And then we married,' said he. 'Don't you remember? And then we had our first little boy, and then Mary, and Nicholas, and Peter, and Christian.'

"'Yes, and how they all grew up to be honest people, and were beloved by everybody.'

"'And their children also have children,' said the old sailor; 'yes, those are our grand-children, full of strength and vigour. It was, methinks about this season that we had our wedding.'

"'Yes, this very day is the fiftieth anniversary of the marriage,' said old Granny, sticking her head between the two old people; who thought it was their neighbour who nodded to them. They looked at each other and held one another by the hand. Soon after came their children, and their grand-children; for they knew well enough that it was the day of the fiftieth anniversary, and had come with their gratulations that very morning; but the old people had forgotten it, although they were able to remember all that had happened many years ago. And the Elderbush sent forth a strong odour in the sun, that was just about to set, and shone right in the old people's faces. They both looked so rosy-cheeked; and the youngest of the grandchildren danced around them, and called out quite delighted, that there was to be something very splendid that evening—they were all to have hot potatoes. And old Nanny nodded in the bush, and shouted 'hurrah!' with the rest."

"But that is no fairy tale," said the little boy, who was listening to the story.

"The thing is, you must understand it," said the narrator; "let us ask old Nanny."

"That was no fairy tale, 'tis true," said old Nanny; "but now it's coming. The most wonderful fairy tales grow out of that which is reality; were that not the case, you know, my magnificent Elderbush could not have grown out of the tea-pot." And then she took the little boy out of bed, laid him on her bosom, and the branches of the Elder Tree, full of flowers, closed around her. They sat in an aerial dwelling, and it flew with them through the air. Oh, it was wondrous beautiful! Old Nanny had grown all of a sudden a young and pretty maiden; but her robe was still the same green stuff with white flowers, which she had worn before. On her bosom she had a real Elderflower, and in her yellow waving hair a wreath of the flowers; her eyes were so large and blue that it was a pleasure to look at them; she kissed the boy, and now they were of the same age and felt alike.

Hand in hand they went out of the bower, and they were standing in the beautiful garden of their home. Near the green lawn papa's walking-stick was tied, and for the little ones it seemed to be endowed with life; for as soon as they got astride it, the round polished knob was turned into a magnificent neighing head, a long black mane fluttered in the breeze, and four slender yet strong legs shot out. The animal was strong and handsome, and away they went at full gallop round the lawn.

"Huzza! Now we are riding miles off," said the boy. "We are riding away to the castle where we were last year!"

And on they rode round the grass-plot; and the little maiden, who, we know, was no one else but old Nanny, kept on crying out, "Now we are in the country! Don't you see the farm-house yonder? And there is an Elder Tree standing beside it; and the cock is scraping away the earth for the hens, look, how he struts! And now we are close to the church. It lies high upon the hill, between the large oak-trees, one of which is half decayed. And now we are by the smithy, where the fire is blazing, and where the half-naked men are banging with their hammers till the sparks fly about. Away! away! To the beautiful country-seat!"

And all that the little maiden, who sat behind on the stick, spoke of, flew by in reality. The boy saw it all, and yet they were only going round the grass-plot. Then they played in a side avenue, and marked out a little garden on the earth; and they took Elder-blossoms from their hair, planted them, and they grew just like those the old people planted when they were children, as related before. They went hand in hand, as the old people had done when they were children; but not to the Round Tower, or to Friedericksberg; no, the little damsel wound her arms round the boy, and then they flew far away through all Denmark. And spring came, and summer; and then it was autumn, and then winter; and a thousand pictures were reflected in the eye and in the heart of the boy; and the little girl always sang to him, "This you will never forget." And during their whole flight the Elder Tree smelt so sweet and odorous; he remarked the roses and the fresh beeches, but the Elder Tree had a more wondrous fragrance, for its flowers hung on the breast of the little maiden; and there, too, did he often lay his head during the flight.

"It is lovely here in spring!" said the young maiden. And they stood in a beech-wood that had just put on its first green, where the woodroof at their feet sent forth its fragrance, and the pale-red anemony looked so pretty among the verdure. "Oh, would it were always spring in the sweetly-smelling Danish beech-forests!"

"It is lovely here in summer!" said she. And she flew past old castles of by-gone days of chivalry, where the red walls and the embattled gables were mirrored in the canal, where the swans were swimming, and peered up into the old cool avenues. In the fields the corn was waving like the sea; in the ditches red and yellow flowers were growing; while wild-drone flowers, and blooming convolvuluses were creeping in the hedges; and towards evening the moon rose round and large, and the haycocks in the meadows smelt so sweetly. "This one never forgets!"

"It is lovely here in autumn!" said the little maiden. And suddenly the atmosphere grew as blue again as before; the forest grew red, and green, and yellow-colored. The dogs came leaping along, and whole flocks of wild-fowl flew over the cairn, where blackberry-bushes were hanging round the old stones. The sea was dark blue, covered with ships full of white sails; and in the barn old women, maidens, and children were sitting picking hops into a large cask; the young sang songs, but the old told fairy tales of mountain-sprites and soothsayers. Nothing could be more charming.

"It is delightful here in winter!" said the little maiden. And all the trees were covered with hoar-frost; they looked like white corals; the snow crackled under foot, as if one had new boots on; and one falling star after the other was seen in the sky. The Christmas-tree was lighted in the room; presents were there, and good-humour reigned. In the country the violin sounded in the room of the peasant; the newly-baked cakes were attacked; even the poorest child said, "It is really delightful here in winter!"

Yes, it was delightful; and the little maiden showed the boy everything; and the Elder Tree still was fragrant, and the red flag, with the white cross, was still waving: the flag under which the old seaman in the New Booths had sailed. And the boy grew up to be a lad, and was to go forth in the wide world-far, far away to warm lands, where the coffee-tree grows; but at his departure the little maiden took an Elder-blossom from her bosom, and gave it him to keep; and it was placed between the leaves of his Prayer-Book; and when in foreign lands he opened the book, it was always at the place where the keepsake-flower lay; and the more he looked at it, the fresher it became; he felt as it were, the fragrance of the Danish groves; and from among the leaves of the flowers he could distinctly see the little maiden, peeping forth with her bright blue eyes—and then she whispered, "It is delightful here in Spring, Summer, Autumn, and Winter"; and a hundred visions glided before his mind.

Thus passed many years, and he was now an old man, and sat with his old wife under the blooming tree. They held each other by the hand, as the old grand-father and grand-mother yonder in the New Booths did, and they talked exactly like them of old times, and of the fiftieth anniversary of their wedding. The little maiden, with the blue eyes, and with Elder-blossoms in her hair, sat in the tree, nodded to both of them, and said, "To-day is the fiftieth anniversary!" And then she took two flowers out of her hair, and kissed them. First, they shone like silver, then like gold; and when they laid them on the heads of the old people, each flower became a golden crown. So there they both sat, like a king and a queen, under the fragrant tree, that looked exactly like an elder: the old man told his wife the story of "Old Nanny," as it had been told him when a boy. And it seemed to both of them it contained much that resembled their own history; and those parts that were like it pleased them best.

"Thus it is," said the little maiden in the tree, "some call me 'Old Nanny,' others a 'Dryad,' but, in reality, my name is 'Remembrance'; 'tis I who sit in the tree that grows and grows! I can remember; I can tell things! Let me see if you have my flower still?"

And the old man opened his Prayer-Book. There lay the Elder-blossom, as fresh as if it had been placed there but a short time before; and Remembrance nodded, and the old people, decked with crowns of gold, sat in the flush of the evening sun. They closed their eyes, and—and—! Yes, that's the end of the story!

The little boy lay in his bed; he did not know if he had dreamed or not, or if he had been listening while someone told him the story. The tea-pot was standing on the table, but no Elder Tree was growing out of it! And the old man, who had been talking, was just on the point of going out at the door, and he did go.

"How splendid that was!" said the little boy. "Mother, I have been to warm countries."

"So I should think," said his mother. "When one has drunk two good cupfuls of Elder-flower tea, 'tis likely enough one goes into warm climates"; and she tucked him up nicely, least he should take cold. "You have had a good sleep while I have been sitting here, and arguing with him whether it was a story or a fairy tale."

"And where is old Nanny?" asked the little boy.

"In the tea-pot," said his mother; "and there she may remain."

~

Hans Christian Andersen (1805–1875) was a Danish author of short stories, novels, plays and poems. His fairy tales are extremely popular around the world and are among the most translated writings in literature, including *The Tinder-Box*, *Little Claus and Big Claus*, *The Princess and the Pea*, *Thumbelina* and *The Ugly Duckling*.

From A Doll's House

Henrik Ibsen

A Doll's House *is a late nineteenth century play set in a Norwegian town. Touching upon themes such as societal expectations, gender roles and identity, the story is about Nora Helmer and her outwardly perfect marriage to Torvald.*

ACT II

(The Christmas tree is in the corner by the piano, stripped of its ornaments and with burnt-down candle-ends on its dishevelled branches. NORA'S cloak and hat are lying on the sofa. She is alone in the room, walking about uneasily. She stops by the sofa and takes up her cloak.)

NORA

(drops her cloak)

Someone is coming now!

(Goes to the door and listens.)

No—it is no one. Of course, no one will come today, Christmas Day—nor tomorrow either. But, perhaps—

(opens the door and looks out)

No, nothing in the letterbox; it is quite empty.

(comes forward)

What rubbish! of course he can't be in earnest about it. Such a thing couldn't happen; it is impossible—I have three little children.

(Enter the NURSE from the room on the left, carrying a big cardboard box.)

NURSE

At last I have found the box with the fancy dress.

NORA

Thanks; put it on the table.

NURSE

(doing so)

But it is very much in want of mending.

NORA

I should like to tear it into a hundred thousand pieces.

NURSE

What an idea! It can easily be put in order—just a little patience.

NORA

Yes, I will go and get Mrs Linde to come and help me with it.

NURSE

What, out again? In this horrible weather? You will catch cold, ma'am, and make yourself ill.

NORA

Well, worse than that might happen. How are the children?

NURSE

The poor little souls are playing with their Christmas presents, but—

NORA

Do they ask much for me?

NURSE

You see, they are so accustomed to have their mamma with them.

NORA

Yes, but, nurse, I shall not be able to be so much with them now as I was before.

NURSE

Oh well, young children easily get accustomed to anything.

NORA

Do you think so? Do you think they would forget their mother if she went away altogether?

NURSE

Good heavens! Went away altogether?

NORA

Nurse, I want you to tell me something I have often wondered about—how could you have the heart to put your own child out among strangers?

NURSE

I was obliged to, if I wanted to be little Nora's nurse.

NORA

Yes, but how could you be willing to do it?

NURSE

What, when I was going to get such a good place by it? A poor girl who has got into trouble should be glad to. Besides, that wicked man didn't do a single thing for me.

NORA

But I suppose your daughter has quite forgotten you.

NURSE

No, indeed she hasn't. She wrote to me when she was confirmed, and when she was married.

NORA

(putting her arms round her neck)
Dear old Anne, you were a good mother to me when I was little.

NURSE

Little Nora, poor dear, had no other mother but me.

NORA

And if my little ones had no other mother, I am sure you would—what nonsense I am talking!

(opens the box)

Go in to them. Now I must go. You will see tomorrow how charming I shall look.

NURSE

I am sure there will be no one at the ball so charming as you, ma'am.

(She goes into the room on the left.)

NORA

(begins to unpack the box, but soon pushes it away from her)

If only I dared go out. If only no one would come. If only I could be sure nothing would happen here in the meantime. Stuff and nonsense! No one will come. Only I mustn't think about it. I will brush my muff. What lovely, lovely gloves! Out of my thoughts, out of my thoughts! One, two, three, four, five, six—

(screams)

Ah! there is someone coming!

(She makes a movement towards the door, but stands irresolute.)

(Enter Mrs Linde from the hall, where she has taken off her cloak and hat.)

NORA

Oh, it's you, Christine. There is no one else out there, is there? How good of you to come!

MRS LINDE

I heard you were up asking for me.

NORA

Yes, I was passing by. As a matter of fact, it is something you could help me with. Let us sit down here on the sofa. Look here. Tomorrow evening there is to be a fancy-dress ball at the Stenborgs', who live above us; and Torvald wants me to go as a Neapolitan fisher-girl, and dance the Tarantella that I learned at Capri.

MRS LINDE

I see; you are going to keep up the character.

NORA

Yes, Torvald wants me to. Look, here is the dress; Torvald had it made for me there, but now it is all so torn, and I haven't any idea—

MRS LINDE

We will easily put that right. It is only some of the trimming come unsewn here and there. Needle and thread? Now then, that's all we want.

NORA

It is nice of you.

MRS LINDE

Something has happened to you since yesterday morning. Nora, what is it?

NORA

(going nearer to her)

Christine! (listens) Hush! there's Torvald come home. Do you mind going in to the children for the present? Torvald can't bear to see dressmaking going on. Let Anne help you.

MRS LINDE

(gathering some of the things together)

Certainly—but I am not going away from here until we have had it out with one another.

(She goes into the room on the left, as HELMER comes in from the hall.)

NORA
(going up to HELMER)
I have wanted you so much, Torvald dear.

HELMER
Was that the dressmaker?

NORA
No, it was Christine; she is helping me to put my dress in order. You will see I shall look quite smart.

HELMER
Wasn't that a happy thought of mine, now?

NORA
Splendid! But don't you think it is nice of me, too, to do as you wish?

HELMER
Nice? Because you do as your husband wishes? Well, well, you little rogue, I am sure you did not mean it in that way. But I am not going to disturb you; you will want to be trying on your dress, I expect.

NORA
I suppose you are going to work.

HELMER
Yes.

(shows her a bundle of papers)
Look at that. I have just been into the bank.
(He turns to go into his room.)

NORA

Torvald.

HELMER

Yes.

NORA

If your little squirrel were to ask you for something very, very prettily—?

HELMER

What then?

NORA

Would you do it?

HELMER

I should like to hear what it is, first.

NORA

Your squirrel would run about and do all her tricks if you would be nice, and do what she wants.

HELMER

Speak plainly.

NORA

Your skylark would chirp about in every room, with her song rising and falling—

HELMER

Well, my skylark does that anyhow.

NORA

I would play the fairy and dance for you in the moonlight, Torvald.

HELMER

Nora—you surely don't mean that request you made to me this morning?

NORA

(going near him)

Yes, Torvald, I beg you so earnestly—

HELMER

Have you really the courage to open up that question again?

NORA

Yes, dear, you must do as I ask; you must let Krogstad keep his post in the bank.

HELMER

My dear Nora, it is his post that I have arranged Mrs Linde shall have.

NORA

Yes, you have been awfully kind about that; but you could just as well dismiss some other clerk instead of Krogstad.

HELMER

This is simply incredible obstinacy! Because you chose to give him a thoughtless promise that you would speak for him, I am expected to—

NORA

That isn't the reason, Torvald. It is for your own sake. This fellow writes in the most scurrilous newspapers; you have told me so yourself. He can do you an unspeakable amount of harm. I am frightened to death of him—

HELMER

Ah, I understand; it is recollections of the past that scare you.

NORA

What do you mean?

HELMER

Naturally you are thinking of your father.

NORA

Yes—yes, of course. Just recall to your mind what these malicious creatures wrote in the papers about papa, and how horribly they slandered him. I believe they would have procured his dismissal if the Department had not sent you over to inquire into it, and if you had not been so kindly disposed and helpful to him.

HELMER

My little Nora, there is an important difference between your father and me. Your father's reputation as a public official was not above suspicion. Mine is, and I hope it will continue to be so, as long as I hold my office.

NORA

You never can tell what mischief these men may contrive. We ought to be so well off, so snug and happy here in our peaceful home, and have no cares—you and I and the children, Torvald! That is why I beg you so earnestly—

HELMER

And it is just by interceding for him that you make it impossible for me to keep him. It is already known at the Bank that I mean to dismiss Krogstad. Is it to get about now that the new manager has changed his mind at his wife's bidding—

NORA

And what if it did?

HELMER

Of course! If only this obstinate little person can get her way! Do you suppose I am going to make myself ridiculous before my whole staff, to let people think that I am a man to be swayed by all sorts of outside influence? I should very soon feel the consequences of it, I can tell you! And besides, there is one thing that makes it quite impossible for me to have Krogstad in the Bank as long as I am manager.

NORA

Whatever is that?

HELMER

His moral failings I might perhaps have overlooked, if necessary—

NORA

Yes, you could—couldn't you?

HELMER

And I hear he is a good worker, too. But I knew him when we were boys. It was one of those rash friendships that so often prove an incubus in afterlife. I may as well tell you plainly, we were once on very intimate terms with one another. But this tactless fellow lays no restraint on himself when other people are present. On the contrary, he thinks it gives him the right to adopt a familiar tone with me, and every minute it is "I say, Helmer, old fellow!" and that sort of thing. I assure you it is extremely painful for me. He would make my position in the Bank intolerable.

NORA

Torvald, I don't believe you mean that.

HELMER

Don't you? Why not?

NORA

Because it is such a narrow-minded way of looking at things.

HELMER

What are you saying? Narrow-minded? Do you think I am narrow-minded?

NORA

No, just the opposite, dear—and it is exactly for that reason.

HELMER

It's the same thing. You say my point of view is narrow-minded, so I must be so too. Narrow-minded! Very well—I must put an end to this.

(He goes to the hall door and calls.) Helen!

NORA

What are you going to do?

HELMER

(looking among his papers)

Settle it.

(Enter MAID.)

Look here; take this letter and go downstairs with it at once. Find a messenger and tell him to deliver it, and be quick. The address is on it, and here is the money.

MAID

Very well, sir.

(She exits with the letter.)

HELMER

(putting his papers together)

Now then, little Miss Obstinate.

NORA

(breathlessly)

Torvald—what was that letter?

HELMER

Krogstad's dismissal.

NORA

Call her back, Torvald! There is still time. Oh Torvald, call her back! Do it for my sake—for your own sake—for the children's sake! Do you hear me, Torvald?

Call her back! You don't know what that letter can bring upon us.

HELMER

It's too late.

NORA

Yes, it's too late.

~

A Norwegian playwright and theatre director known as the father of realism and prose drama, Henrik Ibsen (1828–1906) is known for his revolutionary themes and strong characters. His notable works include *A Doll's House*, *The Wild Duck, Peer Gynt* and *The Lady from the Sea.*

That Spot

Jack London

I don't think much of Stephen Mackaye anymore, though I used to swear by him. I know that in those days I loved him more than my own brother. If ever I meet Stephen Mackaye again, I shall not be responsible for my actions. It passes beyond me that a man with whom I shared food and blanket, and with whom I mushed over the Chilcoot Trail, should turn out the way he did. I always sized Steve up as a square man, a kindly comrade, without an iota of anything vindictive or malicious in his nature. I shall never trust my judgment in men again. Why, I nursed that man through typhoid fever; we starved together on the headwaters of the Stewart; and he saved my life on the Little Salmon. And now, after the years we were together, all I can say of Stephen Mackaye is that he is the meanest man I ever knew.

We started for the Klondike in the fall rush of 1897, and we started too late to get over Chilcoot Pass before the freeze-up.

We packed our outfit on our backs part way over, when the snow began to fly, and then we had to buy dogs in order to sled it the rest of the way. That was how we came to get that Spot. Dogs were high, and we paid one hundred and ten dollars for him. He looked worth it. I say *looked*, because he was one of the finest-appearing dogs I ever saw. He weighed sixty pounds, and he had all the lines of a good sled animal. We never could make out his breed. He wasn't husky, nor Malemute, nor Hudson Bay; he looked like all of them and he didn't look like any of them; and on top of it all he had some of the white man's dog in him, for on one side, in the thick of the mixed yellow-brown-red-and-dirty-white that was his prevailing colour, there was a spot of coal-black as big as a water-bucket. That was why we called him Spot.

He was a good looker all right. When he was in condition his muscles stood out in bunches all over him. And he was the strongest-looking brute I ever saw in Alaska, also the most intelligent-looking. To run your eyes over him, you'd think he could outpull three dogs of his own weight. Maybe he could, but I never saw it. His intelligence didn't run that way. He could steal and forage to perfection; he had an instinct that was positively gruesome for divining when work was to be done and for making a sneak accordingly; and for getting lost and not staying lost he was nothing short of inspired. But when it came to work, the way that intelligence dribbled out of him and left him a mere clot of wobbling, stupid jelly would make your heart bleed.

There are times when I think it wasn't stupidity. Maybe, like some men I know, he was too wise to work. I shouldn't wonder if he put it all over us with that intelligence of his. Maybe he figured it all out and decided that a licking now and again and no work was a whole lot better than work all the time and no licking. He was intelligent enough for such a computation. I tell you, I've sat and looked into that dog's eyes till the shivers ran up and down my spine and the marrow crawled like yeast, what of the intelligence I saw shining out. I can't express myself about that intelligence. It is beyond mere words. I saw it, that's all. At times it was like gazing into a human soul, to look into his eyes; and what I saw there frightened me and started all sorts of ideas in my own mind of reincarnation and all the rest. I tell you I sensed something big in that brute's eyes; there was a message there, but I wasn't big enough myself to catch it. Whatever it was (I know I'm making a fool of myself)—whatever it was, it baffled me. I can't give an inkling of what I saw in that brute's eyes; it wasn't light, it wasn't colour; it was something that moved, away back, when the eyes themselves weren't moving. And I guess I didn't see it move either; I only sensed that it moved. It was an expression—that's what it was—and I got an impression of it. No; it was different from a mere expression; it was more than that. I don't know what it was, but it gave me a feeling of kinship just the same. Oh, no, not sentimental kinship. It was, rather, a kinship of equality. Those eyes never pleaded like a deer's eyes. They challenged. No, it wasn't defiance. It was just a calm assumption of equality. And I don't think it was deliberate. My belief is that it was unconscious on his part. It was there because it was there, and it couldn't help shining out. No, I don't mean shine. It didn't shine; it *moved.* I know I'm talking rot, but if you'd looked into that animal's eyes the way I have, you'd understand. Steve was affected the same way I was. Why, I tried to kill that Spot once—he was no good for anything; and I fell down on it. I led him out into the brush, and he came along slow and unwilling. He knew what was going on. I stopped in a likely place, put my foot on the rope, and pulled my big Colt's. And that dog sat down and looked at me. I tell you he didn't plead. He just looked. And I saw all kinds of incomprehensible things moving, yes, *moving*, in those eyes of his. I didn't really see them move; I thought I saw them, for, as I said before, I guess I only sensed them. And I want to tell you right now that it got beyond me. It was like killing a man, a conscious, brave man, who looked calmly into your gun as much as to say, "Who's afraid?"

Then, too, the message seemed so near that, instead of pulling the trigger quick, I stopped to see if I could catch the message. There it was, right before me, glimmering all around in those eyes of his. And then it was too late. I got scared. I was trembly all over, and my stomach generated a nervous palpitation that made me seasick. I just sat down and looked at the dog, and he looked at me, till I thought I was going crazy. Do you want to know what I did? I threw down the gun and ran back to camp with the fear of God in my heart. Steve laughed at me. But I notice that Steve led Spot into the woods, a week later, for the same purpose, and that Steve came back alone, and a little later Spot drifted back, too.

At any rate, Spot wouldn't work. We paid a hundred and ten dollars for him from the bottom of our sack, and he wouldn't work. He wouldn't even tighten the traces. Steve spoke to him the first time we put him in harness, and he sort of shivered, that was all. Not an ounce on the traces. He just stood still and wobbled, like so much jelly. Steve touched him with the whip. He yelped, but not an ounce. Steve touched him again, a bit harder, and he howled—the regular long wolf howl. Then Steve got mad and gave him half a dozen, and I came on the run from the tent.

I told Steve he was brutal with the animal, and we had some words—the first we'd ever had. He threw the whip down in the snow and walked away mad. I picked it up and went to it. That Spot trembled and wobbled and cowered before ever I swung the lash, and with the first bite of it he howled like a lost soul.

Next he lay down in the snow. I started the rest of the dogs, and they dragged him along while I threw the whip into him. He rolled over on his back and bumped along, his four legs waving in the air, himself howling as though he was going through a sausage machine. Steve came back and laughed at me, and I apologized for what I'd said.

There was no getting any work out of that Spot; and to make up for it, he was the biggest pig-glutton of a dog I ever saw. On top of that, he was the cleverest thief. There was no circumventing him. Many a breakfast we went without our bacon because Spot had been there first. And it was because of him that we nearly starved to death up the Stewart. He figured out the way to break into our meat-cache, and what he didn't eat, the rest of the team did. But he was impartial. He stole from everybody. He was a restless dog, always very busy snooping around or going somewhere. And there was never a camp within five miles that he didn't raid. The worst of it was that they always came back on us to pay his board bill, which was just, being the law of the land; but it was mighty hard on us, especially that first winter on the Chilcoot, when we were busted, paying for whole hams and sides of bacon that we never ate. He could fight, too, that Spot. He could do everything but work. He never pulled a pound, but he was the boss of the whole team. The way he made those dogs stand around was an education. He bullied them, and there was always one or more of them fresh-marked with his fangs. But he was more than a bully. He wasn't afraid of anything that walked on four legs; and I've seen him march, single-handed into a strange team, without any provocation whatever, and put the *kibosh* on the whole outfit. Did I say he could eat? I caught him eating the whip once. That's straight. He started in at the lash, and when I caught him he was down to the handle, and still going.

But he was a good looker. At the end of the first week we sold him for seventy-five dollars to the Mounted Police. They had experienced dog-drivers, and we knew that by the time he'd covered the six hundred miles to Dawson he'd be a good sled-dog. I say we *knew*, for we were just getting acquainted with that Spot. A little later we were not brash enough to know anything where he was concerned. A week later we woke up in the morning to the dangdest dog-fight we'd ever heard. It was that Spot come back and knocking the team into shape. We ate a pretty depressing breakfast, I can tell you; but cheered up two hours afterward when we sold him to an official courier, bound in to Dawson with government despatches. That Spot was only three days in coming back, and, as usual, celebrated his arrival with a rough house.

We spent the winter and spring, after our own outfit was across the pass, freighting other people's outfits; and we made a fat stake. Also, we made money out of Spot. If we sold him once, we sold him twenty times. He always came back, and no one asked for their money. We didn't want the money. We'd have paid handsomely for anyone to take him off our hands for keeps'. We had to get rid of him, and we couldn't give him away, for that would have been suspicious. But he was such a fine looker that we never had any difficulty in selling him. "Unbroke," we'd say, and they'd pay any old price for him. We sold him as low as twenty-five dollars, and once we got a hundred and fifty for him. That particular party returned him in person, refused to take his money back, and the way he abused us was something awful. He said it was cheap at the price to tell us what he thought of us; and we felt he was so justified that we never talked back. But to this day I've never quite regained all the old self-respect that was mine before that man talked to me.

When the ice cleared out of the lakes and river, we put our outfit in a Lake Bennett boat and started for Dawson. We had a good team of dogs, and of course we piled them on top the outfit. That Spot was along—there was no losing him; and a dozen times, the first day, he knocked one or another of the dogs overboard in the course of fighting with them. It was close quarters, and he didn't like being crowded.

"What that dog needs is space," Steve said the second day. "Let's maroon him."

We did, running the boat in at Caribou Crossing for him to jump ashore. Two of the other dogs, good dogs, followed him; and we lost two whole days trying to find them. We never saw those two dogs again; but the quietness and relief we enjoyed made us decide, like the man who refused his hundred and fifty, that it was cheap at the price. For the first time in months Steve and I laughed and whistled and sang. We were as happy as clams. The dark days were over. The nightmare had been lifted. That Spot was gone.

Three weeks later, one morning, Steve and I were standing on the river-bank at Dawson. A small boat was just arriving from Lake Bennett. I saw Steve give a start, and heard him say something that was not nice and that was not under his breath. Then I looked; and there, in the bow of the boat, with ears pricked up, sat Spot. Steve and I sneaked immediately, like beaten curs, like cowards, like absconders from justice. It was this last that the lieutenant of police thought when he saw us sneaking. He surmised that there were law-officers in the boat who were after us. He didn't wait to find out, but kept us in sight, and in the M. & M. saloon got us in a corner. We had a merry time explaining, for we refused to go back to the boat and meet Spot; and finally he held us under guard of another policeman while he went to the boat. After we got clear of him, we started for the cabin, and when we arrived, there was that Spot sitting on the stoop waiting for us. Now how did he know we lived there? There were forty thousand people in Dawson that summer, and how did he save our cabin out of all the cabins? How did he know we were in Dawson, anyway? I leave it to you. But don't forget what I said about his intelligence and that immortal something I have seen glimmering in his eyes.

There was no getting rid of him any more. There were too many people in Dawson who had bought him up on Chilcoot, and the story got around. Half a dozen times we put him on board steamboats going down the Yukon; but he merely went ashore at the first landing and trotted back up the bank. We couldn't sell him, we couldn't kill him (both Steve and I had tried), and nobody else was able to kill him. He bore a charmed life. I've seen him go down in a dogfight on the main street with fifty dogs on top of him, and when they were separated, he'd appear on all his four legs, unharmed, while two of the dogs that had been on top of him would be lying dead.

I saw him steal a chunk of moose-meat from Major Dinwiddie's cache so heavy that he could just keep one jump ahead of Mrs Dinwiddie's squaw cook, who was after him with an axe. As he went up the hill, after the squaw gave up, Major Dinwiddie himself came out and pumped his Winchester into the landscape. He emptied his magazine twice, and never touched that Spot. Then a policeman came along and arrested him for discharging firearms inside the city limits. Major Dinwiddie paid his fine, and Steve and I paid him for the moose-meat at the rate of a dollar a pound, bones and all. That was what he paid for it. Meat was high that year.

I am only telling what I saw with my own eyes. And now I'll tell you something also. I saw that Spot fall through a water-hole. The ice was three and a half feet thick, and the current sucked him under like a straw. Three hundred yards below was the big water-hole used by the hospital. Spot crawled out of the hospital water-hole, licked off the water, bit out the ice that had formed between his toes, trotted up the bank, and whipped a big Newfoundland belonging to the Gold Commissioner.

In the fall of 1898, Steve and I poled up the Yukon on the last water, bound for Stewart River. We took the dogs along, all except Spot. We figured we'd been feeding him long enough. He'd cost us more time and trouble and money and grub than we'd got by selling him on the Chilcoot—especially grub. So Steve and I tied him down in the cabin and pulled our freight. We camped that night at the mouth of Indian River, and Steve and I were pretty facetious over having shaken him. Steve was a funny cuss, and I was just sitting up in the blankets and laughing when a tornado hit camp. The way that Spot walked into those dogs and gave them what-for was hair-raising. Now how did he get loose? It's up to you. I haven't any theory. And how did he get across the Klondike River? That's another facer. And anyway, how did he know we had gone up the Yukon? You see, we went by water, and he couldn't smell our tracks. Steve and I began to get superstitious about that dog. He got on our nerves, too; and, between you and me, we were just a mite afraid of him.

The freeze-up came on when we were at the mouth of Henderson Creek, and we traded him off for two sacks of flour to an outfit that was bound up White River after copper. Now that whole outfit was lost. Never trace nor hide nor hair of men, dogs, sleds, or anything was ever found. They dropped clean out of sight. It became one of the mysteries of the country. Steve and I plugged away up the Stewart, and six weeks afterward that Spot crawled into camp. He was a perambulating skeleton, and could just drag along; but he got there. And what I want to know is, who told him we were up the Stewart? We could have gone to a thousand other places. How did he know? You tell me, and I'll tell you.

No losing him. At the Mayo he started a row with an Indian dog. The buck who owned the dog took a swing at Spot with an axe, missed him, and killed his own dog. Talk about magic and turning bullets aside—I, for one, consider it a blamed sight harder to turn an axe aside with a big buck at the other end of it. And I saw him do it with my own eyes. That buck didn't want to kill his own dog. You've got to show me.

I told you about Spot breaking into our meat cache. It was nearly the death of us. There wasn't any more meat to be killed, and meat was all we had to live on. The moose had gone back several hundred miles and the Indians with them. There we were. Spring was on, and we had to wait for the river to break. We got pretty thin before we decided to eat the dogs, and we decided to eat Spot first. Do you know what that dog did? He sneaked. Now how did he know our minds were made up to eat him? We sat up nights laying for him, but he never came back, and we ate the other dogs. We ate the whole team.

And now for the sequel. You know what it is when a big river breaks up and a few billion tons of ice go out, jamming and milling and grinding. Just in the thick of it, when the Stewart went out, rumbling and roaring, we sighted Spot out in the middle. He'd got caught as he was trying to cross up above somewhere. Steve and I yelled and shouted and ran up and down the bank, tossing our hats in the air. Sometimes we'd stop and hug each other, we were that boisterous, for we saw Spot's finish. He didn't have a chance in a million. He didn't have any chance at all. After the ice-run, we got into a canoe and paddled down to the Yukon, and down the Yukon to Dawson, stopping to feed up for a week at the cabins at the mouth of Henderson Creek. And as we came in to the bank at Dawson, there sat that Spot, waiting for us, his ears pricked up, his tail wagging, his mouth smiling, extending a hearty welcome to us. Now how did he get out of that ice? How did he know we were coming to Dawson, to the very hour and minute, to be out there on the bank waiting for us?

The more I think of that Spot, the more I am convinced that there are things in this world that go beyond science. On no scientific grounds can that Spot be explained. It's psychic phenomena, or mysticism, or something of that sort, I guess, with a lot of Theosophy thrown in. The Klondike is a good country. I might have been there yet, and become a millionaire, if it hadn't been for Spot. He got on my nerves. I stood him for two years altogether, and then I guess my stamina broke. It was the summer of 1899 when I pulled out. I didn't say anything to Steve. I just sneaked. But I fixed it up all right. I wrote Steve a note, and enclosed a package of "rough-on-rats," telling him what to do with it. I was worn down to skin and bone by that Spot, and I was that nervous that I'd jump and look around when there wasn't anybody within hailing distance. But it was astonishing the way I recuperated when I got quit of him. I got back twenty pounds before I arrived in San Francisco, and by the time I'd crossed the ferry to Oakland I was my old self again, so that even my wife looked in vain for any change in me.

Steve wrote to me once, and his letter seemed irritated. He took it kind of hard because I'd left him with Spot. Also, he said he'd used the "rough-on-rats," per directions, and that there was nothing doing. A year went by. I was back in the office and prospering in all ways—even getting a bit fat. And then Steve arrived. He didn't look me up. I read his name in the steamer list, and wondered why. But I didn't wonder long. I got up one morning and found that Spot chained to the gate-post and holding up the milkman. Steve went north to Seattle, I learned, that very morning. I didn't put on any more weight.

My wife made me buy him a collar and tag, and within an hour he showed his gratitude by killing her pet Persian cat. There is no getting rid of that Spot. He will be with me until I die, for he'll never die. My appetite is not so good since he arrived, and my wife says I am looking peaked. Last night that Spot got into Mr Harvey's hen-house (Harvey is my next-door neighbour) and killed nineteen of his fancy-bred chickens. I shall have to pay for them. My neighbours on the other side quarrelled with my wife and then moved out. Spot was the cause of it. And that is why I am disappointed in Stephen Mackaye. I had no idea he was so mean a man.

~

John Griffith Chaney, known to readers as Jack London (1876–1916), was an American short-story, fiction and non-fiction writer who is best known for his novels *Call of the Wild*, *White Fang* and *The Sea Wolf*. Several of his works centre around the Klondike Gold Rush, an event that he experienced first hand.

From Three Men In A Boat

Jerome K. Jerome

Three Men in a Boat *is the story of three friends and their dog who embark on a chaotic boating trip on the Thames as a remedy for their various ailments and to seek some rest and relaxation.*

So, on the following evening, we again assembled, to discuss and arrange our plans. Harris said:

"Now, the first thing to settle is what to take with us. Now, you get a bit of paper and write down, J., and you get the grocery catalogue, George, and somebody give me a bit of pencil, and then I'll make out a list."

That's Harris all over—so ready to take the burden of everything himself, and put it on the backs of other people.

He always reminds me of my poor Uncle Podger. You never saw such a commotion up and down a house, in all your life, as when my Uncle Podger undertook to do a job. A picture would have come home from the frame-maker's, and be standing in the dining-room, waiting to be put up; and Aunt Podger would ask what was to be done with it, and Uncle Podger would say:

"Oh, you leave that to *me*. Don't you, any of you, worry yourselves about that. *I'll* do all that."

And then he would take off his coat, and begin. He would send the girl out for sixpen'orth of nails, and then one of the boys after her to tell her what size to get; and, from that, he would gradually work down, and start the whole house.

"Now you go and get me my hammer, Will," he would shout; "and you bring me the rule, Tom; and I shall want the step-ladder, and I had better have a kitchen-chair, too; and, Jim! you run round to Mr Goggles, and tell him, 'Pa's kind regards, and hopes his leg's better; and will he lend him his spirit-level?' And don't you go, Maria, because I shall want somebody to hold me the light; and when the girl comes back, she must go out again for a bit of picture-cord; and Tom!—where's Tom?—Tom, you come here; I shall want you to hand me up the picture."

And then he would lift up the picture, and drop it, and it would come out of the frame, and he would try to save the glass, and cut himself; and then he would spring round the room, looking for his handkerchief. He could not find his handkerchief, because it was in the pocket of the coat he had taken off, and he did not know where he had put the coat, and all the house had to leave off looking for his tools, and start looking for his coat; while he would dance round and hinder them.

"Doesn't anybody in the whole house know where my coat is? I never came across such a set in all my life—upon my word I didn't. Six of you!—and you can't find a coat that I put down not five minutes ago! Well, of all the—"

Then he'd get up, and find that he had been sitting on it, and would call out:

"Oh, you can give it up! I've found it myself now. Might just as well ask the cat to find anything as expect you people to find it."

And, when half an hour had been spent in tying up his finger, and a new glass had been got, and the tools, and the ladder, and the chair, and the candle had been brought, he would have another go, the whole family, including the girl and the charwoman, standing round in a semi-circle, ready to help. Two people would have to hold the chair, and a third would help him up on it, and hold him there, and a fourth would hand him a nail, and a fifth would pass him up the hammer, and he would take hold of the nail, and drop it.

"There!" he would say, in an injured tone, "now the nail's gone."

And we would all have to go down on our knees and grovel for it, while he would stand on the chair, and grunt, and want to know if he was to be kept there all the evening.

The nail would be found at last, but by that time he would have lost the hammer.

"Where's the hammer? What did I do with the hammer? Great heavens! Seven of you, gaping round there, and you don't know what I did with the hammer!"

We would find the hammer for him, and then he would have lost sight of the mark he had made on the wall, where the nail was to go in, and each of us had to get up on the chair, beside him, and see if we could find it; and we would each discover it in a different place, and he would call us all fools, one after another, and tell us to get down. And he would take the rule, and re-measure, and find that he wanted half thirty-one and three-eighths inches from the corner, and would try to do it in his head, and go mad.

And we would all try to do it in our heads, and all arrive at different results, and sneer at one another. And in the general row, the original number would be forgotten, and Uncle Podger would have to measure it again.

He would use a bit of string this time, and at the critical moment, when the old fool was leaning over the chair at an angle of forty-five, and trying to reach a point three inches beyond what was possible for him to reach, the string would slip, and down he would slide on to the piano, a really fine musical effect being produced by the suddenness with which his head and body struck all the notes at the same time.

And Aunt Maria would say that she would not allow the children to stand round and hear such language.

At last, Uncle Podger would get the spot fixed again, and put the point of the nail on it with his left hand, and take the hammer in his right hand. And, with the first blow, he would smash his thumb, and drop the hammer, with a yell, on somebody's toes.

Aunt Maria would mildly observe that, next time Uncle Podger was going to hammer a nail into the wall, she hoped he'd let her know in time, so that she could make arrangements to go and spend a week with her mother while it was being done.

"Oh! you women, you make such a fuss over everything," Uncle Podger would reply, picking himself up. "Why, I *like* doing a little job of this sort."

And then he would have another try, and, at the second blow, the nail would go clean through the plaster, and half the hammer after it, and Uncle Podger be precipitated against the wall with force nearly sufficient to flatten his nose.

Then we had to find the rule and the string again, and a new hole was made; and, about midnight, the picture would be up—very crooked and insecure, the wall for yards round looking as if it had been smoothed down with a rake, and everybody dead beat and wretched—except Uncle Podger.

"There you are," he would say, stepping heavily off the chair on to the charwoman's corns, and surveying the mess he had made with evident pride. "Why, some people would have had a man in to do a little thing like that!"

Harris will be just that sort of man when he grows up, I know, and I told him so. I said I could not permit him to take so much labour upon himself. I said:

"No; *you* get the paper, and the pencil, and the catalogue, and George write down, and I'll do the work."

The first list we made out had to be discarded. It was clear that the upper reaches of the Thames would not allow of the navigation of a boat sufficiently large to take the things we had set down as indispensable; so we tore the list up, and looked at one another!

George said:

"You know we are on a wrong track altogether. We must not think of the things we could do with, but only of the things that we can't do without."

George comes out really quite sensible at times. You'd be surprised. I call that downright wisdom, not merely as regards the present case, but with reference to our trip up the river of life, generally. How many people, on that voyage, load up the boat till it is ever in danger of swamping with a store of foolish things which they think essential to the pleasure and comfort of the trip, but which are really only useless lumber.

How they pile the poor little craft mast-high with fine clothes and big houses; with useless servants, and a host of swell friends that do not care twopence for them, and that they do not care three ha'pence for; with expensive entertainments that nobody enjoys, with formalities and fashions, with pretence and ostentation, and with—oh, heaviest, maddest lumber of all!—the dread of what will my neighbour think, with luxuries that only cloy, with pleasures that bore, with empty show that, like the criminal's iron crown of yore, makes to bleed and swoon the aching head that wears it!

It is lumber, man—all lumber! Throw it overboard. It makes the boat so heavy to pull, you nearly faint at the oars. It makes it so cumbersome and dangerous to manage, you never know a moment's freedom from anxiety and care, never gain a moment's rest for dreamy laziness—no time to watch the windy shadows skimming lightly o'er the shallows, or the glittering sunbeams flitting in and out among the ripples, or the great trees by the margin looking down at their own image, or the woods all green and golden, or the lilies white and yellow, or the sombre-waving rushes, or the sedges, or the orchis, or the blue forget-me-nots.

Throw the lumber over, man! Let your boat of life be light, packed with only what you need—a homely home and simple pleasures, one or two friends, worth the name, someone to love and someone to love you, a cat, a dog, and a pipe or two, enough to eat and enough to wear, and a little more than enough to drink; for thirst is a dangerous thing.

You will find the boat easier to pull then, and it will not be so liable to upset, and it will not matter so much if it does upset; good, plain merchandise will stand water. You will have time to think as well as to work. Time to drink in life's sunshine—time to listen to the Æolian music that the wind of God draws from the human heart-strings around us—time to—

I beg your pardon, really. I quite forgot.

Well, we left the list to George, and he began it.

"We won't take a tent," suggested George; "we will have a boat with a cover. It is ever so much simpler, and more comfortable."

It seemed a good thought, and we adopted it. I do not know whether you have ever seen the thing I mean. You fix iron hoops up over the boat, and stretch a huge canvas over them, and fasten it down all round, from stem to stern, and it converts the boat into a sort of little house, and it is beautifully cosy, though a trifle stuffy; but there, everything has its drawbacks, as the man said when his mother-in-law died, and they came down upon him for the funeral expenses.

George said that in that case we must take a rug each, a lamp, some soap, a brush and comb (between us), a toothbrush (each), a basin, some tooth-powder, some shaving tackle (sounds like a French exercise, doesn't it?), and a couple of big-towels for bathing. I notice that people always make gigantic arrangements for bathing when they are going anywhere near the water, but that they don't bathe much when they are there.

It is the same when you go to the sea-side. I always determine—when thinking over the matter in London—that I'll get up early every morning, and go and have a dip before breakfast, and I religiously pack up a pair of drawers and a bath towel. I always get red bathing drawers. I rather fancy myself in red drawers. They suit my complexion so. But when I get to the sea I don't feel somehow that I want that early morning bathe nearly so much as I did when I was in town.

On the contrary, I feel more that I want to stop in bed till the last moment, and then come down and have my breakfast. Once or twice virtue has triumphed, and I have got out at six and half-dressed myself, and have taken my drawers and towel, and stumbled dismally off. But I haven't enjoyed it. They seem to keep a specially cutting east wind, waiting for me, when I go to bathe in the early morning; and they pick out all the three-cornered stones, and put them on the top, and they sharpen up the rocks and cover the points over with a bit of sand so that I can't see them, and they take the sea and put it two miles out, so that I have to huddle myself up in my arms and hop, shivering, through six inches of water. And when I do get to the sea, it is rough and quite insulting.

One huge wave catches me up and chucks me in a sitting posture, as hard as ever it can, down on to a rock which has been put there for me. And, before I've said "Oh! Ugh!" and found out what has gone, the wave comes back and carries me out to mid-ocean. I begin to strike out frantically for the shore, and wonder if I shall ever see home and friends again, and wish I'd been kinder to my little sister when a boy (when I was a boy, I mean). Just when I have given up all hope, a wave retires and leaves me sprawling like a star-fish on the sand, and I get up and look back and find that I've been swimming for my life in two feet of water. I hop back and dress, and crawl home, where I have to pretend I liked it.

In the present instance, we all talked as if we were going to have a long swim every morning.

George said it was so pleasant to wake up in the boat in the fresh morning, and plunge into the limpid river. Harris said there was nothing like a swim before breakfast to give you an appetite. He said it always gave him an appetite. George said that if it was going to make Harris eat more than Harris ordinarily ate, then he should protest against Harris having a bath at all.

He said there would be quite enough hard work in towing sufficient food for Harris up against stream, as it was.

I urged upon George, however, how much pleasanter it would be to have Harris clean and fresh about the boat, even if we did have to take a few more hundredweight of provisions; and he got to see it in my light, and withdrew his opposition to Harris's bath.

Agreed, finally, that we should take *three* bath towels, so as not to keep each other waiting.

For clothes, George said two suits of flannel would be sufficient, as we could wash them ourselves, in the river, when they got dirty. We asked him if he had ever tried washing flannels in the river, and he replied: "No, not exactly himself like; but he knew some fellows who had, and it was easy enough;" and Harris and I were weak enough to fancy he knew what he was talking about, and that three respectable young men, without position or influence, and with no experience in washing, could really clean their own shirts and trousers in the river Thames with a bit of soap.

We were to learn in the days to come, when it was too late, that George was a miserable impostor, who could evidently have known nothing whatever about the matter. If you had seen these clothes after—but, as the shilling shockers say, we anticipate.

George impressed upon us to take a change of under-things and plenty of socks, in case we got upset and wanted a change; also plenty of handkerchiefs, as they would do to wipe things, and a pair of leather boots as well as our boating shoes, as we should want them if we got upset.

~

Jerome Klapka Jerome (1859–1927) was an English novelist, humourist and playwright. Best known for his comic masterpiece *Three Men in a Boat*, Jerome is said to have based the main characters on himself and two of his friends. His other works include *The Idle Thoughts of an Idle Fellow*, *Three Men on the Bummel* and *Paul Kelver*.

To Autumn

John Keats

Season of mists and mellow fruitfulness,
Close bosom-friend of the maturing sun;
Conspiring with him how to load and bless
With fruit the vines that round the thatch-eves run;
To bend with apples the moss'd cottage-trees,
And fill all fruit with ripeness to the core;
To swell the gourd, and plump the hazel shells
With a sweet kernel; to set budding more,
And still more, later flowers for the bees,
Until they think warm days will never cease,
For Summer has o'er-brimm'd their clammy cells.

Who hath not seen thee oft amid thy store?
Sometimes whoever seeks abroad may find
Thee sitting careless on a granary floor,
Thy hair soft-lifted by the winnowing wind;
Or on a half-reap'd furrow sound asleep,
Drows'd with the fume of poppies, while thy hook
Spares the next swath and all its twined flowers:

And sometimes like a gleaner thou dost keep
Steady thy laden head across a brook;
Or by a cyder-press, with patient look,
Thou watchest the last oozings hours by hours.

Where are the songs of Spring? Ay, where are they?
Think not of them, thou hast thy music too,—
While barred clouds bloom the soft-dying day,
And touch the stubble-plains with rosy hue;
Then in a wailful choir the small gnats mourn
Among the river sallows, borne aloft
Or sinking as the light wind lives or dies;
And full-grown lambs loud bleat from hilly bourn;
Hedge-crickets sing; and now with treble soft
The red-breast whistles from a garden-croft;
And gathering swallows twitter in the skies.

~

One of the greatest Romantic poets of his time, Englishman John Keats (1795–1821) is best known for his poems "On a Grecian Urn", "To a Nightingale", "La Belle Dame Sans Merci" and "Bright Star", among others. He tragically died of consumption at just twenty-five years of age.

From Gulliver's Travels

Jonathan Swift

Gulliver's Travels *is a satirical work of adventure fiction about a surgeon and seaman who embarks on several voyages to fantastical lands and his experiences with the people and cultures he encounters.*

My father had a small estate in Nottinghamshire; I was the third of five sons. He sent me to Emanuel College in Cambridge at fourteen years old, where I resided three years, and applied myself close to my studies; but the charge of maintaining me, although I had a very scanty allowance, being too great for a narrow fortune, I was bound apprentice to Mr James Bates, an eminent surgeon in London, with whom I continued four years. My father now and then sending me small sums of money, I laid them out in learning navigation, and other parts of the mathematics, useful to those who intend to travel, as I always believed it would be, some time or other, my fortune to do. When I left Mr Bates, I went down to my father: where, by the assistance of him and my uncle John, and some other relations, I got forty pounds, and a promise of thirty pounds a year to maintain me at Leyden: there I studied physic two years and seven months, knowing it would be useful in long voyages.

Soon after my return from Leyden, I was recommended by my good master, Mr Bates, to be surgeon to the Swallow, Captain Abraham Pannel, commander; with whom I continued three years and a half, making a voyage or two into the Levant, and some other parts. When I came back I resolved to settle in London; to which Mr Bates, my master, encouraged me, and by him I was recommended to several patients. I took part of a small house in the Old Jewry; and being advised to alter my condition, I married Mrs Mary Burton, second daughter to Mr Edmund Burton, hosier, in Newgate-street, with whom I received four hundred pounds for a portion.

But my good master Bates dying in two years after, and I having few friends, my business began to fail; for my conscience would not suffer me to imitate the bad practice of too many among my brethren. Having therefore consulted with my wife, and some of my acquaintance, I determined to go again to sea. I was surgeon successively in two ships, and made several voyages, for six years, to the East and West Indies, by which I got some addition to my fortune. My hours of leisure I spent in reading the best authors, ancient and modern, being always provided with a good number of books; and when I was ashore, in observing the manners and dispositions of the people, as well as learning their language; wherein I had a great facility, by the strength of my memory.

The last of these voyages not proving very fortunate, I grew weary of the sea, and intended to stay at home with my wife and family. I removed from the Old Jewry to Fetter Lane, and from thence to Wapping, hoping to get business among the sailors;

but it would not turn to account. After three years expectation that things would mend, I accepted an advantageous offer from Captain William Prichard, master of the Antelope, who was making a voyage to the South Sea. We set sail from Bristol, 4 May, 1699, and our voyage was at first very prosperous.

It would not be proper, for some reasons, to trouble the reader with the particulars of our adventures in those seas; let it suffice to inform him, that in our passage from thence to the East Indies, we were driven by a violent storm to the north-west of Van Diemen's Land. By an observation, we found ourselves in the latitude of 30 degrees 2 minutes south. Twelve of our crew were dead by immoderate labour and ill food; the rest were in a very weak condition. On 5 November, which was the beginning of summer in those parts, the weather being very hazy, the seamen spied a rock within half a cable's length of the ship; but the wind was so strong, that we were driven directly upon it, and immediately split. Six of the crew, of whom I was one, having let down the boat into the sea, made a shift to get clear of the ship and the rock. We rowed, by my computation, about three leagues, till we were able to work no longer, being already spent with labour while we were in the ship. We therefore trusted ourselves to the mercy of the waves, and in about half an hour the boat was overset by a sudden flurry from the north. What became of my companions in the boat, as well as of those who escaped on the rock, or were left in the vessel, I cannot tell; but conclude they were all lost. For my own part, I swam as fortune directed me, and was pushed forward by wind and tide. I often let my legs drop, and could feel no bottom; but when I was almost gone, and able to struggle no longer, I found myself within my depth; and by this time the storm was much abated. The declivity was so small, that I walked near a mile before I got to the shore, which I conjectured was about eight o'clock in the evening. I then advanced forward near half a mile, but could not discover any sign of houses or inhabitants; at least I was in so weak a condition, that I did not observe them. I was extremely tired, and with that, and the heat of the weather, and about half a pint of brandy that I drank as I left the ship, I found myself much inclined to sleep. I lay down on the grass, which was very short and soft, where I slept sounder than ever I remembered to have done in my life, and, as I reckoned, about nine hours; for when I awaked, it was just day-light. I attempted to rise, but was not able to stir: for, as I happened to lie on my back, I found my arms and legs were strongly fastened on each side to the ground; and my hair, which was long and thick, tied down in the same manner. I likewise felt several slender ligatures across my body, from my arm-pits to my thighs. I could only look upwards; the sun began to grow hot, and the light offended my eyes. I heard a confused noise about me; but in the posture I lay, could see nothing except the sky. In a little time I felt something alive moving on my left leg, which advancing gently forward over my breast, came almost up to my chin; when, bending my eyes downwards as much as I could, I perceived it to be a human creature not six inches high, with a bow and arrow in his hands, and a quiver at his back. In the mean time, I felt at least forty more of the same kind (as I conjectured) following the first. I was in the utmost astonishment, and roared so loud, that they all ran back in a fright; and some of them, as I was afterwards told, were hurt with the falls they got by leaping from my sides upon the ground. However, they soon returned, and one of them, who ventured so far as to get a full sight of my face, lifting up his hands and eyes by way of admiration, cried out in a shrill but distinct voice, *Hekinah degul*: the others repeated the same words several times, but then I knew not what they meant. I lay all this while, as the reader may believe, in great uneasiness. At length, struggling to get loose, I had the fortune to break the strings, and wrench out the pegs that fastened my left arm to the ground; for, by lifting it up to my face, I discovered the methods they had taken to bind me, and at the same time with a violent pull, which gave me excessive pain, I a little loosened the strings that tied down my hair on the left side, so that I was just able to turn my head about two inches. But the creatures ran off a second time, before I could seize them; whereupon there was a great shout in a very shrill accent, and after it ceased I heard one of them cry aloud *Tolgo phonac*; when in an instant I felt above a hundred arrows discharged on my left hand, which, pricked me like so many needles; and besides, they shot another flight into the air, as we do bombs in Europe, whereof many, I suppose, fell on my body, (though I felt them not), and some on my face, which I immediately covered with my left hand. When this shower of arrows was over, I fell a groaning with grief and pain; and then striving again to get loose, they discharged another volley larger than the first, and some of them attempted with spears to stick me in the sides; but by good luck I had on a buff jerkin, which they could not pierce. I thought it the most prudent method to lie still, and my design was to continue so till night, when, my left hand being already loose, I could easily free myself: and as for the inhabitants, I had reason to believe I might be a match for the greatest army they could bring against me, if they were all of the same size with him that I saw. But fortune disposed otherwise of me. When the people observed I was quiet, they discharged no more arrows; but, by the noise I heard, I knew their numbers increased; and about four yards from me, over against my right ear, I heard a knocking for above an hour, like that of people at work; when turning my head that way, as well as the pegs and strings would permit me, I saw a stage erected about a foot and a half from the ground, capable of holding four of the inhabitants, with two or three ladders to mount it: from whence one of them, who seemed to be a person of quality, made me a long speech, whereof I understood not one syllable. But I should have mentioned, that before the principal person began his oration, he cried out three times, *Langro dehul san* (these words and the former were afterwards repeated and explained to me); whereupon, immediately, about fifty of the inhabitants came and cut the strings that fastened the left side of my head, which gave me the liberty of turning it to the right, and of observing the person and gesture of him that was to speak. He appeared to be of a middle age, and taller than any of the other three who attended him, whereof one was a page that held up his train, and seemed to be somewhat longer than my middle finger; the other two stood one on each side to support him. He acted every part of an orator, and I could observe many periods of threatenings, and others of promises, pity, and kindness. I answered in a few words, but in the most submissive manner, lifting up my left hand, and both my eyes to the sun, as calling him for a witness; and being almost famished with hunger, having not eaten a morsel for some hours before I left the ship, I found the demands of nature so strong upon me, that I could not forbear showing my impatience (perhaps against the strict rules of decency) by putting my finger frequently to my mouth, to signify that I wanted food. The *hurgo* (for so they call a great lord, as I afterwards learnt) understood me very well. He descended from the stage, and commanded that several ladders should be applied to my sides, on which above a hundred of the inhabitants mounted and walked towards my mouth, laden with baskets full of meat, which had been provided and sent thither by the king's orders, upon the first intelligence he received of me. I observed there was the flesh of several animals, but could not distinguish them by the taste. There were shoulders, legs, and loins, shaped like those of mutton, and very well dressed, but smaller than the wings of a lark. I ate them by two or three at a mouthful, and took three loaves at a time, about the bigness of musket bullets. They supplied me as fast as they could, showing a thousand marks of wonder and astonishment at my bulk and appetite. I then made another sign, that I wanted drink. They found by my eating that a small quantity would not suffice me; and being a most ingenious people, they slung up, with great dexterity, one of their largest hogsheads, then rolled it towards my hand, and beat out the top; I drank it off at a draught, which I might well do, for it did not hold half a pint, and tasted like a small wine of Burgundy, but much more delicious. They brought me a second hogshead, which I drank in the same manner, and made signs for more; but they had none to give me. When I had performed these wonders, they shouted for joy, and danced upon my breast, repeating several times as they did at first, *Hekinah degul.* They made me a sign that I should throw down the two hogsheads, but first warning the people below to stand out of the way, crying aloud, *Borach mevolah*; and when they saw the vessels in the air, there was a universal shout of *Hekinah degul.* I confess I was often tempted, while they were passing backwards and forwards on my body, to seize forty or fifty of the first that came in my reach, and dash them against the ground. But the remembrance of what I had felt, which probably might not be the worst they could do, and the promise of honour I made them—for so I interpreted my submissive behaviour—soon drove out these imaginations. Besides, I now considered myself as bound by the laws of hospitality, to a people who had treated me with so much expense and magnificence. However, in my thoughts I could not sufficiently wonder at the intrepidity of these diminutive mortals, who durst venture to mount and walk upon my body, while one of my hands was at liberty, without trembling at the very sight of so prodigious a creature as I must appear to them. After some time, when they observed that I made no more demands for meat, there appeared before me a person of high rank from his imperial majesty. His excellency, having mounted on the small of my right leg, advanced forwards up to my face, with about a dozen of his retinue; and producing his credentials under the signet royal, which he applied close to my eyes, spoke about ten minutes without any signs of anger, but with a kind of determinate resolution, often pointing forwards, which, as I afterwards found, was towards the capital city, about half a mile distant; whither it was agreed by his majesty in council that I must be conveyed. I answered in few words, but to no purpose, and made a sign with my hand that was loose, putting it to the other (but over his excellency's head for fear of hurting him or his train) and then to my own head and body, to signify that I desired my liberty. It appeared that he understood me well enough, for he shook his head by way of disapprobation, and held his hand in a posture to show that I must be carried as a prisoner. However, he made other signs to let me understand that I should have meat and drink enough, and very good treatment. Whereupon I once more thought of attempting to break my bonds; but again, when I felt the smart of their arrows upon my face and hands, which were all in blisters, and many of the darts still sticking in them, and observing likewise that the number of my enemies increased, I gave tokens to let them know that they might do with me what they pleased. Upon this, the *hurgo* and his train withdrew, with much civility and cheerful countenances. Soon after I heard a general shout, with frequent repetitions of the words *Peplom selan*; and I felt great numbers of people on my left side relaxing the cords to such a degree, that I was able to turn upon my right, and to ease myself with making water; which

I very plentifully did, to the great astonishment of the people; who, conjecturing by my motion what I was going to do, immediately opened to the right and left on that side, to avoid the torrent, which fell with such noise and violence from me. But before this, they had daubed my face and both my hands with a sort of ointment, very pleasant to the smell, which, in a few minutes, removed all the smart of their arrows. These circumstances, added to the refreshment I had received by their victuals and drink, which were very nourishing, disposed me to sleep. I slept about eight hours, as I was afterwards assured; and it was no wonder, for the physicians, by the emperor's order, had mingled a sleepy potion in the hogsheads of wine.

It seems, that upon the first moment I was discovered sleeping on the ground, after my landing, the emperor had early notice of it by an express; and determined in council, that I should be tied in the manner I have related, (which was done in the night while I slept;) that plenty of meat and drink should be sent to me, and a machine prepared to carry me to the capital city.

This resolution perhaps may appear very bold and dangerous, and I am confident would not be imitated by any prince in Europe on the like occasion. However, in my opinion, it was extremely prudent, as well as generous: for, supposing these people had endeavoured to kill me with their spears and arrows, while I was asleep, I should certainly have awaked with the first sense of smart, which might so far have roused my rage and strength, as to have enabled me to break the strings wherewith I was tied; after which, as they were not able to make resistance, so they could expect no mercy.

These people are most excellent mathematicians, and arrived to a great perfection in mechanics, by the countenance and encouragement of the emperor, who is a renowned patron of learning. This prince has several machines fixed on wheels, for the carriage of trees and other great weights. He often builds his largest men of war, whereof some are nine feet long, in the woods where the timber grows, and has them carried on these engines three or four hundred yards to the sea. Five hundred carpenters and engineers were immediately set at work to prepare the greatest engine they had. It was a frame of wood raised three inches from the ground, about seven feet long, and four wide, moving upon twenty-two wheels. The shout I heard was upon the arrival of this engine, which, it seems, set out in four hours after my landing. It was brought parallel to me, as I lay. But the principal difficulty was to raise and place me in this vehicle. Eighty poles, each of one foot high, were erected for this purpose, and very strong cords, of the bigness of packthread, were fastened by hooks to many bandages, which the workmen had girt round my neck, my hands, my body, and my legs. Nine hundred of the strongest men were employed to draw up these cords, by many pulleys fastened on the poles; and thus, in less than three hours, I was raised and slung into the engine, and there tied fast. All this I was told; for, while the operation was performing, I lay in a profound sleep, by the force of that soporiferous medicine infused into my liquor. Fifteen hundred of the emperor's largest horses, each about four inches and a half high, were employed to draw me towards the metropolis, which, as I said, was half a mile distant.

About four hours after we began our journey, I awaked by a very ridiculous accident; for the carriage being stopped a while, to adjust something that was out of order, two or three of the young natives had the curiosity to see how I looked when I was asleep; they climbed up into the engine, and advancing very softly to my face, one of them, an officer in the guards, put the sharp end of his half-pike a good way up into my left nostril, which tickled my nose like a straw, and made me sneeze violently;

whereupon they stole off unperceived, and it was three weeks before I knew the cause of my waking so suddenly. We made a long march the remaining part of the day, and, rested at night with five hundred guards on each side of me, half with torches, and half with bows and arrows, ready to shoot me if I should offer to stir. The next morning at sunrise we continued our march, and arrived within two hundred yards of the city gates about noon. The emperor, and all his court, came out to meet us; but his great officers would by no means suffer his majesty to endanger his person by mounting on my body.

At the place where the carriage stopped there stood an ancient temple, esteemed to be the largest in the whole kingdom; which, having been polluted some years before by an unnatural murder, was, according to the zeal of those people, looked upon as profane, and therefore had been applied to common use, and all the ornaments and furniture carried away. In this edifice it was determined I should lodge. The great gate fronting to the north was about four feet high, and almost two feet wide, through which I could easily creep. On each side of the gate was a small window, not above six inches from the ground: into that on the left side, the king's smith conveyed fourscore and eleven chains, like those that hang to a lady's watch in Europe, and almost as large, which were locked to my left leg with six-and-thirty padlocks. Over against this temple, on the other side of the great highway, at twenty feet distance, there was a turret at least five feet high. Here the emperor ascended, with many principal lords of his court, to have an opportunity of viewing me, as I was told, for I could not see them. It was reckoned that above a hundred thousand inhabitants came out of the town upon the same errand; and, in spite of my guards, I believe there could not be fewer than ten thousand at several times, who mounted my body by the help of ladders. But a proclamation was soon issued, to forbid it upon pain of death. When the workmen found it was impossible for me to break loose, they cut all the strings that bound me; whereupon I rose up, with as melancholy a disposition as ever I had in my life. But the noise and astonishment of the people, at seeing me rise and walk, are not to be expressed. The chains that held my left leg were about two yards long, and gave me not only the liberty of walking backwards and forwards in a semicircle, but, being fixed within four inches of the gate, allowed me to creep in, and lie at my full length in the temple.

~

Jonathan Swift (1667–1745) was an Anglo-Irish writer and satirist who had a diverse career as an author, political journalist and clergyman. His most popular works include *Gulliver's Travels*, *A Modest Proposal* and *A Tale of a Tub*. Through his writing, he often criticized the English beliefs, customs and politics of the time.

From Twenty Thousand Leagues Under the Sea

Jules Verne

Twenty Thousand Leagues Under the Sea *is a science fiction novel about the pursuit of a mysterious sea creature by a professor and his companions.*

An Unknown Species of Whale

This unexpected fall so stunned me that I have no clear recollection of my sensations at the time. I was at first drawn down to a depth of about twenty feet. I am a good swimmer (though without pretending to rival Byron or Edgar Poe, who were masters of the art), and in that plunge I did not lose my presence of mind. Two vigorous strokes brought me to the surface of the water. My first care was to look for the frigate. Had the crew seen me disappear? Had the *Abraham Lincoln* veered round? Would the captain put out a boat? Might I hope to be saved?

The darkness was intense. I caught a glimpse of a black mass disappearing in the east, its beacon lights dying out in the distance. It was the frigate! I was lost.

"Help, help!" I shouted, swimming towards the *Abraham Lincoln* in desperation.

My clothes encumbered me; they seemed glued to my body, and paralyzed my movements.

I was sinking! I was suffocating!

"Help!"

This was my last cry. My mouth filled with water; I struggled against being drawn down the abyss. Suddenly my clothes were seized by a strong hand, and I felt myself quickly drawn up to the surface of the sea; and I heard, yes, I heard these words pronounced in my ear—

"If master would be so good as to lean on my shoulder, master would swim with much greater ease."

I seized with one hand my faithful Conseil's arm.

"Is it you?" said I, "you?"

"Myself," answered Conseil; "and waiting master's orders."

"That shock threw you as well as me into the sea?"

"No; but being in my master's service, I followed him."

The worthy fellow thought that was but natural.

"And the frigate?" I asked.

"The frigate?" replied Conseil, turning on his back; "I think that master had better not count too much on her."

"You think so?"

"I say that, at the time I threw myself into the sea, I heard the men at the wheel say, 'The screw and the rudder are broken.'"

"Broken?"

"Yes, broken by the monster's teeth. It is the only injury the *Abraham Lincoln* has sustained. But it is a bad look out for us—she no longer answers her helm."

"Then we are lost!"

"Perhaps so," calmly answered Conseil. "However, we have still several hours before us, and one can do a good deal in some hours."

Conseil's imperturbable coolness set me up again. I swam more vigorously; but, cramped by my clothes, which stuck to me like a leaden weight, I felt great difficulty in bearing up. Conseil saw this.

"Will master let me make a slit?" said he; and, slipping an open knife under my clothes, he ripped them up from top to bottom very rapidly. Then he cleverly slipped them off me, while I swam for both of us.

Then I did the same for Conseil, and we continued to swim near to each other.

Nevertheless, our situation was no less terrible. Perhaps our disappearance had not been noticed; and if it had been, the frigate could not tack, being without its helm. Conseil argued on this supposition, and laid his plans accordingly. This phlegmatic boy was perfectly self-possessed. We then decided that, as our only chance of safety was being picked up by the *Abraham Lincoln's* boats, we ought to manage so as to wait for them as long as possible. I resolved then to husband our strength, so that both should not be exhausted at the same time; and this is how we managed: while one of us lay on our back, quite still, with arms crossed, and legs stretched out, the other would swim and push the other on in front. This towing business did not last more than ten minutes each; and relieving each other thus, we could swim on for some hours, perhaps till daybreak. Poor chance! but hope is so firmly rooted in the heart of man! Moreover, there were two of us. Indeed I declare (though it may seem improbable) if I sought to destroy all hope—if I wished to despair, I could not.

The collision of the frigate with the cetacean had occurred about eleven o'clock the evening before. I reckoned then we should have eight hours to swim before sunrise, an operation quite practicable if we relieved each other. The sea, very calm, was in our favour. Sometimes I tried to pierce the intense darkness that was only dispelled by the phosphorescence caused by our movements. I watched the luminous waves that broke over my hand, whose mirror-like surface was spotted with silvery rings. One might have said that we were in a bath of quicksilver.

Near one o'clock in the morning, I was seized with dreadful fatigue. My limbs stiffened under the strain of violent cramp. Conseil was obliged to keep me up, and our preservation devolved on him alone. I heard the poor boy pant; his breathing became short and hurried. I found that he could not keep up much longer.

"Leave me! leave me!" I said to him.

"Leave my master? Never!" replied he. "I would drown first."

Just then the moon appeared through the fringes of a thick cloud that the wind was driving to the east. The surface of the sea glittered with its rays. This kindly light reanimated us. My head got better again. I looked at all points of the horizon. I saw the frigate! She was five miles from us, and looked like a dark mass, hardly discernible. But no boats!

I would have cried out. But what good would it have been at such a distance! My swollen lips could utter no sounds. Conseil could articulate some words, and I heard him repeat at intervals, "Help! help!"

Our movements were suspended for an instant; we listened. It might be only a singing in the ear, but it seemed to me as if a cry answered the cry from Conseil.

"Did you hear?" I murmured.

"Yes! Yes!"

And Conseil gave one more despairing call.

This time there was no mistake! A human voice responded to ours! Was it the voice of another unfortunate creature, abandoned in the middle of the ocean, some other victim of the shock sustained by the vessel? Or rather was it a boat from the frigate, that was hailing us in the darkness?

Conseil made a last effort, and, leaning on my shoulder, while I struck out in a despairing effort, he raised himself half out of the water, then fell back exhausted.

"What did you see?"

"I saw—" murmured he; "I saw—but do not talk—reserve all your strength!"

What had he seen? Then, I know not why, the thought of the monster came into my head for the first time! But that voice! The time is past for Jonahs to take refuge in whales' bellies! However, Conseil was towing me again. He raised his head sometimes, looked before us, and uttered a cry of recognition, which was responded to by a voice that came nearer and nearer. I scarcely heard it. My strength was exhausted; my fingers stiffened; my hand afforded me support no longer; my mouth, convulsively opening, filled with salt water. Cold crept over me. I raised my head for the last time, then I sank.

At this moment a hard body struck me. I clung to it: then I felt that I was being drawn up, that I was brought to the surface of the water, that my chest collapsed—I fainted.

It is certain that I soon came to, thanks to the vigorous rubbings that I received. I half opened my eyes.

"Conseil!" I murmured.

"Does master call me?" asked Conseil.

Just then, by the waning light of the moon which was sinking down to the horizon, I saw a face which was not Conseil's and which I immediately recognised.

"Ned!" I cried.

"The same, sir, who is seeking his prize!" replied the Canadian.

"Were you thrown into the sea by the shock to the frigate?"

"Yes, Professor; but more fortunate than you, I was able to find a footing almost directly upon a floating island."

"An island?"

"Or, more correctly speaking, on our gigantic narwhal."

"Explain yourself, Ned!"

"Only I soon found out why my harpoon had not entered its skin and was blunted."

"Why, Ned, why?"

"Because, Professor, that beast is made of sheet iron."

The Canadian's last words produced a sudden revolution in my brain. I wriggled myself quickly to the top of the being, or object, half out of the water, which served us for a refuge. I kicked it. It was evidently a hard impenetrable body, and not the soft substance that forms the bodies of the great marine mammalia. But this hard body might be a bony carapace, like that of the antediluvian animals; and I should be free to class this monster among amphibious reptiles, such as tortoises or alligators.

Well, no! the blackish back that supported me was smooth, polished, without scales. The blow produced a metallic sound; and incredible though it may be, it seemed, I might say, as if it was made of riveted plates.

There was no doubt about it! This monster, this natural phenomenon that had puzzled the learned world, and overthrown and misled the imagination of seamen of both hemispheres, it must be owned, a still more astonishing phenomenon, inasmuch as it was a simply human construction.

We had no time to lose, however. We were lying upon the back of a sort of submarine boat, which appeared (as far as I could judge) like a huge fish of steel. Ned Land's mind was made up on this point. Conseil and I could only agree with him.

Just then a bubbling began at the back of this strange thing (which was evidently propelled by a screw), and it began to move. We had only just time to seize hold of the upper part, which rose about seven feet out of the water, and happily its speed was not great.

"As long as it sails horizontally," muttered Ned Land, "I do not mind; but if it takes a fancy to dive, I would not give two straws for my life."

The Canadian might have said still less. It became really necessary to communicate with the beings, whatever they were, shut up inside the machine. I searched all over the outside for an aperture, a panel, or a man-hole, to use a technical expression; but the lines of the iron rivets, solidly driven into the joints of the iron plates, were clear and uniform. Besides, the moon disappeared then, and left us in total darkness.

At last this long night passed. My indistinct remembrance prevents my describing all the impressions it made. I can only recall one circumstance. During some lulls of the wind and sea, I fancied I heard several times vague sounds, a sort of fugitive harmony produced by words of command. What was then the mystery of this submarine craft, of which the whole world vainly sought an explanation? What kind of beings existed in this strange boat? What mechanical agent caused its prodigious speed?

Daybreak appeared. The morning mists surrounded us, but they soon cleared off. I was about to examine the hull, which formed on deck a kind of horizontal platform, when I felt it gradually sinking.

"Oh! confound it!" cried Ned Land, kicking the resounding plate. "Open, you inhospitable rascals!"

Happily the sinking movement ceased. Suddenly a noise, like iron works violently pushed aside, came from the interior of the boat. One iron plate was moved, a man appeared, uttered an odd cry, and disappeared immediately.

Some moments after, eight strong men, with masked faces, appeared noiselessly, and drew us down into their formidable machine.

Mobilis in Mobili

This forcible abduction, so roughly carried out, was accomplished with the rapidity of lightning. I shivered all over. Whom had we to deal with? No doubt some new sort of pirates, who explored the sea in their own way.

Hardly had the narrow panel closed upon me, when I was enveloped in darkness. My eyes, dazzled with the outer light, could distinguish nothing. I felt my naked feet cling to the rungs of an iron ladder. Ned Land and Conseil, firmly seized, followed me. At the bottom of the ladder, a door opened, and shut after us immediately with a bang.

We were alone. Where, I could not say, hardly imagine. All was black, and such a dense black that, after some minutes, my eyes had not been able to discern even the faintest glimmer.

Meanwhile, Ned Land, furious at these proceedings, gave free vent to his indignation.

"Confound it!" cried he, "here are people who come up to the Scotch for hospitality. They only just miss being cannibals. I should not be surprised at it, but I declare that they shall not eat me without my protesting."

"Calm yourself, friend Ned, calm yourself," replied Conseil, quietly. "Do not cry out before you are hurt. We are not quite done for yet."

"Not quite," sharply replied the Canadian, "but pretty near, at all events. Things look black. Happily, my bowie knife I have still, and I can always see well enough to use it. The first of these pirates who lays a hand on me—"

"Do not excite yourself, Ned," I said to the harpooner, "and do not compromise us by useless violence. Who knows that they will not listen to us? Let us rather try to find out where we are."

I groped about. In five steps I came to an iron wall, made of plates bolted together. Then turning back I struck against a wooden table, near which were ranged several stools. The boards of this prison were concealed under a thick mat of phormium, which deadened the noise of the feet. The bare walls revealed no trace of window or door. Conseil, going round the reverse way, met me, and we went back to the middle of the cabin, which measured about twenty feet by ten. As to its height, Ned Land, in spite of his own great height, could not measure it.

Half an hour had already passed without our situation being bettered, when the dense darkness suddenly gave way to extreme light. Our prison was suddenly lighted—that is to say, it became filled with a luminous matter, so strong that I could not bear it at first. In its whiteness and intensity I recognized that electric light which played round the submarine boat like a magnificent phenomenon of phosphorescence. After shutting my eyes involuntarily, I opened them, and saw that this luminous agent came from a half globe, unpolished, placed in the roof of the cabin.

"At last one can see," cried Ned Land, who, knife in hand, stood on the defensive.

"Yes," said I; "but we are still in the dark about ourselves."

"Let master have patience," said the imperturbable Conseil.

The sudden lighting of the cabin enabled me to examine it minutely. It only contained a table and five stools. The invisible door might be hermetically sealed. No noise was heard. All seemed dead in the interior of this boat. Did it move, did it float on the surface of the ocean, or did it dive into its depths? I could not guess.

A noise of bolts was now heard, the door opened, and two men appeared.

One was short, very muscular, broad-shouldered, with robust limbs, strong head, an abundance of black hair, thick moustache, a quick penetrating look, and the vivacity which characterizes the population of Southern France.

The second stranger merits a more detailed description. A disciple of Gratiolet or Engel would have read his face like an open book. I made out his prevailing qualities directly: self-confidence, because his head was well set on his shoulders, and his black eyes looked around with cold assurance; calmness, for his skin, rather pale, showed his coolness of blood; energy, evinced by the rapid contraction of his lofty brows; and courage, because his deep breathing denoted great power of lungs.

Whether this person was thirty-five or fifty years of age, I could not say. He was tall, had a large forehead, straight nose, a clearly cut mouth, beautiful teeth, with fine taper hands, indicative of a highly nervous temperament. This man was certainly the most admirable specimen I had ever met. One particular feature was his eyes, rather far from each other, and which could take in nearly a quarter of the horizon at once.

This faculty—(I verified it later)—gave him a range of vision far superior to Ned Land's. When this stranger fixed upon an object, his eyebrows met, his large eyelids closed around so as to contract the range of his vision, and he looked as if he magnified the objects lessened by distance, as if he pierced those sheets of water so opaque to our eyes, and as if he read the very depths of the seas.

The two strangers, with caps made from the fur of the sea otter, and shod with sea boots of seal's skin, were dressed in clothes of a particular texture, which allowed free movement of the limbs. The taller of the two, evidently the chief on board, examined us with great attention, without saying a word; then turning to his companion, talked with him in an unknown tongue. It was a sonorous, harmonious, and flexible dialect, the vowels seeming to admit of very varied accentuation.

The other replied by a shake of the head, and added two or three perfectly incomprehensible words. Then he seemed to question me by a look.

I replied in good French that I did not know his language; but he seemed not to understand me, and my situation became more embarrassing.

"If master were to tell our story," said Conseil, "perhaps these gentlemen may understand some words."

I began to tell our adventures, articulating each syllable clearly, and without omitting one single detail. I announced our names and rank, introducing in person Professor Aronnax, his servant Conseil, and master Ned Land, the harpooner.

The man with the soft calm eyes listened to me quietly, even politely, and with extreme attention; but nothing in his countenance indicated that he had understood my story. When I finished, he said not a word. There remained one resource, to speak English. Perhaps they would know this almost universal language. I knew it, as well as the German language—well enough to read it fluently, but not to speak it correctly. But, anyhow, we must make ourselves understood.

"Go on in your turn," I said to the harpooner; "speak your best Anglo-Saxon, and try to do better than I."

Ned did not beg off, and recommenced our story.

To his great disgust, the harpooner did not seem to have made himself more intelligible than I had. Our visitors did not stir. They evidently understood neither the language of Arago nor of Faraday.

Very much embarrassed, after having vainly exhausted our speaking resources, I knew not what part to take, when Conseil said—

"If master will permit me, I will relate it in German."

But in spite of the elegant terms and good accent of the narrator, the German language had no success. At last, nonplussed, I tried to remember my first lessons, and to narrate our adventures in Latin, but with no better success. This last attempt being of no avail, the two strangers exchanged some words in their unknown language, and retired.

The door shut.

"It is an infamous shame," cried Ned Land, who broke out for the twentieth time. "We speak to those rogues in French, English, German, and Latin, and not one of them has the politeness to answer!"

"Calm yourself," I said to the impetuous Ned, "anger will do no good."

"But do you see, Professor," replied our irascible companion, "that we shall absolutely die of hunger in this iron cage?"

"Bah!" said Conseil, philosophically; "we can hold out some time yet."

"My friends," I said, "we must not despair. We have been worse off than this. Do me the favour to wait a little before forming an opinion upon the commander and crew of this boat."

"My opinion is formed," replied Ned Land, sharply. "They are rascals."

"Good! and from what country?"

"From the land of rogues!"

"My brave Ned, that country is not clearly indicated on the map of the world; but I admit that the nationality of the two strangers is hard to determine. Neither English, French, nor German, that is quite certain. However, I am inclined to think that the commander and his companion were born in low latitudes. There is southern blood in them. But I cannot decide by their appearance whether they are Spaniards, Turks, Arabians, or Indians. As to their language, it is quite incomprehensible."

"There is the disadvantage of not knowing all languages," said Conseil, "or the disadvantage of not having one universal language."

As he said these words, the door opened. A steward entered. He brought us clothes, coats and trousers, made of a stuff I did not know. I hastened to dress myself, and my companions followed my example. During that time, the steward—dumb, perhaps deaf—had arranged the table, and laid three plates.

"This is something like," said Conseil.

"Bah!" said the rancorous harpooner, "what do you suppose they eat here? Tortoise liver, filleted shark, and beefsteaks from sea-dogs."

"We shall see," said Conseil.

The dishes, of bell metal, were placed on the table, and we took our places. Undoubtedly we had to do with civilized people, and, had it not been for the electric light which flooded us, I could have fancied I was in the dining-room of the Adelphi Hotel at Liverpool, or at the Grand Hotel in Paris. I must say, however, that there was neither bread nor wine. The water was fresh and clear, but it was water, and did not suit Ned Land's taste. Amongst the dishes which were brought to us, I recognized several fish delicately dressed; but of some, although excellent, I could give no opinion, neither could I tell to what kingdom they belonged, whether animal or vegetable. As to the dinner service, it was elegant, and in perfect taste. Each utensil, spoon, fork, knife, plate, had a letter engraved on it, with a motto above it, of which this is an exact facsimile:

MOBILIS IN MOBILIN.

The letter N was no doubt the initial of the name of the enigmatical person, who commanded at the bottom of the sea.

Ned and Conseil did not reflect much. They devoured the food, and I did likewise. I was, besides, reassured as to our fate; and it seemed evident that our hosts would not let us die of want.

However, everything has an end, everything passes away, even the hunger of people who have not eaten for fifteen hours. Our appetites satisfied, we felt overcome with sleep.

"Faith! I shall sleep well," said Conseil.

"So shall I," replied Ned Land.

My two companions stretched themselves on the cabin carpet, and were soon sound asleep. For my own part, too many thoughts crowded my brain, too many insoluble questions pressed upon me, too many fancies kept my eyes half open. Where were we? What strange power carried us on? I felt—or rather fancied I felt—the machine sinking down to the lowest beds of the sea. Dreadful nightmares beset me; I saw in these mysterious asylums a world of unknown animals, amongst which this submarine boat seemed to be of the same kind, living, moving, and formidable as they. Then my brain grew calmer, my imagination wandered into vague unconsciousness, and I soon fell into a deep sleep.

~

Jules Verne (1828–1905) was a French author widely regarded as the 'father of modern science fiction'. His famous novels include *Around the World in Eighty Days*, *Twenty Thousand Leagues Under the Sea* and *Journey to the Centre of the Earth*. In total, Verne wrote sixty-five such sci-fi books as part of a collection called *Les Voyages Extraordinaires*.

The Locket

Kate Chopin

I

One night in autumn a few men were gathered about a fire on the slope of a hill. They belonged to a small detachment of Confederate forces and were awaiting orders to march. Their gray uniforms were worn beyond the point of shabbiness. One of the men was heating something in a tin cup over the embers. Two were lying at full length a little distance away, while a fourth was trying to decipher a letter and had drawn close to the light. He had unfastened his collar and a good bit of his flannel shirt front.

"What's that you got around your neck, Ned?" asked one of the men lying in the obscurity.

Ned—or Edmond—mechanically fastened another button of his shirt and did not reply. He went on reading his letter.

"Is it your sweetheart's picture?"

"'Taint no gal's picture," offered the man at the fire. He had removed his tin cup and was engaged in stirring its grimy contents with a small stick. "That's a charm; some kind of hoodoo business that one o' them priests gave him to keep him out o' trouble. I know them Cath'lics. That's how come Frenchy got permoted an never got a scratch sence he's been in the ranks. Hey, French! aint I right?" Edmond looked up absently from his letter.

"What is it?" he asked.

"Aint that a charm you got round your neck?"

"It must be, Nick," returned Edmond with a smile. "I don't know how I could have gone through this year and a half without it."

The letter had made Edmond heart sick and home sick. He stretched himself on his back and looked straight up at the blinking stars. But he was not thinking of them nor of anything but a certain spring day when the bees were humming in the clematis; when a girl was saying good bye to him. He could see her as she unclasped from her neck the locket which she fastened about his own. It was an old fashioned golden locket bearing miniatures of her father and mother with their names and the date of their marriage. It was her most precious earthly possession. Edmond could feel again the folds of the girl's soft white gown, and see the droop of the angel-sleeves as she circled her fair arms about his neck. Her sweet face, appealing, pathetic, tormented by the pain of parting, appeared before him as vividly as life. He turned over, burying his face in his arm and there he lay, still and motionless.

The profound and treacherous night with its silence and semblance of peace settled upon the camp. He dreamed that the fair Octavie brought him a letter. He had no chair to offer her and was pained and embarrassed at the condition of his garments. He was ashamed of the poor food which comprised the dinner at which he begged her to join them.

He dreamt of a serpent coiling around his throat, and when he strove to grasp it the slimy thing glided away from his clutch. Then his dream was clamor.

"Git your duds! you! Frenchy!" Nick was bellowing in his face. There was what appeared to be a scramble and a rush rather than any regulated movement. The hill side was alive with clatter and motion; with sudden up-springing lights among the pines. In the east the dawn was unfolding out of the darkness. Its glimmer was yet dim in the plain below.

"What's it all about?" wondered a big black bird perched in the top of the tallest tree. He was an old solitary and a wise one, yet he was not wise enough to guess what it was all about. So all day long he kept blinking and wondering.

The noise reached far out over the plain and across the hills and awoke the little babes that were sleeping in their cradles. The smoke curled up toward the sun and shadowed the plain so that the stupid birds thought it was going to rain; but the wise one knew better.

"They are children playing a game," thought he. "I shall know more about it if I watch long enough."

At the approach of night they had all vanished away with their din and smoke. Then the old bird plumed his feathers. At last he had understood! With a flap of his great, black wings he shot downward, circling toward the plain.

A man was picking his way across the plain. He was dressed in the garb of a clergyman. His mission was to administer the consolations of religion to any of the prostrate figures in whom there might yet linger a spark of life. A negro[1] accompanied him, bearing a bucket of water and a flask of wine.

---

1 Author's original text; all such instances retained for authenticity

There were no wounded here; they had been borne away. But the retreat had been hurried and the vultures and the good Samaritans would have to look to the dead.

There was a soldier—a mere boy—lying with his face to the sky. His hands were clutching the sward on either side and his finger nails were stuffed with earth and bits of grass that he had gathered in his despairing grasp upon life. His musket was gone; he was hatless and his face and clothing were begrimed. Around his neck hung a gold chain and locket. The priest, bending over him, unclasped the chain and removed it from the dead soldier's neck. He had grown used to the terrors of war and could face them unflinchingly; but its pathos, someway, always brought the tears to his old, dim eyes.

The angelus was ringing half a mile away. The priest and the negro knelt and murmured together the evening benediction and a prayer for the dead.

II

The peace and beauty of a spring day had descended upon the earth like a benediction. Along the leafy road which skirted a narrow, tortuous stream in central Louisiana, rumbled an old fashioned cabriolet, much the worse for hard and rough usage over country roads and lanes. The fat, black horses went in a slow, measured trot, notwithstanding constant urging on the part of the fat, black coachman. Within the vehicle were seated the fair Octavie and her old friend and neighbor, Judge Pillier, who had come to take her for a morning drive.

Octavie wore a plain black dress, severe in its simplicity. A narrow belt held it at the waist and the sleeves were gathered into close fitting wristbands. She had discarded her hoopskirt and appeared not unlike a nun. Beneath the folds of her bodice nestled the old locket. She never displayed it now. It had returned to her sanctified in her eyes; made precious as material things sometimes are by being forever identified with a significant moment of one's existence.

A hundred times she had read over the letter with which the locket had come back to her. No later than that morning she had again pored over it. As she sat beside the window, smoothing the letter out upon her knee, heavy and spiced odors stole in to her with the songs of birds and the humming of insects in the air.

She was so young and the world was so beautiful that there came over her a sense of unreality as she read again and again the priest's letter. He told of that autumn day drawing to its close, with the gold and the red fading out of the west, and the night gathering its shadows to cover the faces of the dead. Oh! She could not believe that one of those dead was her own! with visage uplifted to the gray sky in an agony of supplication. A spasm of resistance and rebellion seized and swept over her. Why was the spring here with its flowers and its seductive breath if he was dead! Why was she here! What further had she to do with life and the living!

Octavie had experienced many such moments of despair, but a blessed resignation had never failed to follow, and it fell then upon her like a mantle and enveloped her.

"I shall grow old and quiet and sad like poor Aunt Tavie," she murmured to herself as she folded the letter and replaced it in the secretary. Already she gave herself a little demure air like her Aunt Tavie. She walked with a slow glide in unconscious imitation of Mademoiselle Tavie whom some youthful affliction had robbed of earthly compensation while leaving her in possession of youth's illusions.

As she sat in the old cabriolet beside the father of her dead lover, again there came to Octavie the terrible sense of loss which had assailed her so often before. The soul of her youth clamored for its rights; for a share in the world's glory and exultation. She leaned back and drew her veil a little closer about her face. It was an old black veil of her Aunt Tavie's. A whiff of dust from the road had blown in and she wiped her cheeks and her eyes with her soft, white handkerchief, a homemade handkerchief, fabricated from one of her old fine muslin petticoats.

"Will you do me the favor, Octavie," requested the judge in the courteous tone which he never abandoned, "to remove that veil which you wear. It seems out of harmony, someway, with the beauty and promise of the day."

The young girl obediently yielded to her old companion's wish and unpinning the cumbersome, sombre drapery from her bonnet, folded it neatly and laid it upon the seat in front of her.

"Ah! that is better; far better!" he said in a tone expressing unbounded relief. "Never put it on again, dear." Octavie felt a little hurt; as if he wished to debar her from share and parcel in the burden of affliction which had been placed upon all of them. Again she drew forth the old muslin handkerchief.

They had left the big road and turned into a level plain which had formerly been an old meadow. There were clumps of thorn trees here and there, gorgeous in their spring radiance. Some cattle were grazing off in the distance in spots where the grass was tall and luscious. At the far end of the meadow was the towering lilac hedge, skirting the lane that led to Judge Pillier's house, and the scent of its heavy blossoms met them like a soft and tender embrace of welcome.

As they neared the house the old gentleman placed an arm around the girl's shoulders and turning her face up to him he said: "Do you not think that on a day like this, miracles might happen? When the whole earth is vibrant with life, does it not seem to you, Octavie, that heaven might for once relent and give us back our dead?" He spoke very low, advisedly, and impressively.

In his voice was an old quaver which was not habitual and there was agitation in every line of his visage. She gazed at him with eyes that were full of supplication and a certain terror of joy.

They had been driving through the lane with the towering hedge on one side and the open meadow on the other. The horses had somewhat quickened their lazy pace. As they turned into the avenue leading to the house, a whole choir of feathered songsters fluted a sudden torrent of melodious greeting from their leafy hiding places.

Octavie felt as if she had passed into a stage of existence which was like a dream, more poignant and real than life. There was the old gray house with its sloping eaves. Amid the blur of green, and dimly, she saw familiar faces and heard voices as if they came from far across the fields, and Edmond was holding her. Her dead Edmond; her living Edmond, and she felt the beating of his heart against her and the agonizing rapture of his kisses striving to awake her. It was as if the spirit of life and the awakening spring had given back the soul to her youth and bade her rejoice.

It was many hours later that Octavie drew the locket from her bosom and looked at Edmond with a questioning appeal in her glance.

"It was the night before an engagement," he said. "In the hurry of the encounter, and the retreat next day, I never missed it till the fight was over. I thought of course I had lost it in the heat of the struggle, but it was stolen."

"Stolen," she shuddered, and thought of the dead soldier with his face uplifted to the sky in an agony of supplication.

Edmond said nothing; but he thought of his messmate; the one who had lain far back in the shadow; the one who had said nothing.

~

Kate Chopin (1850–1904), was an American author known for her novels and short stories, which often centred around feminist themes and issues surrounding traditional gender roles. One of the first feminist authors of her time, Chopin is best known for her novel *The Awakening* and short stories *Désirée's Baby* and *The Story of an Hour*.

The Fly

Katherine Mansfield

"Y'are very snug in here," piped old Mr Woodifield, and he peered out of the great, green leather armchair by his friend the boss's desk as a baby peers out of its pram. His talk was over; it was time for him to be off. But he did not want to go. Since he had retired, since his stroke, the wife and the girls kept him boxed up in the house every day of the week except Tuesday. On Tuesday he was dressed up and brushed and allowed to cut back to the City for the day. Though what he did there the wife and girls couldn't imagine. Made a nuisance of himself to his friends, they supposed... Well, perhaps so. All the same, we cling to our last pleasures as the tree clings to its last leaves. So there sat old Woodifield, smoking a cigar and staring almost greedily at the boss, who rolled in his office chair, stout, rosy, five years older than he, and still going strong, still at the helm. It did one good to see him.

Wistfully, admiringly, the old voice added, "It's snug in here, upon my word!"

"Yes, it's comfortable enough," agreed the boss, and he flipped the *Financial Times* with a paper-knife. As a matter of fact he was proud of his room; he liked to have it admired, especially by old Woodifield. It gave him a feeling of deep, solid satisfaction to be planted there in the midst of it in full view of that frail old figure in the muffler.

"I've had it done up lately," he explained, as he had explained for the past—how many?—weeks. "New carpet," and he pointed to the bright red carpet with a pattern of large white rings. "New furniture," and he nodded towards the massive bookcase and the table with legs like twisted treacle. "Electric heating!" He waved almost exultantly towards the five transparent, pearly sausages glowing so softly in the tilted copper pan.

But he did not draw old Woodifield's attention to the photograph over the table of a grave-looking boy in uniform standing in one of those spectral photographers' parks with photographers' storm-clouds behind him. It was not new. It had been there for over six years.

"There was something I wanted to tell you," said old Woodifield, and his eyes grew dim remembering. "Now what was it? I had it in my mind when I started out this morning." His hands began to tremble, and patches of red showed above his beard.

Poor old chap, he's on his last pins, thought the boss. And, feeling kindly, he winked at the old man, and said jokingly, "I tell you what. I've got a little drop of something here that'll do you good before you go out into the cold again. It's beautiful stuff. It wouldn't hurt a child." He took a key off his watch-chain, unlocked a cupboard below his desk, and drew forth a dark, squat bottle. "That's the medicine," said he. "And the man from whom I got it told me on the strict Q.T. it came from the cellars at Windsor Cassel."

Old Woodifield's mouth fell open at the sight. He couldn't have looked more surprised if the boss had produced a rabbit.

"It's whisky, ain't it?" he piped, feebly.

The boss turned the bottle and lovingly showed him the label. Whisky it was.

"D'you know," said he, peering up at the boss wonderingly, "they won't let me touch it at home." And he looked as though he was going to cry.

"Ah, that's where we know a bit more than the ladies," cried the boss, swooping across for two tumblers that stood on the table with the water-bottle, and pouring a generous finger into each. "Drink it down. It'll do you good. And don't put any water with it. It's sacrilege to tamper with stuff like this. Ah!" He tossed off his, pulled out his handkerchief, hastily wiped his moustaches, and cocked an eye at old Woodifield, who was rolling his in his chaps.

The old man swallowed, was silent a moment, and then said faintly, "It's nutty!"

But it warmed him; it crept into his chill old brain—he remembered.

"That was it," he said, heaving himself out of his chair. "I thought you'd like to know. The girls were in Belgium last week having a look at poor Reggie's grave, and they happened to come across your boy's. They're quite near each other, it seems."

Old Woodifield paused, but the boss made no reply. Only a quiver in his eyelids showed that he heard.

"The girls were delighted with the way the place is kept," piped the old voice. "Beautifully looked after. Couldn't be better if they were at home. You've not been across, have yer?"

"No, no!" For various reasons the boss had not been across.

"There's miles of it," quavered old Woodifield, "and it's all as neat as a garden. Flowers growing on all the graves. Nice broad paths." It was plain from his voice how much he liked a nice broad path.

The pause came again. Then the old man brightened wonderfully.

"D'you know what the hotel made the girls pay for a pot of jam?" he piped. "Ten francs! Robbery, I call it. It was a little pot, so Gertrude says, no bigger than a half-crown. And she hadn't taken more than a spoonful when they charged her ten francs. Gertrude brought the pot away with her to teach 'em a lesson. Quite right, too; it's trading on our feelings. They think because we're over there having a look around we're ready to pay anything. That's what it is." And he turned towards the door.

"Quite right, quite right!" cried the boss, though what was quite right he hadn't the least idea. He came round by his desk, followed the shuffling footsteps to the door, and saw the old fellow out. Woodifield was gone.

For a long moment the boss stayed, staring at nothing, while the grey-haired office messenger, watching him, dodged in and out of his cubby-hole like a dog that expects to be taken for a run. Then: "I'll see nobody for half an hour, Macey," said the boss. "Understand? Nobody at all."

"Very good, sir."

The door shut, the firm heavy steps recrossed the bright carpet, the fat body plumped down in the spring chair, and leaning forward, the boss covered his face with his hands. He wanted, he intended, he had arranged to weep...

It had been a terrible shock to him when old Woodifield sprang that remark upon him about the boy's grave. It was exactly as though the earth had opened and he had seen the boy lying there with Woodifield's girls staring down at him. For it was strange. Although over six years had passed away, the boss never thought of the boy except as lying unchanged, unblemished in his uniform, asleep for ever. "My son!" groaned the boss. But no tears came yet. In the past, in the first months and even years after the boy's death, he had only to say those words to be overcome by such grief that nothing short of a violent fit of weeping could relieve him. Time, he had declared then, he had told everybody, could make no difference. Other men perhaps might recover, might live their loss down, but not he. How was it possible? His boy was an only son. Ever since his birth the boss had worked at building up this business for him; it had no other meaning if it was not for the boy. Life itself had come to have no other meaning. How on earth could he have slaved, denied himself, kept going all those years without the promise for ever before him of the boy's stepping into his shoes and carrying on where he left off?

And that promise had been so near being fulfilled. The boy had been in the office learning the ropes for a year before the war. Every morning they had started off together; they had come back by the same train. And what congratulations he had received as the boy's father! No wonder; he had taken to it marvellously. As to his popularity with the staff, every man jack of them down to old Macey couldn't make enough of the boy. And he wasn't in the least spoilt. No, he was just his bright, natural self, with the right word for everybody, with that boyish look and his habit of saying, "Simply splendid!"

But all that was over and done with as though it never had been. The day had come when Macey had handed him the telegram that brought the whole place crashing about his head. "Deeply regret to inform you…" And he had left the office a broken man, with his life in ruins.

Six years ago, six years... How quickly time passed! It might have happened yesterday. The boss took his hands from his face; he was puzzled. Something seemed to be wrong with him. He wasn't feeling as he wanted to feel. He decided to get up and have a look at the boy's photograph. But it wasn't a favourite photograph of his; the expression was unnatural. It was cold, even stern-looking. The boy had never looked like that.

At that moment the boss noticed that a fly had fallen into his broad inkpot, and was trying feebly but desperately to clamber out again. Help! help! said those struggling legs. But the sides of the inkpot were wet and slippery; it fell back again and began to swim. The boss took up a pen, picked the fly out of the ink, and shook it on to a piece of blotting-paper. For a fraction of a second it lay still on the dark patch that oozed round it. Then the front legs waved, took hold, and, pulling its small sodden body up it began the immense task of cleaning the ink from its wings. Over and under, over and under, went a leg along a wing, as the stone goes over and under the scythe. Then there was a pause, while the fly, seeming to stand on the tips of its toes, tried to expand first one wing and then the other. It succeeded at last, and, sitting down, it began, like a minute cat, to clean its face. Now one could imagine that the little front legs rubbed against each other lightly, joyfully. The horrible danger was over; it had escaped; it was ready for life again.

But just then the boss had an idea. He plunged his pen back into the ink, leaned his thick wrist on the blotting paper, and as the fly tried its wings down came a great heavy blot. What would it make of that? What indeed! The little beggar seemed absolutely cowed, stunned, and afraid to move because of what would happen next. But then, as if painfully, it dragged itself forward. The front legs waved, caught hold, and, more slowly this time, the task began from the beginning.

He's a plucky little devil, thought the boss, and he felt a real admiration for the fly's courage. That was the way to tackle things; that was the right spirit. Never say die; it was only a question of... But the fly had again finished its laborious task, and the boss had just time to refill his pen, to shake fair and square on the new-cleaned body yet another dark drop. What about it this time? A painful moment of suspense followed. But behold, the front legs were again waving; the boss felt a rush of relief. He leaned over the fly and said to it tenderly, "You artful little b..." And he actually had the brilliant notion of breathing on it to help the drying process. All the same, there was something timid and weak about its efforts now, and the boss decided that this time should be the last, as he dipped the pen into the inkpot.

It was. The last blot on the soaked blotting-paper, and the draggled fly lay in it and did not stir. The back legs were stuck to the body; the front legs were not to be seen.

"Come on," said the boss. "Look sharp!" And he stirred it with his pen—in vain. Nothing happened or was likely to happen. The fly was dead.

The boss lifted the corpse on the end of the paper-knife and flung it into the waste-paper basket. But such a grinding feeling of wretchedness seized him that he felt positively frightened. He started forward and pressed the bell for Macey.

"Bring me some fresh blotting-paper," he said, sternly, "and look sharp about it." And while the old dog padded away he fell to wondering what it was he had been thinking about before. What was it? It was... He took out his handkerchief and passed it inside his collar. For the life of him he could not remember.

~

Katherine Mansfield (1888–1923) was an influential short story writer known to have been an acquaintance of

Virginia Woolf, and the only person whose writing Woolf was jealous of. Born in New Zealand, Mansfield later spent time in England and France, where she wrote *The Garden Party*, and *Other Stories*, *The Dove's Nest* and *Bliss and Other Stories*.

From War And Peace

Leo Tolstoy

War and Peace is set against the backdrop of Napoleon's invasion of Russia and the war that followed thereafter. The plot revolves around members of the Russian aristocracy and examines how they were impacted by the events.

BOOK TWO: 1805

In October, 1805, a Russian army was occupying the villages and towns of the Archduchy of Austria, and yet other regiments freshly arriving from Russia were settling near the fortress of Braunau and burdening the inhabitants on whom they were quartered. Braunau was the headquarters of the commander in chief, Kutúzov.

On 11 October, 1805, one of the infantry regiments that had just reached Braunau had halted half a mile from the town, waiting to be inspected by the commander in chief. Despite the un-Russian appearance of the locality and surroundings—fruit gardens, stone fences, tiled roofs, and hills in the distance—and despite the fact that the inhabitants (who gazed with curiosity at the soldiers) were not Russians, the regiment had just the appearance of any Russian regiment preparing for an inspection anywhere in the heart of Russia.

On the evening of the last day's march an order had been received that the commander in chief would inspect the regiment on the march. Though the words of the order were not clear to the regimental commander, and the question arose whether the troops were to be in marching order or not, it was decided at a consultation between the battalion commanders to present the regiment in parade order, on the principle that it is always better to "bow too low than not bow low enough." So the soldiers, after a twenty-mile march, were kept mending and cleaning all night long without closing their eyes, while the adjutants and company commanders calculated and reckoned, and by morning the regiment—instead of the straggling, disorderly crowd it had been on its last march the day before—presented a well-ordered array of two thousand men each of whom knew his place and his duty, had every button and every strap in place, and shone with cleanliness. And not only externally was all in order, but had it pleased the commander in chief to look under the uniforms he would have found on every man a clean shirt, and in every knapsack the appointed number of articles, "awl, soap, and all," as the soldiers say. There was only one circumstance concerning which no one could be at ease. It was the state of the soldiers' boots. More than half the men's boots were in holes. But this defect was not due to any fault of the regimental commander, for in spite of repeated demands boots had not been issued by the Austrian commissariat, and the regiment had marched some seven hundred miles.

The commander of the regiment was an elderly, choleric, stout, and thick-set general with grizzled eyebrows and whiskers, and wider from chest to back than across the shoulders. He had on a brand-new uniform showing the creases where it had been folded and thick gold epaulettes which seemed to stand rather than lie down on his massive shoulders. He had the air of a man happily performing one of the most solemn duties of his life. He walked about in front of the line and at every step pulled himself up, slightly arching his back. It was plain that the commander admired his regiment, rejoiced in it, and that his whole mind was engrossed by it, yet his strut seemed to indicate that, besides military matters, social interests and the fair sex occupied no small part of his thoughts.

"Well, Michael Mítrich, sir?" he said, addressing one of the battalion commanders who smilingly pressed forward (it was plain that they both felt happy). "We had our hands full last night. However, I think the regiment is not a bad one, eh?"

The battalion commander perceived the jovial irony and laughed.

"It would not be turned off the field even on the Tsarítsin Meadow."

"What?" asked the commander.

At that moment, on the road from the town on which signalers had been posted, two men appeared on horse back. They were an aide-de-camp followed by a Cossack.

The aide-de-camp was sent to confirm the order which had not been clearly worded the day before, namely, that the commander in chief wished to see the regiment just in the state in which it had been on the march: in their greatcoats, and packs, and without any preparation whatever.

A member of the Hofkriegsrath from Vienna had come to Kutúzov the day before with proposals and demands for him to join up with the army of the Archduke Ferdinand and Mack, and Kutúzov, not considering this junction advisable, meant, among other arguments in support of his view, to show the Austrian general the wretched state in which the troops arrived from Russia. With this object he intended to meet the regiment; so the worse the condition it was in, the better pleased the commander in chief would be. Though the aide-de-camp did not know these circumstances, he nevertheless delivered the definite order that the men should be in their greatcoats and in marching order, and that the commander in chief would otherwise be dissatisfied. On hearing this the regimental commander hung his head, silently shrugged his shoulders, and spread out his arms with a choleric gesture.

"A fine mess we've made of it!" he remarked.

"There now! Didn't I tell you, Michael Mítrich, that if it was said 'on the march' it meant in greatcoats?" said he reproachfully to the battalion commander. "Oh, my God!" he added, stepping resolutely forward. "Company commanders!" he shouted in a voice accustomed to command. "Sergeants major!... How soon will he be here?" he asked the aide-de-camp with a respectful politeness evidently relating to the personage he was referring to.

"In an hour's time, I should say."

"Shall we have time to change clothes?"

"I don't know, General..."

The regimental commander, going up to the line himself, ordered the soldiers to change into their greatcoats. The company commanders ran off to their companies, the sergeants major began bustling (the greatcoats were not in very good condition), and instantly the squares that had up to then been in regular order and silent began to sway and stretch and hum with voices. On all sides soldiers were running to and fro, throwing up their knapsacks with a jerk of their shoulders and pulling the straps over their heads, unstrapping their overcoats and drawing the sleeves on with upraised arms.

In half an hour all was again in order, only the squares had become gray instead of black. The regimental commander walked with his jerky steps to the front of the regiment and examined it from a distance.

"Whatever is this? This!" he shouted and stood still. "Commander of the third company!"

"Commander of the third company wanted by the general!... commander to the general... third company to the commander." The words passed along the lines and an adjutant ran to look for the missing officer.

When the eager but misrepeated words had reached their destination in a cry of: "The general to the third company," the missing officer appeared from behind his company and, though he was a middle-aged man and not in the habit of running, trotted awkwardly stumbling on his toes toward the general. The captain's face showed the uneasiness of a schoolboy who is told to repeat a lesson he has not learned. Spots appeared on his nose, the redness of which was evidently due to intemperance, and his mouth twitched nervously. The general looked the captain up and down as he came up panting, slackening his pace as he approached.

"You will soon be dressing your men in petticoats! What is this?" shouted the regimental commander, thrusting forward his jaw and pointing at a soldier in the ranks of the third company in a greatcoat of bluish cloth, which contrasted with the others. "What have you been after? The commander in chief is expected and you leave your place? Eh? I'll teach you to dress the men in fancy coats for a parade... Eh...?"

The commander of the company, with his eyes fixed on his superior, pressed two fingers more and more rigidly to his cap, as if in this pressure lay his only hope of salvation.

"Well, why don't you speak? Whom have you got there dressed up as a Hungarian?" said the commander with an austere gibe.

"Your excellency..."

"Well, your excellency, what? Your excellency! But what about your excellency?... nobody knows."

"Your excellency, it's the officer Dólokhov, who has been reduced to the ranks," said the captain softly.

"Well? Has he been degraded into a field marshal, or into a soldier? If a soldier, he should be dressed in regulation uniform like the others."

"Your excellency, you gave him leave yourself, on the march."

"Gave him leave? Leave? That's just like you young men," said the regimental commander cooling down a little. "Leave indeed... One says a word to you and you... What?" he added with renewed irritation, "I beg you to dress your men decently."

And the commander, turning to look at the adjutant, directed his jerky steps down the line. He was evidently pleased at his own display of anger and walking up to the regiment wished to find a further excuse for wrath. Having snapped at an officer for an unpolished badge, at another because his line was not straight, he reached the third company.

"H-o-o-w are you standing? Where's your leg? Your leg?" shouted the commander with a tone of suffering in his voice, while there were still five men between him and Dólokhov with his bluish-gray uniform.

Dólokhov slowly straightened his bent knee, looking straight with his clear, insolent eyes in the general's face.

"Why a blue coat? Off with it... Sergeant major! Change his coat... the ras..." he did not finish.

"General, I must obey orders, but I am not bound to endure..." Dólokhov hurriedly interrupted.

"No talking in the ranks!... No talking, no talking!"

"Not bound to endure insults," Dólokhov concluded in loud, ringing tones.

The eyes of the general and the soldier met. The general became silent, angrily pulling down his tight scarf.

"I request you to have the goodness to change your coat," he said as he turned away.

"He's coming!" shouted the signaler at that moment.

The regimental commander, flushing, ran to his horse, seized the stirrup with trembling hands, threw his body across the saddle, righted himself, drew his saber, and with a happy and resolute countenance, opening his mouth awry, prepared to shout. The regiment fluttered like a bird preening its plumage and became motionless.

"Att-ention!" shouted the regimental commander in a soul-shaking voice which expressed joy for himself, severity for the regiment, and welcome for the approaching chief.

Along the broad country road, edged on both sides by trees, came a high, light blue Viennese *calèche*, slightly creaking on its springs and drawn by six horses at a smart trot. Behind the *calèche* galloped the suite and a convoy of Croats. Beside Kutúzov sat an Austrian general, in a white uniform that looked strange among the Russian black ones. The *calèche* stopped in front of the regiment. Kutúzov and the Austrian general were talking in low voices and Kutúzov smiled slightly as treading heavily he stepped down from the carriage just as if those two thousand men breathlessly gazing at him and the regimental commander did not exist.

The word of command rang out, and again the regiment quivered, as with a jingling sound it presented arms. Then amidst a dead silence the feeble voice of the commander in chief was heard. The regiment roared, "Health to your ex... len... len... lency!" and again all became silent. At first Kutúzov stood still while the regiment moved; then he and the general in white, accompanied by the suite, walked between the ranks.

From the way the regimental commander saluted the commander in chief and devoured him with his eyes, drawing himself up obsequiously, and from the way he walked through the ranks behind the generals, bending forward and hardly able to restrain his jerky movements, and from the way he darted forward at every word or gesture of the commander in chief, it was evident that he performed his duty as a subordinate with even greater zeal than his duty as a commander. Thanks to the strictness and assiduity of its commander the regiment, in comparison with others that had reached Braunau at the same time, was in splendid condition. There were only 217 sick and stragglers. Everything was in good order except the boots.

Kutúzov walked through the ranks, sometimes stopping to say a few friendly words to officers he had known in the Turkish war, sometimes also to the soldiers. Looking at their boots he several times shook his head sadly, pointing them out to the Austrian general with an expression which seemed to say that he was not blaming anyone, but could not help noticing what a bad state of things it was. The regimental commander ran forward on each such occasion, fearing to miss a single word of the commander in chief's regarding the regiment. Behind Kutúzov, at a distance that allowed every softly spoken word to be heard, followed some twenty men of his suite. These gentlemen talked among themselves and sometimes laughed. Nearest of all to the commander in chief walked a handsome adjutant. This was Prince Bolkónski. Beside him was his comrade Nesvítski, a tall staff officer, extremely stout, with a kindly, smiling, handsome face and moist eyes. Nesvítski could hardly keep from laughter provoked by a swarthy hussar officer who walked beside him. This hussar, with a grave face and without a smile or a change in the expression of his fixed eyes, watched the regimental commander's back and mimicked his every movement. Each time the commander started and bent forward, the hussar started and bent forward in exactly the same manner. Nesvítski laughed and nudged the others to make them look at the wag.

Kutúzov walked slowly and languidly past thousands of eyes which were starting from their sockets to watch their chief. On reaching the third company he suddenly stopped. His suite, not having expected this, involuntarily came closer to him.

"Ah, Timókhin!" said he, recognizing the red-nosed captain who had been reprimanded on account of the blue greatcoat.

One would have thought it impossible for a man to stretch himself more than Timókhin had done when he was reprimanded by the regimental commander, but now that the commander in chief addressed him he drew himself up to such an extent that it seemed he could not have sustained it had the commander in chief continued to look at him, and so Kutúzov, who evidently understood his case and wished him nothing but good, quickly turned away, a scarcely perceptible smile flitting over his scarred and puffy face.

"Another Ismail comrade," said he. "A brave officer! Are you satisfied with him?" he asked the regimental commander.

And the latter—unconscious that he was being reflected in the hussar officer as in a looking glass—started, moved forward, and answered: "Highly satisfied, your excellency!"

"We all have our weaknesses," said Kutúzov smiling and walking away from him. "He used to have a predilection for Bacchus."

The regimental commander was afraid he might be blamed for this and did not answer. The hussar at that moment noticed the face of the red-nosed captain and his drawn-in stomach, and mimicked his expression and pose with such exactitude that

Nesvítski could not help laughing. Kutúzov turned round. The officer evidently had complete control of his face, and while Kutúzov was turning managed to make a grimace and then assume a most serious, deferential, and innocent expression.

The third company was the last, and Kutúzov pondered, apparently trying to recollect something. Prince Andrew stepped forward from among the suite and said in French:

"You told me to remind you of the officer Dólokhov, reduced to the ranks in this regiment."

"Where is Dólokhov?" asked Kutúzov.

Dólokhov, who had already changed into a soldier's gray greatcoat, did not wait to be called. The shapely figure of the fair-haired soldier, with his clear blue eyes, stepped forward from the ranks, went up to the commander in chief, and presented arms.

"Have you a complaint to make?" Kutúzov asked with a slight frown.

"This is Dólokhov," said Prince Andrew.

"Ah!" said Kutúzov. "I hope this will be a lesson to you. Do your duty. The Emperor is gracious, and I shan't forget you if you deserve well."

The clear blue eyes looked at the commander in chief just as boldly as they had looked at the regimental commander, seeming by their expression to tear open the veil of convention that separates a commander in chief so widely from a private.

"One thing I ask of your excellency," Dólokhov said in his firm, ringing, deliberate voice. "I ask an opportunity to atone for my fault and prove my devotion to His Majesty the Emperor and to Russia!"

Kutúzov turned away. The same smile of the eyes with which he had turned from Captain Timókhin again flitted over his face. He turned away with a grimace as if to say that everything Dólokhov had said to him and everything he could say had long been known to him, that he was weary of it and it was not at all what he wanted. He turned away and went to the carriage.

The regiment broke up into companies, which went to their appointed quarters near Braunau, where they hoped to receive boots and clothes and to rest after their hard marches.

"You won't bear me a grudge, Prokhór Ignátych?" said the regimental commander, overtaking the third company on its way to its quarters and riding up to Captain Timókhin who was walking in front. (The regimental commander's face now that the inspection was happily over beamed with irrepressible delight.) "It's in the Emperor's service... it can't be helped... one is sometimes a bit hasty on parade... I am the first to apologize, you know me!... He was very pleased!" And he held out his hand to the captain.

"Don't mention it, General, as if I'd be so bold!" replied the captain, his nose growing redder as he gave a smile which showed where two front teeth were missing that had been knocked out by the butt end of a gun at Ismail.

"And tell Mr Dólokhov that I won't forget him—he may be quite easy. And tell me, please—I've been meaning to ask—how is he behaving himself, and in general..."

"As far as the service goes he is quite punctilious, your excellency; but his character..." said Timókhin.

"And what about his character?" asked the regimental commander.

"It's different on different days," answered the captain. "One day he is sensible, well educated, and good-natured, and the next he's a wild beast... In Poland, if you please, he nearly killed a Jew."

"Oh, well, well!" remarked the regimental commander. "Still, one must have pity on a young man in misfortune. You know he has important connections... Well, then, you just..."

"I will, your excellency," said Timókhin, showing by his smile that he understood his commander's wish.

"Well, of course, of course!"

The regimental commander sought out Dólokhov in the ranks and, reining in his horse, said to him:

"After the next affair... epaulettes."

Dólokhov looked round but did not say anything, nor did the mocking smile on his lips change.

"Well, that's all right," continued the regimental commander. "A cup of vodka for the men from me," he added so that the soldiers could hear. "I thank you all! God be praised!" and he rode past that company and overtook the next one.

"Well, he's really a good fellow, one can serve under him," said Timókhin to the subaltern beside him.

"In a word, a hearty one..." said the subaltern, laughing (the regimental commander was nicknamed *King of Hearts*).

The cheerful mood of their officers after the inspection infected the soldiers. The company marched on gaily. The soldiers' voices could be heard on every side.

"And they said Kutúzov was blind of one eye?"

"And so he is! Quite blind!"

"No, friend, he is sharper-eyed than you are. Boots and leg bands... he noticed everything..."

"When he looked at my feet, friend... well, thinks I..."

"And that other one with him, the Austrian, looked as if he were smeared with chalk—as white as flour! I suppose they polish him up as they do the guns."

"I say, Fédeshon!... Did he say when the battles are to begin? You were near him. Everybody said that Buonaparte himself was at Braunau."

"Buonaparte himself!... Just listen to the fool, what he doesn't know! The Prussians are up in arms now. The Austrians, you see, are putting them down. When they've been put down, the war with Buonaparte will begin. And he says Buonaparte is in Braunau! Shows you're a fool. You'd better listen more carefully!"

"What devils these quartermasters are! See, the fifth company is turning into the village already... they will have their buckwheat cooked before we reach our quarters."

"Give me a biscuit, you devil!"

"And did you give me tobacco yesterday? That's just it, friend! Ah, well, never mind, here you are."

"They might call a halt here or we'll have to do another four miles without eating."

"Wasn't it fine when those Germans gave us lifts! You just sit still and are drawn along."

"And here, friend, the people are quite beggarly. There they all seemed to be Poles—all under the Russian crown—but here they're all regular Germans."

"Singers to the front" came the captain's order.

And from the different ranks some twenty men ran to the front. A drummer, their leader, turned round facing the singers, and flourishing his arm, began a long-drawn-out soldiers' song, commencing with the words: *"Morning dawned, the sun was rising,"* and concluding: *"On then, brothers, on to glory, led by Father Kámenski."* This song had been composed in the Turkish campaign and now being sung in Austria, the only change being that the words "Father Kámenski" were replaced by "Father Kutúzov."

Having jerked out these last words as soldiers do and waved his arms as if flinging something to the ground, the drummer—a lean, handsome soldier of forty—looked sternly at the singers and screwed up his eyes. Then having satisfied himself that all eyes were fixed on him, he raised both arms as if carefully lifting some invisible but precious object above his head and, holding it there for some seconds, suddenly flung it down and began:

"Oh, my bower, oh, my bower...!"

"Oh, my bower new...!" chimed in twenty voices, and the castanet player, in spite of the burden of his equipment, rushed out to the front and, walking backwards before the company, jerked his shoulders and flourished his castanets as if threatening someone. The soldiers, swinging their arms and keeping time spontaneously, marched with long steps. Behind the company the sound of wheels, the creaking of springs, and the tramp of horses' hoofs were heard. Kutúzov and his suite were returning to the town. The commander in chief made a sign that the men should continue to march at ease, and he and all his suite showed pleasure at the sound of the singing and the sight of the dancing soldier and the gay and smartly marching men. In the second file from the right flank, beside which the carriage passed the company, a blue-eyed soldier involuntarily attracted notice. It was Dólokhov marching with particular grace and boldness in time to the song and looking at those driving past as if he pitied all who were not at that moment marching with the company. The hussar cornet of Kutúzov's suite who had mimicked the regimental commander, fell back from the carriage and rode up to Dólokhov.

Hussar cornet Zherkóv had at one time, in Petersburg, belonged to the wild set led by Dólokhov. Zherkóv had met Dólokhov abroad as a private and had not seen fit to recognize him. But now that Kutúzov had spoken to the gentleman ranker, he addressed him with the cordiality of an old friend.

"My dear fellow, how are you?" said he through the singing, making his horse keep pace with the company.

"How am I?" Dólokhov answered coldly. "I am as you see."

The lively song gave a special flavor to the tone of free and easy gaiety with which Zherkóv spoke, and to the intentional coldness of Dólokhov's reply.

"And how do you get on with the officers?" inquired Zherkóv.

"All right. They are good fellows. And how have you wriggled onto the staff?"

"I was attached; I'm on duty."

Both were silent.

"She let the hawk fly upward from her wide right sleeve," went the song, arousing an involuntary sensation of courage and cheerfulness. Their conversation would probably have been different but for the effect of that song.

"Is it true that Austrians have been beaten?" asked Dólokhov.

"The devil only knows! They say so."

"I'm glad," answered Dólokhov briefly and clearly, as the song demanded.

"I say, come round some evening and we'll have a game of faro!" said Zherkóv.

"Why, have you too much money?"

"Do come."

"I can't. I've sworn not to. I won't drink and won't play till I get reinstated."

"Well, that's only till the first engagement."

"We shall see."

They were again silent.

"Come if you need anything. One can at least be of use on the staff..."

Dólokhov smiled. "Don't trouble. If I want anything, I won't beg—I'll take it!"

"Well, never mind; I only..."

"And I only..."

"Good-by."

"Good health..."

"It's a long, long way. To my native land..."

Zherkóv touched his horse with the spurs; it pranced excitedly from foot to foot uncertain with which to start, then settled down, galloped past the company, and overtook the carriage, still keeping time to the song.

~

Leo Tolstoy (1828–1910) is best known to the world because of *War and Peace*, his epic in prose, an extract of which you just read, and *Anna Karenina*, one of the most splendid novels in any language. During his lifetime Tolstoy also wrote enough shorter works to fill many volumes, including "The Cossacks" and "Family Happiness".

The Jumping Frog

Mark Twain

In compliance with the request of a friend of mine, who wrote me from the East, I called on good-natured, garrulous old Simon Wheeler, and inquired after my friend's friend, Leonidas W. Smiley, as requested to do, and I hereunto append the result. I have a lurking suspicion that *Leonidas W.* Smiley is a myth; that my friend never knew such a personage; and that he only conjectured that if I asked old Wheeler about him, it would remind him of his infamous *Jim* Smiley, and he would go to work and bore me to death with some exasperating reminiscence of him as long and as tedious as it should be useless to me. If that was the design, it succeeded.

I found Simon Wheeler dozing comfortably by the bar-room stove of the dilapidated tavern in the decaying mining camp of Angel's, and I noticed that he was fat and bald-headed, and had an expression of winning gentleness and simplicity upon his tranquil countenance. He roused up, and gave me good-day. I told him a friend of mine had commissioned me to make some inquiries about a cherished companion of his boyhood named *Leonidas W.* Smiley—*Rev. Leonidas W.* Smiley, a young minister of the Gospel, who he had heard was at one time a resident of Angel's Camp. I added that if Mr Wheeler could tell me anything about this Rev. Leonidas W. Smiley, I would feel under many obligations to him.

Simon Wheeler backed me into a corner and blockaded me there with his chair, and then sat down and reeled off the monotonous narrative which follows this paragraph. He never smiled, he never frowned, he never changed his voice from the gentle-flowing key to which he tuned his initial sentence, he never betrayed the slightest suspicion of enthusiasm; but all through the interminable narrative there ran a vein of impressive earnestness and sincerity, which showed me plainly that, so far from his imagining that there was anything ridiculous or funny about his story, he regarded it as a really important matter, and admired its two heroes as men of transcendent genius in *finesse.* I let him go on in his own way, and never interrupted him once.

"Rev. Leonidas W. H'm, Reverend Le—well, there was a feller here once by the name of *Jim* Smiley, in the winter of '49—or maybe it was the spring of '50—I don't recollect exactly, somehow, though what makes me think it was one or the other is because I remember the big flume warn't finished when he first come to the camp; but anyway, he was the curiosest man about always betting on anything that turned up you ever see, if he could get anybody to bet on the other side; and if he couldn't he'd change sides. Any way that suited the other man would suit *him*—any way just so's he got a bet, *he* was satisfied. But still he was lucky, uncommon lucky; he 'most always come out winner. He was always ready and laying for a chance; there couldn't be no solit'ry thing mentioned but that feller'd offer to bet on it, and take ary side you please, as I was just telling you. If there was a horse-race, you'd find him flush or you'd find him busted at the end of it; if there was a dogfight, he'd bet on it; if there was a cat-fight, he'd bet on it; if there was a chicken-fight, he'd bet on it; why, if there was two birds setting on a fence, he would bet you which one would fly first; or if there was a camp-meeting, he would be there reg'lar to bet on Parson Walker, which he judged to be the best exhorter about here, and so he was, too, and a good man. If he even see a straddle-bug start to go anywheres, he would bet you how long it would take him to get to—to wherever he was going to, and if you took him up, he would foller that straddle-bug to Mexico but what he would find out where he was bound for and how long he was on the road. Lots of the boys here has seen that Smiley, and can tell you about him. Why, it never made no difference to *him*—he'd bet on *any* thing—the dangdest feller. Parson Walker's wife laid very sick once, for a good while, and it seemed as if they warn't going to save her; but one morning he come in, and Smiley up and asked him how she was, and he said she was consid'able better—thank the Lord for his inf'nite mercy—and coming on so smart that with the blessing of Prov'dence she'd get well yet; and Smiley, before he thought, says: 'Well, I'll resk two-and-a-half she don't anyway.'

"Thish-yer Smiley had a mare—the boys called her the fifteen-minute nag, but that was only in fun, you know, because, of course, she was faster than that—and he used to win money on that horse, for all she was so slow and always had the asthma, or the distemper, or the consumption, or something of that kind. They used to give her two or three hundred yards start, and then pass her under way; but always at the fag end of the race she'd get excited and desperate like, and come cavorting and straddling up, and scattering her legs around limber, sometimes in the air, and sometimes out to one side among the fences, and kicking up m-o-r-e dust and raising m-o-r-e racket with her coughing and sneezing and blowing her nose—and *always* fetch up at the stand just about a neck ahead, as near as you could cipher it down.

"And he had a little small bull-pup, that to look at him you'd think he warn't worth a cent but to set around and look ornery and lay for a chance to steal something. But as soon as money was up on him he was a different dog; his under-jaw'd begin to stick out like the fo'castle of a steamboat, and his teeth would uncover and shine like the furnaces. And a dog might tackle him and bully-rag him, and bite him, and throw him over his shoulder two or three times, and Andrew Jackson—which was the name of the pup—Andrew Jackson would never let on but what *he* was satisfied, and hadn't expected nothing else—and the bets being doubled and doubled on the other side all the time, till the money was all up; and then all of a sudden he would grab that other dog jest by the j'int of his hind leg and freeze to it—not chaw, you understand, but only just grip and hang on till they throwed up the sponge, if it was a year. Smiley always come out winner on that pup, till he harnessed a dog once that didn't have no hind legs, because they'd been sawed off in a circular saw, and when the thing had gone along far enough, and the money was all up, and he come to make a snatch for his pet holt, he see in a minute how he'd been imposed on, and how the other dog had him in the door, so to speak, and he 'peared surprised, and then he looked sorter discouraged-like and didn't try no more to win the fight, and so he got shucked out bad. He give Smiley a look, as much as to say his heart was broke, and it was *his* fault, for putting up a dog that hadn't no hind legs for him to take holt of, which was his main dependence in a fight, and then he limped off a piece and laid down and died.

It was a good pup, was that Andrew Jackson, and would have made a name for hisself if he'd lived, for the stuff was in him and he had genius—I know it, because he hadn't no opportunities to speak of, and it don't stand to reason that a dog could make such a fight as he could under them circumstances if he hadn't no talent. It always makes me feel sorry when I think of that last fight of his'n, and the way it turned out.

"Well, thish-yer Smiley had rat-tarriers, and chicken cocks, and tomcats, and all them kind of things, till you couldn't rest, and you couldn't fetch nothing for him to bet on but he'd match you. He ketched a frog one day, and took him home, and said he cal'lated to educate him; and so he never done nothing for three months but set in his back yard and learn that frog to jump. And you bet you he *did* learn him, too. He'd give him a little punch behind, and the next minute you'd see that frog whirling in the air like a doughnut—see him turn one summerset, or maybe a couple, if he got a good start, and come down flat-footed and all right, like a cat. He got him up so in the matter of ketching flies, and kep' him in practice so constant, that he'd nail a fly every time as fur as he could see him. Smiley said all a frog wanted was education, and he could do 'most anything—and I believe him. Why, I've seen him set Dan'l Webster down here on this floor—Dan'l Webster was the name of the frog—and sing out, 'Flies, Dan'l, flies!' and quicker'n you could wink he'd spring straight up and snake a fly off'n the counter there, and flop down on the floor ag'in as solid as a gob of mud, and fall to scratching the side of his head with his hind foot as indifferent as if he hadn't no idea he'd been doin' any more'n any frog might do. You never see a frog so modest and straightfor'ard as he was, for all he was so gifted. And when it come to fair and square jumping on a dead level, he could get over more ground at one straddle than any animal of his breed you ever see. Jumping on a dead level was his strong suit, you understand; and when it come to that, Smiley would ante up money on him as long as he had a red. Smiley was monstrous proud of his frog, and well he might be, for fellers that had travelled and been everywheres all said he laid over any frog that ever *they* see.

"Well, Smiley kep' the beast in a little lattice box, and he used to fetch him down-town sometimes and lay for a bet. One day a feller—a stranger in the camp, he was—come acrost him with his box, and says:

"'What might it be that you've got in the box?'

"And Smiley says, sorter indifferent-like: 'It might be a parrot, or it might be a canary, maybe, but it ain't—it's only just a frog.'

"And the feller took it, and looked at it careful, and turned it round this way and that, and says: 'H'm—so 'tis. Well, what's *he* good for?'

"'Well,' Smiley says, easy and careless, 'he's good enough for *one* thing, I should judge—he can outjump any frog in Calaveras county.'

"The feller took the box again, and took another long, particular look, and give it back to Smiley, and says, very deliberate, 'Well,' he says, 'I don't see no p'ints about that frog that's any better'n any other frog.'

"'Maybe you don't,' Smiley says. 'Maybe you understand frogs and maybe you don't understand 'em; maybe you've had experience, and maybe you ain't only a amature, as it were. Anyways, I've got *my* opinion, and I'll resk forty dollars that he can outjump any frog in Calaveras county.'

"And the feller studied a minute, and then says, kinder sad like, 'Well, I'm only a stranger here, and I ain't got no frog; but if I had a frog, I'd bet you.'

"And then Smiley says, 'That's all right—that's all right—if you'll hold my box a minute, I'll go and get you a frog.' And so the feller took the box, and put up his forty dollars along with Smiley's, and set down to wait.

"So he set there a good while thinking and thinking to hisself, and then he got the frog out and prized his mouth open and took a teaspoon and filled him full of quail shot—filled him pretty near up to his chin—and set him on the floor. Smiley he went to the swamp and slopped around in the mud for a long time, and finally he ketched a frog, and fetched him in, and give him to this feller, and says:

"'Now, if you're ready, set him alongside of Dan'l, with his forepaws just even with Dan'l's, and I'll give the word.' Then he says, 'One—two—three—*git!*' and him and the feller touched up the frogs from behind, and the new frog hopped off lively, but Dan'l give a heave, and hysted up his shoulders—so—like a Frenchman, but it warn't no use—he couldn't budge; he was planted as solid as a church, and he couldn't no more stir than if he was anchored out. Smiley was a good deal surprised, and he was disgusted too, but he didn't have no idea what the matter was, of course.

"The feller took the money and started away; and when he was going out at the door, he sorter jerked his thumb over his shoulder—so—at Dan'l, and says again, very deliberate, 'Well,' he says, '*I* don't see no p'ints about that frog that's any better'n any other frog.'

"Smiley he stood scratching his head and looking down at Dan'l a long time, and at last he says, 'I do wonder what in the nation that frog throw'd off for—I wonder if there ain't something the matter with him—he 'pears to look mighty baggy, somehow.' And he ketched Dan'l by the nap of the neck, and hefted him, and says, 'Why, blame my cats if he don't weigh five pound!' and turned him upside down and he belched out a double handful of shot. And then he see how it was, and he was the maddest man—he set the frog down and took out after that feller, but he never ketched him. And—"

[Here Simon Wheeler heard his name called from the front yard, and got up to see what was wanted.] And turning to me as he moved away, he said: "Just set where you are, stranger, and rest easy—I ain't going to be gone a second."

But, by your leave, I did not think that a continuation of the history of the enterprising vagabond *Jim* Smiley would be likely to afford me much information concerning the Rev. *Leonidas W.* Smiley, and so I started away.

At the door I met the sociable Wheeler returning, and he button-holed me and recommenced:

"Well, thish-yer Smiley had a yeller one-eyed cow that didn't have no tail, only just a short stump like a bannanner, and—"

However, lacking both time and inclination, I did not wait to hear about the afflicted cow, but took my leave.

~

Samuel Langhorne Clemens (1835–1910), known by his pen name Mark Twain, was an American journalist, humourist, lecturer and novelist popular for his works of fiction *Adventures of Huckleberry Finn*, *The Adventures of Tom Sawyer*, *The Prince and the Pauper* and non-fiction *Life on the Mississippi* and *Is Shakespeare Dead*?

From Frankenstein or, the Modern Prometheus

Mary Shelley

Frankenstein; Or, The Modern Prometheus *is an early nineteenth century Gothic novel about an explorer on an expedition to the Arctic regions in search of truth, knowledge and science. It is written in the epistolary form.*

Elizabeth and I were brought up together; there was not quite a year difference in our ages. I need not say that we were strangers to any species of disunion or dispute. Harmony was the soul of our companionship, and the diversity and contrast that subsisted in our characters drew us nearer together. Elizabeth was of a calmer and more concentrated disposition; but, with all my ardour, I was capable of a more intense application and was more deeply smitten with the thirst for knowledge. She busied herself with following the aerial creations of the poets; and in the majestic and wondrous scenes which surrounded our Swiss home—the sublime shapes of the mountains, the changes of the seasons, tempest and calm, the silence of winter, and the life and turbulence of our Alpine summers—she found ample scope for admiration and delight. While my companion contemplated with a serious and satisfied spirit the magnificent appearances of things, I delighted in investigating their causes. The world was to me a secret which I desired to divine. Curiosity, earnest research to learn the hidden laws of nature, gladness akin to rapture, as they were unfolded to me, are among the earliest sensations I can remember.

On the birth of a second son, my junior by seven years, my parents gave up entirely their wandering life and fixed themselves in their native country. We possessed a house in Geneva, and a *campagne* on Belrive, the eastern shore of the lake, at the distance of rather more than a league from the city. We resided principally in the latter, and the lives of my parents were passed in considerable seclusion. It was my temper to avoid a crowd and to attach myself fervently to a few. I was indifferent, therefore, to my school-fellows in general; but I united myself in the bonds of the closest friendship to one among them. Henry Clerval was the son of a merchant of Geneva. He was a boy of singular talent and fancy. He loved enterprise, hardship, and even danger for its own sake. He was deeply read in books of chivalry and romance. He composed heroic songs and began to write many a tale of enchantment and knightly adventure. He tried to make us act plays and to enter into masquerades, in which the characters were drawn from the heroes of Roncesvalles, of the Round Table of King Arthur, and the chivalrous train who shed their blood to redeem the holy sepulchre from the hands of the infidels.

No human being could have passed a happier childhood than myself. My parents were possessed by the very spirit of kindness and indulgence. We felt that they were not the tyrants to rule our lot according to their caprice, but the agents and creators of all the many delights which we enjoyed. When I mingled with other families I distinctly discerned how peculiarly fortunate my lot was, and gratitude assisted the development of filial love.

My temper was sometimes violent, and my passions vehement; but by some law in my temperature they were turned not towards childish pursuits but to an eager desire to learn, and not to learn all things indiscriminately. I confess that neither the structure of languages, nor the code of governments, nor the politics of various states possessed attractions for me. It was the secrets of heaven and earth that I desired to learn; and whether it was the outward substance of things or the inner spirit of nature and the mysterious soul of man that occupied me, still my inquiries were directed to the metaphysical, or in its highest sense, the physical secrets of the world.

Meanwhile Clerval occupied himself, so to speak, with the moral relations of things. The busy stage of life, the virtues of heroes, and the actions of men were his theme; and his hope and his dream was to become one among those whose names are recorded in story as the gallant and adventurous benefactors of our species. The saintly soul of Elizabeth shone like a shrine-dedicated lamp in our peaceful home. Her sympathy was ours; her smile, her soft voice, the sweet glance of her celestial eyes, were ever there to bless and animate us. She was the living spirit of love to soften and attract; I might have become sullen in my study, rough through the ardour of my nature, but that she was there to subdue me to a semblance of her own gentleness. And Clerval—could aught ill entrench on the noble spirit of Clerval? Yet he might not have been so perfectly humane, so thoughtful in his generosity, so full of kindness and tenderness amidst his passion for adventurous exploit, had she not unfolded to him the real loveliness of beneficence and made the doing good the end and aim of his soaring ambition.

I feel exquisite pleasure in dwelling on the recollections of childhood, before misfortune had tainted my mind and changed its bright visions of extensive usefulness into gloomy and narrow reflections upon self. Besides, in drawing the picture of my early days, I also record those events which led, by insensible steps, to my after tale of misery, for when I would account to myself for the birth of that passion which afterwards ruled my destiny I find it arise, like a mountain river, from ignoble and almost forgotten sources; but, swelling as it proceeded, it became the torrent which, in its course, has swept away all my hopes and joys.

Natural philosophy is the genius that has regulated my fate; I desire, therefore, in this narration, to state those facts which led to my predilection for that science. When I was thirteen years of age we all went on a party of pleasure to the baths near Thonon; the inclemency of the weather obliged us to remain a day confined to the inn. In this house I chanced to find a volume of the works of Cornelius Agrippa. I opened it with apathy; the theory which he attempts to demonstrate and the wonderful facts which he relates soon changed this feeling into enthusiasm. A new light seemed to dawn upon my mind, and bounding with joy, I communicated my discovery to my father. My father looked carelessly at the title page of my book and said, "Ah! Cornelius Agrippa! My dear Victor, do not waste your time upon this; it is sad trash."

If, instead of this remark, my father had taken the pains to explain to me that the principles of Agrippa had been entirely exploded and that a modern system of science had been introduced which possessed much greater powers than the ancient, because the powers of the latter were chimerical, while those of the former were real and practical, under such circumstances I should certainly have thrown Agrippa aside and have contented my imagination, warmed as it was, by returning with greater ardour to my former studies. It is even possible that the train of my ideas would never have received the fatal impulse that led to my ruin. But the cursory glance my father had taken of my volume by no means assured me that he was acquainted with its contents, and I continued to read with the greatest avidity.

When I returned home my first care was to procure the whole works of this author, and afterwards of Paracelsus and Albertus Magnus. I read and studied the wild fancies of these writers with delight; they appeared to me treasures known to few besides myself. I have described myself as always having been imbued with a fervent longing to penetrate the secrets of nature. In spite of the intense labour and wonderful discoveries of modern philosophers, I always came from my studies discontented and unsatisfied. Sir Isaac Newton is said to have avowed that he felt like a child picking up shells beside the great and unexplored ocean of truth. Those of his successors in each branch of natural philosophy with whom I was acquainted appeared even to my boy's apprehensions as tyros engaged in the same pursuit.

The untaught peasant beheld the elements around him and was acquainted with their practical uses. The most learned philosopher knew little more. He had partially unveiled the face of Nature, but her immortal lineaments were still a wonder and a mystery. He might dissect, anatomise, and give names; but, not to speak of a final cause, causes in their secondary and tertiary grades were utterly unknown to him. I had gazed upon the fortifications and impediments that seemed to keep human beings from entering the citadel of nature, and rashly and ignorantly I had repined.

But here were books, and here were men who had penetrated deeper and knew more. I took their word for all that they averred, and I became their disciple. It may appear strange that such should arise in the eighteenth century; but while I followed the routine of education in the schools of Geneva, I was, to a great degree, self-taught with regard to my favourite studies. My father was not scientific, and I was left to struggle with a child's blindness, added to a student's thirst for knowledge. Under the guidance of my new preceptors I entered with the greatest diligence into the search of the philosopher's stone and the elixir of life; but the latter soon obtained my undivided attention. Wealth was an inferior object, but what glory would attend the discovery if I could banish disease from the human frame and render man invulnerable to any but a violent death!

Nor were these my only visions. The raising of ghosts or devils was a promise liberally accorded by my favourite authors, the fulfilment of which I most eagerly sought; and if my incantations were always unsuccessful, I attributed the failure rather to my own inexperience and mistake than to a want of skill or fidelity in my instructors. And thus for a time I was occupied by exploded systems, mingling, like an unadept, a thousand contradictory theories and floundering desperately in a very slough of multifarious knowledge, guided by an ardent imagination and childish reasoning, till an accident again changed the current of my ideas.

When I was about fifteen years old we had retired to our house near Belrive, when we witnessed a most violent and terrible thunderstorm. It advanced from behind the mountains of Jura, and the thunder burst at once with frightful loudness from various quarters of the heavens. I remained, while the storm lasted, watching its progress with curiosity and delight. As I stood at the door, on a sudden I beheld a stream of fire issue from an old and beautiful oak which stood about twenty yards from our house; and so soon as the dazzling light vanished, the oak had disappeared, and nothing remained but a blasted stump. When we visited it the next morning, we found the tree shattered in a singular manner. It was not splintered by the shock, but entirely reduced to thin ribbons of wood. I never beheld anything so utterly destroyed.

Before this I was not unacquainted with the more obvious laws of electricity. On this occasion a man of great research in natural philosophy was with us, and excited by this catastrophe, he entered on the explanation of a theory which he had formed on the subject of electricity and galvanism, which was at once new and astonishing to me. All that he said threw greatly into the shade Cornelius Agrippa, Albertus Magnus, and Paracelsus, the lords of my imagination; but by some fatality the overthrow of these men disinclined me to pursue my accustomed studies. It seemed to me as if nothing would or could ever be known. All that had so long engaged my attention suddenly grew despicable. By one of those caprices of the mind which we are perhaps most subject to in early youth, I at once gave up my former occupations, set down natural history and all its progeny as a deformed and abortive creation, and entertained the greatest disdain for a would-be science which could never even step within the threshold of real knowledge. In this mood of mind I betook myself to the mathematics and the branches of study appertaining to that science as being built upon secure foundations, and so worthy of my consideration.

Thus strangely are our souls constructed, and by such slight ligaments are we bound to prosperity or ruin. When I look back, it seems to me as if this almost miraculous change of inclination and will was the immediate suggestion of the guardian angel of my life—the last effort made by the spirit of preservation to avert the storm that was even then hanging in the stars and ready to envelop me. Her victory was announced by an unusual tranquillity and gladness of soul which followed the relinquishing of my ancient and latterly tormenting studies. It was thus that I was to be taught to associate evil with their prosecution, happiness with their disregard.

It was a strong effort of the spirit of good, but it was ineffectual. Destiny was too potent, and her immutable laws had decreed my utter and terrible destruction.

When I had attained the age of seventeen my parents resolved that I should become a student at the university of Ingolstadt. I had hitherto attended the schools of Geneva, but my father thought it necessary for the completion of my education that I should be made acquainted with other customs than those of my native country. My departure was therefore fixed at an early date, but before the day resolved upon could arrive, the first misfortune of my life occurred—an omen, as it were, of my future misery.

Elizabeth had caught the scarlet fever; her illness was severe, and she was in the greatest danger. During her illness many arguments had been urged to persuade my mother to refrain from attending upon her. She had at first yielded to our entreaties, but when she heard that the life of her favourite was menaced, she could no longer control her anxiety. She attended her sickbed; her watchful attentions triumphed over the malignity of the distemper—Elizabeth was saved, but the consequences of this imprudence were fatal to her preserver. On the third day my mother sickened; her fever was accompanied by the most alarming symptoms, and the looks of her medical attendants prognosticated the worst event. On her deathbed the fortitude and benignity of this best of women did not desert her. She joined the hands of Elizabeth and myself. "My children," she said, "my firmest hopes of future happiness were placed on the prospect of your union. This expectation will now be the consolation of your father.

Elizabeth, my love, you must supply my place to my younger children. Alas! I regret that I am taken from you; and, happy and beloved as I have been, is it not hard to quit you all? But these are not thoughts befitting me; I will endeavour to resign myself cheerfully to death and will indulge a hope of meeting you in another world."

She died calmly, and her countenance expressed affection even in death. I need not describe the feelings of those whose dearest ties are rent by that most irreparable evil, the void that presents itself to the soul, and the despair that is exhibited on the countenance. It is so long before the mind can persuade itself that she whom we saw every day and whose very existence appeared a part of our own can have departed for ever—that the brightness of a beloved eye can have been extinguished and the sound of a voice so familiar and dear to the ear can be hushed, never more to be heard. These are the reflections of the first days; but when the lapse of time proves the reality of the evil, then the actual bitterness of grief commences. Yet from whom has not that rude hand rent away some dear connection? And why should I describe a sorrow which all have felt, and must feel? The time at length arrives when grief is rather an indulgence than a necessity; and the smile that plays upon the lips, although it may be deemed a sacrilege, is not banished. My mother was dead, but we had still duties which we ought to perform; we must continue our course with the rest and learn to think ourselves fortunate whilst one remains whom the spoiler has not seized.

My departure for Ingolstadt, which had been deferred by these events, was now again determined upon. I obtained from my father a respite of some weeks. It appeared to me sacrilege so soon to leave the repose, akin to death, of the house of mourning and to rush into the thick of life. I was new to sorrow, but it did not the less alarm me. I was unwilling to quit the sight of those that remained to me, and above all, I desired to see my sweet Elizabeth in some degree consoled.

She indeed veiled her grief and strove to act the comforter to us all. She looked steadily on life and assumed its duties with courage and zeal. She devoted herself to those whom she had been taught to call her uncle and cousins. Never was she so enchanting as at this time, when she recalled the sunshine of her smiles and spent them upon us. She forgot even her own regret in her endeavours to make us forget.

The day of my departure at length arrived. Clerval spent the last evening with us. He had endeavoured to persuade his father to permit him to accompany me and to become my fellow student, but in vain. His father was a narrow-minded trader and saw idleness and ruin in the aspirations and ambition of his son. Henry deeply felt the misfortune of being debarred from a liberal education. He said little, but when he spoke I read in his kindling eye and in his animated glance a restrained but firm resolve not to be chained to the miserable details of commerce.

We sat late. We could not tear ourselves away from each other nor persuade ourselves to say the word "Farewell!" It was said, and we retired under the pretence of seeking repose, each fancying that the other was deceived; but when at morning's dawn I descended to the carriage which was to convey me away, they were all there—my father again to bless me, Clerval to press my hand once more, my Elizabeth to renew her entreaties that I would write often and to bestow the last feminine attentions on her playmate and friend.

I threw myself into the chaise that was to convey me away and indulged in the most melancholy reflections. I, who had ever been surrounded by amiable companions, continually engaged in endeavouring to bestow mutual pleasure—I was now alone. In the university whither I was going I must form my own friends and be my own protector. My life had hitherto been remarkably secluded and domestic, and this had given me invincible repugnance to new countenances. I loved my brothers, Elizabeth, and Clerval; these were "old familiar faces," but I believed myself totally unfitted for the company of strangers. Such were my reflections as I commenced my journey; but as I proceeded, my spirits and hopes rose. I ardently desired the acquisition of knowledge. I had often, when at home, thought it hard to remain during my youth cooped up in one place and had longed to enter the world and take my station among other human beings. Now my desires were complied with, and it would, indeed, have been folly to repent.

I had sufficient leisure for these and many other reflections during my journey to Ingolstadt, which was long and fatiguing. At length the high white steeple of the town met my eyes. I alighted and was conducted to my solitary apartment to spend the evening as I pleased.

The next morning I delivered my letters of introduction and paid a visit to some of the principal professors. Chance—or rather the evil influence, the Angel of Destruction, which asserted omnipotent sway over me from the moment I turned my reluctant steps from my father's door—led me first to M. Krempe, professor of natural philosophy. He was an uncouth man, but deeply imbued in the secrets of his science. He asked me several questions concerning my progress in the different branches of science appertaining to natural philosophy. I replied carelessly, and partly in contempt, mentioned the names of my alchemists as the principal authors I had studied. The professor stared. "Have you," he said, "really spent your time in studying such nonsense?"

I replied in the affirmative. "Every minute," continued M. Krempe with warmth, "every instant that you have wasted on those books is utterly and entirely lost. You have burdened your memory with exploded systems and useless names. Good God! In what desert land have you lived, where no one was kind enough to inform you that these fancies which you have so greedily imbibed are a thousand years old and as musty as they are ancient? I little expected, in this enlightened and scientific age, to find a disciple of Albertus Magnus and Paracelsus. My dear sir, you must begin your studies entirely anew."

So saying, he stepped aside and wrote down a list of several books treating of natural philosophy which he desired me to procure, and dismissed me after mentioning that in the beginning of the following week he intended to commence a course of lectures upon natural philosophy in its general relations, and that M. Waldman, a fellow professor, would lecture upon chemistry the alternate days that he omitted.

I returned home not disappointed, for I have said that I had long considered those authors useless whom the professor reprobated; but I returned not at all the more inclined to recur to these studies in any shape. M. Krempe was a little squat man with a gruff voice and a repulsive countenance; the teacher, therefore, did not prepossess me in favour of his pursuits. In rather a too philosophical and connected a strain, perhaps, I have given an account of the conclusions I had come to concerning them in my early years. As a child I had not been content with the results promised by the modern professors of natural science. With a confusion of ideas only to be accounted for by my extreme youth and my want of a guide on such matters, I had retrod the steps of knowledge along the paths of time and exchanged the discoveries of recent inquirers for the dreams of forgotten alchemists. Besides, I had a contempt for the uses of modern natural philosophy. It was very different when the masters of the science sought immortality and power; such views, although futile, were grand; but now the scene was changed. The ambition of the inquirer seemed to limit itself to the annihilation of those visions on which my interest in science was chiefly founded. I was required to exchange chimeras of boundless grandeur for realities of little worth.

Such were my reflections during the first two or three days of my residence at Ingolstadt, which were chiefly spent in becoming acquainted with the localities and the principal residents in my new abode. But as the ensuing week commenced, I thought of the information which M. Krempe had given me concerning the lectures. And although I could not consent to go and hear that little conceited fellow deliver sentences out of a pulpit, I recollected what he had said of M. Waldman, whom I had never seen, as he had hitherto been out of town.

Partly from curiosity and partly from idleness, I went into the lecturing room, which M. Waldman entered shortly after. This professor was very unlike his colleague. He appeared about fifty years of age, but with an aspect expressive of the greatest benevolence; a few grey hairs covered his temples, but those at the back of his head were nearly black. His person was short but remarkably erect and his voice the sweetest I had ever heard. He began his lecture by a recapitulation of the history of chemistry and the various improvements made by different men of learning, pronouncing with fervour the names of the most distinguished discoverers. He then took a cursory view of the present state of the science and explained many of its elementary terms. After having made a few preparatory experiments, he concluded with a panegyric upon modern chemistry, the terms of which I shall never forget:

"The ancient teachers of this science," said he, "promised impossibilities and performed nothing. The modern masters promise very little; they know that metals cannot be transmuted and that the elixir of life is a chimera but these philosophers, whose hands seem only made to dabble in dirt, and their eyes to pore over the microscope or crucible, have indeed performed miracles. They penetrate into the recesses of nature and show how she works in her hiding-places. They ascend into the heavens; they have discovered how the blood circulates, and the nature of the air we breathe. They have acquired new and almost unlimited powers; they can command the thunders of heaven, mimic the earthquake, and even mock the invisible world with its own shadows."

Such were the professor's words—rather let me say such the words of the fate—enounced to destroy me. As he went on I felt as if my soul were grappling with a palpable enemy; one by one the various keys were touched which formed the mechanism of my being; chord after chord was sounded, and soon my mind was filled with one thought, one conception, one purpose. So much has been done, exclaimed the soul of Frankenstein—more, far more, will I achieve; treading in the steps already marked, I will pioneer a new way, explore unknown powers, and unfold to the world the deepest mysteries of creation.

I closed not my eyes that night. My internal being was in a state of insurrection and turmoil; I felt that order would thence arise, but I had no power to produce it. By degrees, after the morning's dawn, sleep came. I awoke, and my yesternight's thoughts were as a dream. There only remained a resolution to return to my ancient studies and to devote myself to a science for which I believed myself to possess a natural talent. On the same day I paid M. Waldman a visit. His manners in private were even more mild and attractive than in public, for there was a certain dignity in his mien during his lecture which in his own house was replaced by the greatest affability and kindness. I gave him pretty nearly the same account of my former pursuits as I had given to his fellow professor. He heard with attention the little narration concerning my studies and smiled at the names of Cornelius Agrippa and Paracelsus, but without the contempt that M. Krempe had exhibited. He said that "These were men to whose indefatigable zeal modern philosophers were indebted for most of the foundations of their knowledge. They had left to us, as an easier task, to give new names and arrange in connected classifications the facts which they in a great degree had been the instruments of bringing to light. The labours of men of genius, however erroneously directed, scarcely ever fail in ultimately turning to the solid advantage of mankind." I listened to his statement, which was delivered without any presumption or affectation, and then added that his lecture had removed my prejudices against modern chemists; I expressed myself in measured terms, with the modesty and deference due from a youth to his instructor, without letting escape (inexperience in life would have made me ashamed) any of the enthusiasm which stimulated my intended labours. I requested his advice concerning the books I ought to procure.

"I am happy," said M. Waldman, "to have gained a disciple; and if your application equals your ability, I have no doubt of your success. Chemistry is that branch of natural philosophy in which the greatest improvements have been and may be made; it is on that account that I have made it my peculiar study; but at the same time, I have not neglected the other branches of science. A man would make but a very sorry chemist if he attended to that department of human knowledge alone. If your wish is to become really a man of science and not merely a petty experimentalist, I should advise you to apply to every branch of natural philosophy, including mathematics."

He then took me into his laboratory and explained to me the uses of his various machines, instructing me as to what I ought to procure and promising me the use of his own when I should have advanced far enough in the science not to derange their mechanism. He also gave me the list of books which I had requested, and I took my leave.

Thus ended a day memorable to me; it decided my future destiny.

~

Mary Wollstonecraft Shelley (1797–1851) was an English author best known for *Frankenstein, or the Modern Prometheus*, a novel with Gothic themes. Her other works include *The Last Man*, *Mathilde*, *Falkner* and *History of a Six Weeks' Tour*, which is an account of her travels to France with poet Percy B. Shelley.

From Chitra: A Play In One Act

Rabindranath Tagore

Chitra: A Play in One Act *is a dance-drama adaptation of a story from the Mahabharata—of the warrior princess Chitrangada and Arjuna, the Pandava brother.*

SCENE VIII

VILLAGERS

Who will protect us now?

ARJUNA

Why, by what danger are you threatened?

VILLAGERS

The robbers are pouring from the northern hills like a mountain flood to devastate our village.

ARJUNA

Have you in this kingdom no warden?

VILLAGERS

Princess Chitra was the terror of all evil doers. While she was in this happy land we feared natural deaths, but had no other fears. Now she has gone on a pilgrimage, and none knows where to find her.

ARJUNA

Is the warden of this country a woman?

VILLAGERS

Yes, she is our father and mother in one.

(Exeunt)

(Enter CHITRA)

CHITRA

Why are you sitting all alone?

ARJUNA

I am trying to imagine what kind of woman Princess Chitra may be.
I hear so many stories of her from all sorts of men.

CHITRA

Ah, but she is not beautiful. She has no such lovely eyes as mine, dark as death. She can pierce any target she will, but not our hero's heart.

ARJUNA

They say that in valour she is a man, and a woman in tenderness.

CHITRA

That, indeed, is her greatest misfortune. When a woman is merely a woman; when she winds herself round and round men's hearts with her smiles and sobs and services and caressing endearments; then she is happy. Of what use to her are learning and great achievements? Could you have seen her only yesterday in the court of the Lord Shiva's temple by the forest path, you would have passed by without deigning to look at her. But have you grown so weary of woman's beauty that you seek in her for a man's strength?

With green leaves wet from the spray of the foaming waterfall, I have made our noonday bed in a cavern dark as night. There the cool of the soft green mosses thick on the black and dripping stone, kisses your eyes to sleep. Let me guide you thither.

ARJUNA

Not today, beloved.

CHITRA

Why not today?

ARJUNA

I have heard that a horde of robbers has neared the plains.
Needs must I go and prepare my weapons to protect the frightened villagers.

CHITRA

You need have no fear for them. Before she started on her pilgrimage, Princess Chitra had set strong guards at all the frontier passes.

ARJUNA

Yet permit me for a short while to set about a Kshatriya's work.
With new glory will I ennoble this idle arm, and make of it a pillow more worthy of your head.

CHITRA

What if I refuse to let you go, if I keep you entwined in my arms? Would you rudely snatch yourself free and leave me? Go then! But you must know that the liana, once broken in two, never joins again. Go, if your thirst is quenched. But, if not, then remember that the goddess of pleasure is fickle, and waits for no man. Sit for a while, my lord! Tell me what uneasy thoughts tease you. Who occupied your mind today? Is it Chitra?

ARJUNA

Yes, it is Chitra. I wonder in fulfilment of what vow she has gone on her pilgrimage. Of what could she stand in need?

CHITRA

Her needs? Why, what has she ever had, the unfortunate creature? Her very qualities are as prison walls, shutting her woman's heart in a bare cell. She is obscured, she is unfulfilled. Her womanly love must content itself dressed in rags; beauty is denied her. She is like the spirit of a cheerless morning, sitting upon the stony mountain peak, all her light blotted out by dark clouds. Do not ask me of her life. It will never sound sweet to man's ear.

ARJUNA

I am eager to learn all about her. I am like a traveller come to a strange city at midnight. Domes and towers and garden-trees look vague and shadowy, and the dull moan of the sea comes fitfully through the silence of sleep. Wistfully he waits for the morning to reveal to him all the strange wonders. Oh, tell me her story.

CHITRA

What more is there to tell?

ARJUNA

I seem to see her, in my mind's eye, riding on a white horse, proudly holding the reins in her left hand, and in her right a bow, and like the Goddess of Victory dispensing glad hope all round her. Like a watchful lioness she protects the litter at her dugs with a fierce love. Woman's arms, though adorned with naught but unfettered strength, are beautiful! My heart is restless, fair one, like a serpent reviving from his long winter's sleep. Come, let us both race on swift horses side by side, like twin orbs of light sweeping through space. Out from this slumbrous prison of green gloom, this dank, dense cover of perfumed intoxication, choking breath.

CHITRA

Arjuna, tell me true, if, now at once, by some magic I could shake myself free from this voluptuous softness, this timid bloom of beauty shrinking from the rude and healthy touch of the world, and fling it from my body like borrowed clothes, would you be able to bear it? If I stand up straight and strong with the strength of a daring heart spurning the wiles and arts of twining weakness, if I hold my head high like a tall young mountain fir, no longer trailing in the dust like a liana, shall I then appeal to man's eye? No, no, you could not endure it. It is better that I should keep spread about me all the dainty playthings of fugitive youth, and wait for you in patience. When it pleases you to return, I will smilingly pour out for you the wine of pleasure in the cup of this beauteous body. When you are tired and satiated with this wine, you can go to work or play; and when I grow old I will accept humbly and gratefully whatever corner is left for me. Would it please your heroic soul if the playmate of the night aspired to be the helpmeet of the day, if the left arm learnt to share the burden of the proud right arm?

ARJUNA

I never seem to know you aright. You seem to me like a goddess hidden within a golden image. I cannot touch you, I cannot pay you my dues in return for your priceless gifts. Thus my love is incomplete. Sometimes in the enigmatic depth of your sad look, in your playful words mocking at their own meaning, I gain glimpses of a being trying to rend asunder the languorous grace of her body, to emerge in a chaste fire of pain through a vaporous veil of smiles. Illusion is the first appearance of Truth. She advances towards her lover in disguise. But a time

comes when she throws off her ornaments and veils and stands clothed in naked dignity. I grope for that ultimate you, that bare simplicity of truth.
Why these tears, my love? Why cover your face with your hands? Have I pained you, my darling? Forget what I said. I will be content with the present. Let each separate moment of beauty come to me like a bird of mystery from its unseen nest in the dark bearing a message of music. Let me for ever sit with my hope on the brink of its realization, and thus end my days.

SCENE IX

CHITRA

(cloaked)

My lord, has the cup been drained to the last drop? Is this, indeed, the end? No, when all is done something still remains, and that is my last sacrifice at your feet. I brought from the garden of heaven flowers of incomparable beauty with which to worship you, god of my heart. If the rites are over, if the flowers have faded, let me throw them out of the temple.
(unveiling in her original male attire) Now, look at your worshipper with gracious eyes.
I am not beautifully perfect as the flowers with which I worshipped. I have many flaws and blemishes. I am a traveller in the

great world-path, my garments are dirty, and my feet are bleeding with thorns. Where should I achieve flower-beauty, the unsullied loveliness of a moment's life? The gift that I proudly bring you is the heart of a woman. Here have all pains and joys gathered, the hopes and fears and shames of a daughter of the dust; here love springs up struggling toward immortal life. Herein lies an imperfection which yet is noble and grand. If the flower-service is finished, my master, accept this as your servant for the days to come!

I am Chitra, the king's daughter. Perhaps you will remember the day when a woman came to you in the temple of Shiva, her body loaded with ornaments and finery. That shameless woman came to court you as though she were a man. You rejected her; you did well. My lord, I am that woman. She was my disguise. Then by the boon of gods I obtained for a year the most radiant form that a mortal ever wore, and wearied my hero's heart with the burden of that deceit. Most surely I am not that woman.

I am Chitra. No goddess to be worshipped, nor yet the object of common pity to be brushed aside like a moth with indifference. If you deign to keep me by your side in the path of danger and daring, if you allow me to share the great duties of your life, then you will know my true self. If your babe, whom I am nourishing in my womb be born a son, I shall myself teach him to be a second Arjuna, and send him to you when the time comes, and then at last you will truly know me. Today I can only offer you Chitra, the daughter of a king.

ARJUNA

Beloved, my life is full.

~

Rabindranath Tagore (1861–1941) was the first non-European to win the Nobel Prize in Literature. A poet, writer and preeminent thinker, he composed the Indian national anthem. Some of his best-known works are short stories like *The Runaway* and *Gitanjali*, his award-winning poetry collection. There are museums across India that celebrate his life and work, and universities have been named in his honour.

The Boy Who was Caught

S. Mukerji

Nothing is more common in India than seeing a ghost. Every one of us has seen ghost at some period of his existence; and if we have not actually seen one, some other person has, and has given us such a vivid description that we cannot but believe to be true what we hear.

This is, however, my own experience. I am told others have observed the phenomenon before.

When we were boys at school we used, among other things, to discuss ghosts. Most of my fellow students asserted that they did not believe in ghosts, but I was one of those who not only believed in their existence but also in their power to do harm to human beings if they liked. Of course, I was in the minority. As a matter of fact I knew that all those who said that they did not believe in ghosts told a lie. They believed in ghosts as much as I did, only they had not the courage to admit their weakness and differ boldly from the sceptics. Among the lot of unbelievers was one Ram Lal, a student of the Fifth Standard, who swore that he did not believe in ghosts and further that he would do anything to convince us that they did not exist.

It was, therefore, at my suggestion that he decided to go one moon-light night and hammer down a wooden peg into the soft sandy soil of the Hindoo Burning Ghat, it being well known that the ghosts generally put in a visible appearance at a burning ghat on a moon-light night. (A burning ghat is the place where dead bodies of Hindoos are cremated).

It was the warm month of April and the river had shrunk into the size of a nullah or drain. The real pukka ghat (the bathing place, built of bricks and lime) was about 200 yards from the water of the main stream, with a stretch of sand between.

The ghats are only used in the morning when people come to bathe, and in the evening they are all deserted. After a game of football on the school grounds we sometimes used to come and sit on the pukka ghat for an hour and return home after nightfall.

Now, it was 23 April and a bright moon-light night, every one of us (there were about a dozen) had told the people at home that there was a function at the school and he might be late. On this night, it was arranged that the ghost test should take place.

The boy who had challenged the ghost, Ram Lal, was to join us at the pukka ghat at 8 pm; and then while we waited there he would walk across the sand and drive the peg into the ground at the place where a dead body had been cremated that very morning. We were to supply the peg and the hammer. (I had to pay the school gardener two annas for the loan of a peg and a hammer).

Well, we procured the peg and the hammer and proceeded to the pukka ghat. If the gardener had known what we required the peg and the hammer for, I am sure he would not have lent these to us.

Though I was a firm believer in ghosts yet I did not expect that Ram Lal would be caught. What I hoped for was that he would not turn up at the trysting place. But to my disappointment Ram Lal did turn up and at the appointed hour too. He came boasting as usual, took the peg and the hammer and started across the sand saying that he would break the head of any ghost who might venture within the reach of the hammerhead. Well, he went along and we waited for his return at the pukka ghat. It was a glorious night, the whole expanse of sand was shining in the bright moon-light.

On and on went Ram Lal with the peg in his left hand and the hammer in his right. He was dressed in the usual upcountry Indian style, in a long coat or Achkan which reached well below his knees and fluttered in the breeze.

As he went on his pace slackened. When he had gone about half the distance he stopped and looked back. We hoped he would return. He put down the hammer and the peg, sat down on the sand facing us, took off his shoes. Only some sand had got in. He took up the peg and hammer and walked on.

But then we felt that his courage was oozing away. Another fifty yards and he again stopped, and looked back at us.

Another fifty yards remained. Will he return? No! he again proceeded, but we could clearly see that his steps were less jaunty than when he had started. We knew that he was trembling, we knew that he would have blessed us to call him back. But we would not yield, neither would he. Looking in our direction at every step he proceeded and reached the burning ghat. He reached the identical spot where the pyre had been erected in the morning.

There was very little breeze,—not a mouse stirring. Not a soul was within 200 yards of him and he could not expect much help from us. How poor Ram Lal's heart must have palpitated! When we see Ram Lal now how we feel that we should burst.

Well, Ram Lal knelt down, fixed the peg in the wet sandy soil and began hammering. After each stroke he looked at us and at the river and in all directions. He struck blow after blow and we counted about thirty. That his hands had become nerveless we would understand, for otherwise a dozen strokes should have been enough to make the peg vanish in the soft sandy soil.

The peg went in and only about a couple of inches remained visible above the surface; and then Ram Lal thought of coming back. He was kneeling still. He tried to stand up, gave out a shrill cry for help and fell down face foremost.

It must have been his cry for help that made us forget our fear of the ghost, and we all ran at top speed towards the ghat. It was rather difficult to run fast on the sand but we managed it as well as we could, and stopped only when we were about half a dozen yards from the unconscious form of Ram Lal.

There he lay senseless as if gone to sleep. Our instinct told us that he was not dead. We thanked God, and each one of us sent up a silent prayer. Then we cried for help and a boatman who lived a quarter of a mile away came up. He took up Ram Lal in his arms and as he was doing it *tr—rrrrrrrrr—* went Ram Lal's long coat. The unfortunate lad had hammered the skirt of his long coat along with the peg into the ground.

We took Ram Lal to his house and explained to his mother that he had a bad fall in the football field, and there we left him.

The next morning at school, one student, who was a neighbour of Ram Lal, told us that the whole mischief had become known.

Ram Lal, it appears, got high fever immediately after we had left him and about midnight he became delirious and in that condition he disclosed everything in connection with his adventure at the ghat.

In the evening we went to see him. His parents were very angry with us.

The whole story reached the ears of the school authorities and we got, what I thought I richly deserved (for having allowed any mortal being to defy a ghost) but what I need not say.

Ram Lal is now a grown up young man. He holds a responsible government appointment and I meet him sometimes when he comes to tour in our part of the Province.

I always ask him if he has seen a ghost since we met last.

In this connection it will not be out of place to mention two simple stories one from my own experience and another told by a friend.

I shall tell my friend's story first, in his own words.

"I used to go for a bath in the Ganges early every morning. I used to start from home at 4 o'clock in the morning and walked down to the Ganges which was about 3 miles from my house. The bath took about an hour and then I used to come back in my carriage which went for me at about six in the morning.

"On this eventful morning when I awoke it was brilliant moonlight and so I thought it was dawn.

"I started from home without looking at the clock and when I was about a mile and a half from home and about the same distance from the river I realized that I was rather early. The policeman under the railway bridge told me that it was only 2 o'clock. I knew that I should have to cross the small *maidan* through which the road ran and I remembered that there was a rumour that a ghost had sometimes been seen in the *maidan* and on the road. This however did not make me nervous, because I really did not believe in ghosts; but all the same I wished I could have gone back. But then in going back I should have to pass the policeman and he would think that I was afraid; so I decided to go on.

"When I entered the *maidan* a creepy sensation came over me. My first idea was that I was being followed, but I did not dare look back, all the same I went on with quick steps.

"My next idea was that a gust of wind swept past me, and then I thought that a huge form was passing over the trees which lined the road.

"By this time I was in the middle of the *maidan* about half a mile from the nearest human being.

"And then, horror of horrors, the huge form came down from the trees and stood in the middle of the road about a hundred yards ahead of me, barring my way.

"I instinctively moved to the side—but did not stop. By the time I reached the spot, I had left the metalled portion of the road and was actually passing under the road-side trees allowing their thick trunks to intervene between me and the huge form standing in the middle of the road. I did not look at it, but I was sure it was extending a gigantic arm towards me. It could not, however, catch me and I walked on with vigorous strides. After I had passed the figure I nearly ran under the trees, my heart beating like a sledge hammer within me.

"After a couple of minutes I saw two glaring eyes in front of me. This I thought was the end. The eyes were advancing towards me at a rapid pace and then I heard a shout like that of a cow in distress. I stopped where I was. I hoped the ghost would pass along the road overlooking me. But when the ghost was within say fifty yards of me it gave another howl and I knew that it had seen me. A cry for help escaped my lips and I fainted.

"When I regained consciousness I found myself on the grassy foot-path by the side of the road, about 4 or 5 human beings hovering about me and a motor car standing near.

"Then the whole mystery became clear as day-light. The eyes that I had seen were the headlights of the 24 H.P. Silent Knight

Minerva of Captain ——. He had gone on a pleasure-trip to the next station and was returning home with two friends and his wife in his motor car when in that part of the road he saw something like a man standing in the middle of the road and sounded his horn. As the figure in the middle of the road would not move aside he slowed down and then heard my cry.

"The rest the reader may guess. The figure that had loomed so large with an outstretched arm was only a municipal danger signal erected in the middle of the road. A red lamp had been placed on the top of the erection but it had been blown out."

This was the whole story of my friend. It shows how even our prosaic but overwrought imagination sometimes gives to airy nothings a local habitation and a name. My own personal experience which I shall describe now will also, I am sure, be interesting.

It was on a brilliant moon-light night in the month of June that we were sleeping in the open court-yard of our house.

Of course, the court-yard had a wall all round with a partition in the middle; on one side of the partition slept three girls of the family and on the other were the younger male members, four in number.

It was our custom to have a long chat after dinner and before retiring to bed.

On this particular night the talk had been about ghosts. Of course, the girls are always ready to believe everything and so when we left them we knew that they would not sleep very comfortably that night. We retired to our part of the court-yard, but we could overhear the conversation of the girls. One was trying to convince the other two that ghosts did not exist and if they did exist they never came into contact with human beings.

Then we fell asleep.

How long we had slept we did not know, but a sudden cry from, one of the girls awoke us and within three seconds we were across the low partition wall, and with her. She was sitting up in bed pointing with her fingers. Following the direction we saw in the clear moonlight the figure of a short woman standing in the corner of the court-yard about 20 yards from us pointing her finger at something (not towards us).

We looked in that direction bub could see nothing peculiar there.

Our first idea was that it was one of the maid-servants, who had heard our after-dinner conversation, playing the ghost. But this particular ghostly lady was very short, much shorter than any servant in the establishment. After some, hesitation all (four) of us advanced towards the ghost. I remember how my heart throbbed as I advanced with the other three boys.

Then we laughed loud and long.

What do you think it was?

It was only the Lawn Tennis net wrapped round the pole standing against the wall. The handle of the ratchet arrangement looked like an extending finger.

But from a distance in the moon-light it looked exactly like a short woman draped in white.

This story again shows what trick our imagination plays with us at times.

Talking of ghosts reminds me of a very funny story told by a friend of my grand-father—a famous medical man of Calcutta.

This famous doctor was once sent for to treat a gentleman at Agra. This gentleman was a rich Marwari who was suffering from indigestion. When the doctor reached Agra he was lodged in very comfortable quarters and a number of horses and carriages was placed at his disposal.

He was informed that the patient had been treated by all the local and provincial practitioners but without any result.

The doctor who was as clever a man of the world as of medicine, at once saw that there was really nothing the matter with the patient. He was really suffering from a curious malady which could in a phrase be called—"want of physical exercise."

Agra, the city after which the Province is named, abounds in old magnificent buildings which it takes the tourist a considerable time to see, and the Doctor, of course, was enjoying all the sights in the meantime.

He also prescribed a number of medicines which proved of no avail. The Doctor had anticipated it, and so he had decided what medicine he would prescribe next.

During the sight-seeing excursions into the environs of the city the doctor had discovered a large pukka well not far from a main street and at a distance of 3 miles from his patient's house.

This was a very old disused well and it was generally rumoured that a ghost dwelt in it. So nobody would go near the well at night. Of course, there was a lot of stories as to what the ghost looked like and how he came out at times and stood on the brink and all that,—but the doctor really did not believe any of these. He, however, believed that this ghost, (whether there really was any or not in that well) would cure his patient.

So one morning when he saw his patient he said "Lalla Saheb—I have found out the real cause of your trouble—it is a ghost whom you have got to propitiate and unless you do that you will never get well—and no medicine will help you and your digestion will never improve."

"A Ghost?" asked the patient.

"A Ghost!" exclaimed the people around.

"A Ghost" said the doctor sagely.

"What shall I have to do?" inquired the patient, anxiously—

"You will have to go every morning to that well (indicating the one mentioned above), and throw a basketful of flowers in" said the doctor.

"I shall do that every day" said the patient.

"Then we shall begin from to-morrow" said the doctor.

The next morning everybody had been ready to start long before the doctor was out of bed. He came at last and all got up to start. Then a big landau and pair drew up to take the doctor and the patient to the abode of the ghost in the well. Just as the patient was thinking of getting in the doctor said "We don't require a carriage Lalla Saheb—we shall all have to walk—and bare-footed too, and between you and me we shall have to carry the basket of flowers also."

The patient was really troubled. Never indeed in his life had he walked a mile—not to say of three—and that, bare-footed and carrying a basket of flowers in his hands. However he had to do it. It was a goodly procession. The big millionaire—the big doctor with a large number of followers walking bare-footed—caused amazement and amusement to all who saw them.

It took them a full hour and a half to reach the well—and there the doctor pronounced the *mantra* in Sanskrit and the flowers were thrown in. The *mantra* (charm) was in Sanskrit, the doctor who knew a little of the language had taken great pains to compose it the night before and even then it was not grammatically quite correct.

At last the party returned, but not on foot. The journey back was performed in the carriages that had followed the patient and his doctor. From that day the practice was followed regularly. The patient's health began to improve and he began to regain his power of digestion fast. In a month he was all right; but he never discontinued the practice of going to the well and throwing in a basketful of flowers with his own hands. He had also learnt the *mantra* (the mystic charm) by heart; but the doctor had sworn him to secrecy and he told it to nobody. Shoes with felt sole were soon procured from England (it being 40 years before any Indian Rope Sole Shoe Factory came into existence) and thus the inconvenience of walking this distance bare-footed was easily obviated.

After a month's further stay the doctor came away from Agra having earned a fabulous fee, and he always received occasional letters and presents from his patient who never discontinued the practice of visiting the well till his death about 17 years later.

"The three-mile walk is all that he requires" said the doctor to his friends (among whom evidently my grand-father was one) on his return from Agra, "and since he has got used to it now he won't discontinue even if he comes to know of the deception I have practised on him—and I have cured his indigestion after all."

The patient, of course, never discovered the fraud. He never gave the matter his serious consideration. His friends, who were as ignorant and prejudiced as he himself was, believed in the *ghost* as much as he did himself. The medical practitioners of Agra who probably were in the Doctor's secret never told him anything—and if they had told him anything they would probably have heard language from *Our patient* that could not well be described as quite parliamentary, for they had all tried to cure him and failed.

This series of stories will prove how much "imagination" works upon the external organs of a human being.

If a person goes about with the idea that there is a ghost somewhere about he will probably see the ghost in everything.

But has it ever struck the reader that sometimes horses and dogs do not quite enjoy going to a place which is reputed to be haunted?

In a village in Bengal not far from my home there is a big Jack-fruit tree which is said to be haunted.

I visited this place once—the local zamindar had sent me his elephant. The Gomashta (estate manager) who knew that I had come to see the haunted tree, told me that I should probably see nothing during the day, but the elephant would not go near the tree.

I passed the tree. It was about 3 miles from the Railway Station. There was nothing extraordinary about it. This was about 11 o'clock in the morning. Then I went to the Shooting Box (usually called the Cutchery or Court house—where the zamindars and their servants put up when they pay a visit to this part of their possessions) to have my bath and breakfast most hospitably provided by my generous host. I ordered the elephant to be put under this tree, and this was done though the people there told me that the elephant would not remain there long.

At about 2 P.M. I heard an extraordinary noise from the tree.

It was only the elephant. It was wailing and was looking as bad as it possibly could.

We all went there but found nothing. The elephant was not ill.

I ordered it to be taken away from under the tree. As soon as the chain was removed from the animal's foot it rushed away like a race horse and would not stop within 200 yards of the tree. I was vastly amused. I had never seen an elephant running before. But under the tree we found nothing. What made the elephant so afraid has remained a secret.

The servants told me (what I had heard before) that it was only elephants, horses and dogs that did not stay long under that tree. No human eyes have ever seen anything supernatural or fearful there.

~

Very little is known about S. Mukerji, an Indian author and journalist, and the author credited with a compilation of some of the best horror stories set in small-town India.

From Far from the Madding Crowd

Thomas Hardy

Set against the backdrop of Victorian England, Far from the Madding Crowd *revolves around its heroine Bathsheba Everdene, a headstrong, ambitious girl, and her farmer friend Gabriel Oak. The novel addresses themes such as rural life and human relationships.*

A GIRL ON HORSEBACK—CONVERSATION

The sluggish day began to break. Even its position terrestrially is one of the elements of a new interest, and for no particular reason save that the incident of the night had occurred there. Oak went again into the plantation. Lingering and musing here, he heard the steps of a horse at the foot of the hill, and soon there appeared in view an auburn pony with a girl on its back, ascending by the path leading past the cattle-shed. She was the young woman of the night before. Gabriel instantly thought of the hat she had mentioned as having lost in the wind; possibly she had come to look for it. He hastily scanned the ditch and after walking about ten yards along it found the hat among the leaves. Gabriel took it in his hand and returned to his hut. Here he ensconced himself, and peeped through the loophole in the direction of the rider's approach.

She came up and looked around—then on the other side of the hedge. Gabriel was about to advance and restore the missing article when an unexpected performance induced him to suspend the action for the present. The path, after passing the cowshed, bisected the plantation. It was not a bridle-path—merely a pedestrian's track, and the boughs spread horizontally at a height not greater than seven feet above the ground, which made it impossible to ride erect beneath them. The girl, who wore no riding-habit, looked around for a moment, as if to assure herself that all humanity was out of view, then dexterously dropped backwards flat upon the pony's back, her head over its tail, her feet against its shoulders, and her eyes to the sky. The rapidity of her glide into this position was that of a kingfisher—its noiselessness that of a hawk. Gabriel's eyes had scarcely been able to follow her. The tall lank pony seemed used to such doings, and ambled along unconcerned. Thus she passed under the level boughs.

The performer seemed quite at home anywhere between a horse's head and its tail, and the necessity for this abnormal attitude having ceased with the passage of the plantation, she began to adopt another, even more obviously convenient than the first. She had no side-saddle, and it was very apparent that a firm seat upon the smooth leather beneath her was unattainable sideways. Springing to her accustomed perpendicular like a bowed sapling, and satisfying herself that nobody was in sight, she seated herself in the manner demanded by the saddle, though hardly expected of the woman, and trotted off in the direction of Tewnell Mill.

Oak was amused, perhaps a little astonished, and hanging up the hat in his hut, went again among his ewes. An hour passed, the girl returned, properly seated now, with a bag of bran in front of her. On nearing the cattle-shed she was met by a boy bringing a milking-pail, who held the reins of the pony whilst she slid off. The boy led away the horse, leaving the pail with the young woman.

Soon soft spirts alternating with loud spirts came in regular succession from within the shed, the obvious sounds of a person milking a cow. Gabriel took the lost hat in his hand, and waited beside the path she would follow in leaving the hill.

She came, the pail in one hand, hanging against her knee. The left arm was extended as a balance, enough of it being shown bare to make Oak wish that the event had happened in the summer, when the whole would have been revealed. There was a bright air and manner about her now, by which she seemed to imply that the desirability of her existence could not be questioned; and this rather saucy assumption failed in being offensive because a beholder felt it to be, upon the whole, true. Like exceptional emphasis in the tone of a genius, that which would have made mediocrity ridiculous was an addition to recognized power. It was with some surprise that she saw Gabriel's face rising like the moon behind the hedge.

The adjustment of the farmer's hazy conceptions of her charms to the portrait of herself she now presented him with was less a diminution than a difference. The starting point selected by the judgment was her height. She seemed tall, but the pail was a small one, and the hedge diminutive; hence, making allowance for error by comparison with these, she could have been not above the height to be chosen by women as best. All features of consequence were severe and regular. It may have been observed by persons who go about the shires with eyes for beauty, that in Englishwoman a classically formed face is seldom found to be united with a figure of the same pattern, the highly finished features being generally too large for the remainder of the frame; that a graceful and proportionate figure of eight heads usually goes off into random facial curves. Without throwing a Nymphean tissue over a milkmaid, let it be said that here criticism checked itself as out of place, and looked at her proportions with a long consciousness of pleasure. From the contours of her figure in its upper part, she must have had a beautiful neck and shoulders; but since her infancy nobody had ever seen them. Had she been put into a low dress she would have run and thrust her head into a bush. Yet she was not a shy girl by any means; it was merely her instinct to draw the line dividing the seen from the unseen higher than they do it in towns.

That the girl's thoughts hovered about her face and form as soon as she caught Oak's eyes conning the same page was natural, and almost certain. The self-consciousness shown would have been vanity if a little more pronounced, dignity if a little less. She brushed her face with her hand, as if Gabriel had been irritating its pink surface by actual touch, and the free air of her previous movements was reduced at the same time to a chastened phase of itself. Yet it was the man who blushed, the maid not at all.

"I found a hat," said Oak.

"It is mine," said she, and, from a sense of proportion, kept down to a small smile an inclination to laugh distinctly: "it flew away last night."

"One o'clock this morning?"

"Well—it was." She was surprised. "How did you know?" she said.

"I was here."

"You are Farmer Oak, are you not?"

"That or thereabouts. I'm lately come to this place."

"A large farm?" she inquired, casting her eyes round, and swinging back her hair, which was black in the shaded hollows of its mass; but it being now an hour past sunrise the rays touched its prominent curves with a colour of their own.

"No; not large. About a hundred." (In speaking of farms the word "acres" is omitted by the natives, by analogy to such old expressions as "a stag of ten.")

"I wanted my hat this morning," she went on. "I had to ride to Tewnell Mill."

"Yes you had."

"How do you know?"

"I saw you."

"Where?" she inquired, a misgiving bringing every muscle of her lineaments and frame to a standstill.

"Here—going through the plantation, and all down the hill," said Farmer Oak, with an aspect excessively knowing with regard to some matter in his mind, as he gazed at a remote point in the direction named, and then turned back to meet his colloquist's eyes.

A perception caused him to withdraw his own eyes from hers as suddenly as if he had been caught in a theft. Recollection of the strange antics she had indulged in when passing through the trees was succeeded in the girl by a nettled palpitation, and that by a hot face. It was a time to see a woman redden who was not given to reddening as a rule; not a point in the milkmaid but was of the deepest rose-colour. From the Maiden's Blush, through all varieties of the Provence down to the Crimson Tuscany, the countenance of Oak's acquaintance quickly graduated; whereupon he, in considerateness, turned away his head.

The sympathetic man still looked the other way, and wondered when she would recover coolness sufficient to justify him in facing her again. He heard what seemed to be the flitting of a dead leaf upon the breeze, and looked. She had gone away.

With an air between that of Tragedy and Comedy Gabriel returned to his work.

Five mornings and evenings passed. The young woman came regularly to milk the healthy cow or to attend to the sick one, but never allowed her vision to stray in the direction of Oak's person. His want of tact had deeply offended her—not by seeing what he could not help, but by letting her know that he had seen it. For, as without law there is no sin, without eyes there is no indecorum; and she appeared to feel that Gabriel's espial had made her an indecorous woman without her own connivance. It was food for great regret with him; it was also a *contretemps* which touched into life a latent heat he had experienced in that direction.

The acquaintanceship might, however, have ended in a slow forgetting, but for an incident which occurred at the end of the same week. One afternoon it began to freeze, and the frost increased with evening, which drew on like a stealthy tightening of bonds. It was a time when in cottages the breath of the sleepers freezes to the sheets; when round the drawing-room fire of a thick-walled mansion the sitters' backs are cold, even whilst their faces are all aglow. Many a small bird went to bed supperless that night among the bare boughs.

As the milking-hour drew near, Oak kept his usual watch upon the cowshed. At last he felt cold, and shaking an extra quantity of bedding round the yearling ewes he entered the hut and heaped more fuel upon the stove. The wind came in at the bottom of the door, and to prevent it Oak laid a sack there and wheeled the cot round a little more to the south. Then the wind spouted in at a ventilating hole—of which there was one on each side of the hut.

Gabriel had always known that when the fire was lighted and the door closed one of these must be kept open—that chosen being always on the side away from the wind. Closing the slide to windward, he turned to open the other; on second thoughts the farmer considered that he would first sit down leaving both closed for a minute or two, till the temperature of the hut was a little raised. He sat down.

His head began to ache in an unwonted manner, and, fancying himself weary by reason of the broken rests of the preceding nights, Oak decided to get up, open the slide, and then allow himself to fall asleep. He fell asleep, however, without having performed the necessary preliminary.

How long he remained unconscious Gabriel never knew. During the first stages of his return to perception peculiar deeds seemed to be in course of enactment. His dog was howling, his head was aching fearfully—somebody was pulling him about, hands were loosening his neckerchief.

On opening his eyes he found that evening had sunk to dusk in a strange manner of unexpectedness. The young girl with the remarkably pleasant lips and white teeth was beside him. More than this—astonishingly more—his head was upon her lap, his face and neck were disagreeably wet, and her fingers were unbuttoning his collar.

"Whatever is the matter?" said Oak, vacantly.

She seemed to experience mirth, but of too insignificant a kind to start enjoyment.

"Nothing now," she answered, "since you are not dead. It is a wonder you were not suffocated in this hut of yours."

"Ah, the hut!" murmured Gabriel. "I gave ten pounds for that hut. But I'll sell it, and sit under thatched hurdles as they did in old times, and curl up to sleep in a lock of straw! It played me nearly the same trick the other day!" Gabriel, by way of emphasis, brought down his fist upon the floor.

"It was not exactly the fault of the hut," she observed in a tone which showed her to be that novelty among women—one who finished a thought before beginning the sentence which was to convey it. "You should, I think, have considered, and not have been so foolish as to leave the slides closed."

"Yes I suppose I should," said Oak, absently. He was endeavouring to catch and appreciate the sensation of being thus with her, his head upon her dress, before the event passed on into the heap of bygone things. He wished she knew his impressions; but he would as soon have thought of carrying an odour in a net as of attempting to convey the intangibilities of his feeling in the coarse meshes of language. So he remained silent.

She made him sit up, and then Oak began wiping his face and shaking himself like a Samson. "How can I thank 'ee?" he said at last, gratefully, some of the natural rusty red having returned to his face.

"Oh, never mind that," said the girl, smiling, and allowing her smile to hold good for Gabriel's next remark, whatever that might prove to be.

"How did you find me?"

"I heard your dog howling and scratching at the door of the hut when I came to the milking (it was so lucky, Daisy's milking is almost over for the season, and I shall not come here after this week or the next). The dog saw me, and jumped over to me, and laid hold of my skirt. I came across and looked round the hut the very first thing to see if the slides were closed. My uncle has a hut like this one, and I have heard him tell his shepherd not to go to sleep without leaving a slide open. I opened the door, and there you were like dead. I threw the milk over you, as there was no water, forgetting it was warm, and no use."

"I wonder if I should have died?" Gabriel said, in a low voice, which was rather meant to travel back to himself than to her.

"Oh no!" the girl replied. She seemed to prefer a less tragic probability; to have saved a man from death involved talk that should harmonize with the dignity of such a deed—and she shunned it.

"I believe you saved my life, Miss—I don't know your name. I know your aunt's, but not yours."

"I would just as soon not tell it—rather not. There is no reason either why I should, as you probably will never have much to do with me."

"Still, I should like to know."

"You can inquire at my aunt's—she will tell you."

"My name is Gabriel Oak."

"And mine isn't. You seem fond of yours in speaking it so decisively, Gabriel Oak."

"You see, it is the only one I shall ever have, and I must make the most of it."

"I always think mine sounds odd and disagreeable."

"I should think you might soon get a new one."

"Mercy!—how many opinions you keep about you concerning other people, Gabriel Oak."

"Well, Miss—excuse the words—I thought you would like them. But I can't match you, I know, in mapping out my mind upon my tongue. I never was very clever in my inside. But I thank you. Come, give me your hand."

She hesitated, somewhat disconcerted at Oak's old-fashioned earnest conclusion to a dialogue lightly carried on. "Very well," she said, and gave him her hand, compressing her lips to a demure impassivity. He held it but an instant, and in his fear of being too demonstrative, swerved to the opposite extreme, touching her fingers with the lightness of a small-hearted person.

"I am sorry," he said the instant after.

"What for?"

"Letting your hand go so quick."

"You may have it again if you like; there it is." She gave him her hand again.

Oak held it longer this time—indeed, curiously long. "How soft it is—being winter time, too—not chapped or rough or anything!" he said.

"There—that's long enough," said she, though without pulling it away. "But I suppose you are thinking you would like to kiss it? You may if you want to."

"I wasn't thinking of any such thing," said Gabriel, simply; "but I will—"

"That you won't!" She snatched back her hand.

Gabriel felt himself guilty of another want of tact.

"Now find out my name," she said, teasingly; and withdrew.

~

Thomas Hardy (1840–1928) was one of the most celebrated English novelists whose works depict the stark reality of the members of the British working class of his time, and their social issues. His famous novels, which continue to be studied and read widely, include *The Mayor of Casterbridge*, *Tess of the d'Urbervilles*, *Jude the Obscure* and *Far from the Madding Crowd*.

Daffodils

William Wordsworth

I wandered lonely as a cloud
That floats on high o'er vales and hills,
When all at once I saw a crowd,
A host, of golden daffodils;
Beside the lake, beneath the trees,
Fluttering and dancing in the breeze.

Continuous as the stars that shine
And twinkle on the milky way,
They stretched in never-ending line
Along the margin of a bay:
Ten thousand saw I at a glance,
Tossing their heads in sprightly dance.

The waves beside them danced; but they
Out-did the sparkling waves in glee:
A poet could not but be gay,
In such a jocund company:
I gazed—and gazed—but little thought
What wealth the show to me had brought:

For oft, when on my couch I lie
In vacant or in pensive mood,
They flash upon that inward eye
Which is the bliss of solitude;
And then my heart with pleasure fills,
And dances with the daffodils.

~

William Wordsworth (1770–1850) is credited as the co-founder of the English Romantic movement along with fellow poet Samuel Taylor Coleridge, with whom he wrote one of his most famous poetry collections, *Lyrical Ballads*. He is celebrated mostly for his ballads and elegies, including "Tintern Abbey", "Lucy Gray" and "The Prelude", and his essay "The Preface to Lyrical Ballads".

ALSO IN THE CLASSICS SERIES

Best Classic Short Stories for Children brings together some of the most well-known and beloved stories by authors like O. Henry, Oscar Wilde and Saki, and extracts from children's classics such as *The Railway Children* and *Little Women*. With a mix of genres including science fiction, mystery and ghost stories, and a host of popular characters such as Oliver Twist, Sherlock Holmes, Jane Eyre and Dracula, this is the perfect introduction to a range of classic literature.

Authors featured in this anthology include Charles Dickens, Charlotte Brontë, Rabindranath Tagore, Rudyard Kipling, Louisa May Alcott and Anton Chekhov among others.

Available in hardback and paperback!

Evergreen Classic Short Stories brings together some of the most popular and beloved stories by celebrated authors like Guy de Maupassant, James Joyce and Rudyard Kipling, and extracts from classics such as *Pride and Prejudice and The Great Gatsby*. With a mix of genres including mystery, romance, crime and supernatural, and a host of popular characters such as Tom Sawyer, Sherlock Holmes, Mr Darcy and Jo March, this is the perfect book to immerse yourself in a range of classic literature.

Authors featured in this anthology include Agatha Christie, Emily Bronte, Rabindranath Tagore, Emily Dickinson, F. Scott Fitzgerald and Edgar Allan Poe among others.

Available in hardback and paperback.

LOOK OUT FOR MORE IN

THE CLASSICS SERIES